ROBERTS & MACLAY

THE
A **TOM WAGNER** ADVENTURE
SACRED
WEAPON

Thriller

Translator: Edwin Miles / Copyeditor: Philip Yaeger

Imprint: Independently published / ISBN 9798565200942

Cover Art by reinhardfenzl.com

Cover Art was created with images from: depositphotos.com
(portokalis, marchello74, ccaetano, _Ansud_, fightingfear, I_gorZh,
iLexx) and Shutterstock.com (Gio.tto)

www.robertsmaclay.com

office@robertsmaclay.com

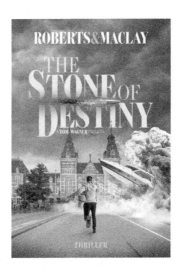

Get the free Tom Wagner adventure
"The Stone of Destiny"

— LEARN MORE AT THE END OF THE BOOK

"They that take the sword shall perish with the sword."

— From "Brockes Passion," Part i

Score by Georg Philipp Telemann (1681-1767)

Text by Barthold Heinrich Brockes (1680 - 1747)

1

Jacinto Guerra had to take a big step to avoid stumbling over the corpses of the three guards that lay in front of him on the floor of the church. He had just removed the Shroud of Turin from the glass cabinet at the altar. Taking care not to damage it, he rolled it up.

He paused in his work for a moment and listened. On a pew beside him, the baroque strains of Georg Philipp Telemann's "Musique de table" emanated from the small JBL Bluetooth speaker he had set up. He was particularly fond of the rondo. One of his companions, the one with a scar slashed across his right cheek, approached him and reached out to take the shroud. Guerra's hand shot up, stopping Scarface in his tracks. He required concentration, and absolute silence. He would not hesitate for a split second to cut the throat of anyone who dared disturb the sublime passage in which the flutes alternated with the orchestra, as if in a dialogue. Scarface knew this and froze in mid-movement, his eyes wide and fixed on Guerra. At almost six foot six, Guerra was a giant

—muscular, his face cruel, its lines carved too deeply for his forty-something years. He did not look like a man sensitive enough to love music. He looked, in fact, like the killer he was. And yet there he stood, immersed in the music as if in a trance. With the patience of an angel, Scarface waited until the rondo was over and Guerra returned to the world around him.

"Into the backpack, soldier!" Guerra handed the roll of cloth to the man, whose name simply would not stick in his head. For him, he was simply Scarface.

"That's Italians for you," Scarface said. "When they put the real shroud on display and run thousands of tourists through here like cattle, security's tighter than Fort Knox."

"And at night there's just a couple of watchmen, and they didn't slow us down for long," said Guerra, glancing again at the three bodies. Scarface nodded and packed the shroud—measuring almost fifteen feet by four unrolled—into the leather document roll made especially to protect it.

"You can reset the alarm system," Guerra said to the third man. "Let's tell not only the good people of Turin but the whole world that another sacred relic's been stolen. If we're going to this much trouble to collect all this Catholic junk, we ought to at least make sure we get a little PR out of it." He spoke the last sentence more to himself than to anyone else.

Guerra gazed through the nave of the cathedral and regretted that he hadn't had the time to finish his work properly. For him, "finish it properly" meant finish it the way he had the previous week, when he had stolen the Crown of Thorns from Notre Dame: with an inferno that made headlines around the globe. That was their mission: to attract attention. Inspire fear. Sow terror. The Notre Dame fire had been the perfect start, and Guerra had no intention of deviating from that perfection in the projects still to come.

"Okay. Alarm system's up and running again. It'll go off in ten," said the second of the two mercenaries, neither of whom had any idea of the real plan, and presumably had no interest in it either.

"Perfect." Guerra tilted his head slightly, the order to go. Men of this caliber needed no lengthy thank-you speeches. A gesture of respect, soldier to soldier, and the timely transfer of the fee was quite enough. No need to go on about it.

Purposefully, but without haste, the three men made their way to the cathedral exit. Just before they left the church by the side entrance leading to the Piazza San Giovanni, they pulled off the woolen masks they wore with a synchronized movement. The black garments that, together with the masks, had marked them as criminals, transformed in a moment into the robes of priests. The three Heckler & Koch pistols they carried vanished into the large side pockets of their soutanes.

The square beside the cathedral was dark and silent. It had rained heavily not long before, and the streets were wet and fetid—the usual stink that congealed in a big city when it was too humid. The streetlamps had gone off for a few hours in this part of Turin. Guerra smiled, reminded once again of just how far their influence reached. One call was enough, and the switch would be thrown just for them. Sometimes their schemes were just a little too easy. But the thought was abruptly interrupted.

"Padre, can you spare a few cents for me? I haven't eaten for days."

Guerra, by nature, was a stranger to fright and surprise. His pulse barely rippled when he heard the child's voice behind him. The other two men, obviously, took the unexpected intrusion less lightly, sudden uncertainty on their faces.

Guerra raised both hands and indicated to them to wait a moment. He went down on one knee before the boy and looked him in the eye. The youngster looked to be about twelve years old. "What are you doing out here all alone in the middle of the night?" Guerra asked in a gentle voice that took his two companions by surprise.

The boy looked into Guerra's cold, gray eyes. "I broke out of the orphanage a few weeks ago. All the rules they had bugged me. I read a book in the library just a little while ago, about Tom Sawyer and Huckleberry Finn, and I want to be just as free as them," the boy said.

There was pride in the boy's eyes. Guerra turned down the corners of his mouth and nodded appreciatively.

"So you're someone who doesn't like to stick to the rules, are you? A little mutineer, am I right?"

"Yes," said the boy, his eyes radiant. "I have a dream. I want to be a race car driver and earn a ton of money. I don't need school for that, or any teacher or master to tell me what I can or can't do."

Guerra's companions were growing nervous. The alarm inside the cathedral would go off soon, and the whole area would be buzzing with *carabinieri* before they knew it. One of the men tapped frantically at his watch. Guerra ignored them and calmly went on talking to the boy.

"What's your name, my son?" Guerra grinned almost imperceptibly. He was starting to enjoy the role of priest.

"Raffaele," the boy replied hastily.

Guerra ran his hand over the boy's head, mussing his hair a little. The youngster clucked his tongue and looked at Guerra with a broad grin.

"Rules are important, Raffaele. Otherwise, the world would get completely out of control, and everyone would do whatever they felt like doing. Most people in this world aren't mature enough to deal with freedom. They need rules, they need laws they can follow. People are simply too stupid for freedom. They need a strong hand that shows them what they're supposed to do."

Raffaele nodded but didn't say anything. He did not understand exactly what the padre was trying to tell him. Guerra looked around to his two companions and slowly rose from his crouch. He looked down at the boy and reached into the pocket of his soutane. Raffaele's eyes grew large. "Thank you, Padre!" he said, before Guerra's hand had reemerged. He plainly thought that the priest was going to give him a few euros and that he could finally get himself something to eat. Then everything happened at once: Guerra pressed his pistol to the boy's head and pulled the trigger without a moment's hesitation. The suppressor turned the cold-blooded act into a harmless "pfft." Raffaele's head tipped back and his skinny body slumped to the ground. Guerra's companions, who had seen a lot in their mercenary lives, looked at Guerra with horror and a little disgust.

"No witnesses," Guerra said, betraying no emotion. Without turning around, he strode off toward the corner of Via IV Marzo, where they had left the old Alfa Romeo 156.

2

"Paging passenger Tom Wagner for Austrian Airlines Flight AUA158 to Vienna. Passenger Tom Wagner, please proceed to Gate D7."

With a start, Tom came to his senses and looked around in confusion. It took him a few seconds to realize that he had nodded off in the VIP lounge at Milan Airport.

"I repeat: Passenger Tom Wagner, please go immediately to Gate D7."

He shook his head. "Can't anyone say my name right? My father was American. It's not pronounced 'Vahg-ner'," he mumbled in annoyance. He'd been traveling for more than twenty-four hours: first the flight from Acapulco to Miami, then a seven-hour wait for his connection to Milan, and now another four hours had passed . . . three more and he could finally put his feet up at home. Fortunately, Tom had been blessed with the enviable ability of being able to take a nap wherever he happened to be. On the other hand, this same talent had landed him in hot water more than once.

Tom calmly gathered his things and glanced at the screens in the lounge, where a news program was being broadcast. The Shroud of Turin had been stolen the previous night, joining a growing list of purloined relics. In the past week, in addition to the shroud, thieves had stolen the Crown of Thorns from Notre Dame, the bones of the Three Wise Men from Cologne Cathedral, and the Holy Nails from Rome and Monza. On the news, they were speculating that Arab extremists were behind the raids. At the same time, however, people were glad that Cologne Cathedral had not fallen victim to arson the way Notre Dame had. The unusually high number of airplane hijackings in recent weeks was also being put down to ISIS.

Tom was just about to head for the gate when he stopped mid-stride. His gaze was locked on the forearm of a man who was just helped himself to an espresso from the VIP lounge buffet. The man's sleeve had slipped up a little, revealing a tattoo:

It was a symbol Tom hadn't seen for years, but it was burned indelibly into his memory. Nothing in the world would ever make him forget the first and—until today—the last time he had seen that symbol. From one instant to the next, his life had become a living hell. The car bomb that had killed his parents. The explosion that had made Tom an orphan. The actual memories of that day in Syria were dim in Tom's mind. Pain, tears and desperation smothered almost everything that had happened. But one thing had stuck in little Tom's memory: the man with the jubilant smile who suddenly stood beside him as he stumbled in tears through the rubble, the man wearing the exact same tattoo, who had put his arm around Tom and leaned down to him. He had pointed to the countless bodies, the blood-soaked soil and body parts strewn all around that surreal scene. "Remember one thing: what you see here is what happens when someone sticks their nose into things that are none of their business." Then he had straightened up again, clapped Tom on the shoulder and left, laughing.

Tom would never forget the day, the face, the voice, or the tattoo. Or the music. For a reason Tom could not understand, he associated the death of his parents with a piece of music that had been stuck in his head all these years. The tattoo and that piece of music had stalked him in his sleep, fueling years of nightmares. Now all of it had come back into his life with no warning, like a punch to the gut.

Twenty-five years later: the same man, the same tattoo. Tom felt the heat rise inside him. He stared at the man in astonishment and did not move an inch. His head was spinning. He tried to pull himself together, to separate his emotions from his rational mind. His emotional side wanted to grab hold of the man then and there, confront him, knock him down, even kill him. The rational side—the elite fighter, the officer of the Austrian antiterrorist unit Cobra—stopped him from doing anything so foolish.

Another announcement: "Passenger Tom Wagner for Austrian Airlines Flight AUA158 to Vienna. Passenger Tom Wagner, please proceed to Gate D7 at once."

The tattooed man calmly departed the VIP lounge and Tom could do nothing but follow him. He slid his phone from his pocket and, as unobtrusively as possible, took several pictures of him. He immediately sent the pictures to his friend Noah. Noah would run the images through facial recognition, and would no doubt come up with a match.

For now, there wasn't much else Tom could do. The man was on the way to his gate. Tom followed him as far as the security checkpoint, but was unable to discover the man's destination. Still, he knew Noah would find something. Since he'd been confined to a wheelchair Noah had become a true IT wizard. No code, no firewall, no encryption could keep him out. And in the course of his career, he'd built up an extensive network, with dependable contacts among the Americans, the Israelis, even the Russians and Arabs. Noah would find the guy; Tom was sure of it.

"This is the final call for passenger Tom Wagner for Austrian Airlines flight AUA158 to Vienna. Passenger Tom Wagner, please proceed to Gate D7 immediately. You are delaying takeoff."

He glanced at the departures board and quickly found which way he had to go. He broke into a run—he really could not afford to miss this flight. He had an assignment waiting for him in Vienna starting early the next day. Another boring assignment, as usual, but that was his job. His thoughts still with the unknown man, he took a left, raced down the escalator two steps at a time, ignored the moving walkway so beloved of lazy passengers, and spotted his gate about a hundred yards ahead. The waiting area was completely empty. Tom waved to the woman at the ticket desk, who screwed up her face in annoyance.

3

Tom was one of those people who didn't have the slightest problem being in a plane; even the strongest turbulence didn't rattle him. The man in the seat next to him, however, wasn't so lucky. On the corpulent side, he dug the fingers of one hand into the armrest and clutched a plastic cup of whiskey and cola in the other—judging by the color, more whiskey than cola.

"I *hate* turbulence," the man beside Tom muttered, his eyes squeezed almost shut. Perspiration collected on his balding scalp; even his glasses were a little misted over. He lifted the cup to his lips, drained it in a gulp, and looked around immediately for the flight attendant. "My very own fear-of-flying cure," he said, glancing at Tom. When he saw the flight attendant coming, he lifted the cup in her direction and pointed at it. When she returned with the requested drink, the man reached for it greedily, crushing Tom slightly in his seat.

"Denise," Tom read on the flight attendant's name tag. She was attractive, dark-haired, in her late twenties, and probably one of the very few women who actually looked good in the ridiculous, bright red Austrian Airlines uniform.

"Something for you, sir?" she asked Tom, with an entrancing smile. She had noticed the good-looking man with the collar-length, tousled, dark-blond hair and the three-day beard as soon as he boarded. She liked men with chiseled, almost cruel features, but who could still manage a charming smile.

Tom, arranging himself in his seat, declined politely.

"Perhaps a pillow or a blanket?"

Tom shook his head. "No, thank you."

"Let me know if there's anything I can do for you," she said with another smile, and she grazed his shoulder gently with her hand as she moved on.

"The chick's got her eye on you, big time. A blind man could see that," the man beside him murmured, then slurped at his drink.

Tom ignored him. He leaned back and closed his eyes. The last thing he needed right now was a fling. He tried not to speculate about the man with the tattoo, but only partially succeeded. His vacation, the sun, the beach, the cliff diving, the Mexican women . . . all of it was pushed aside by the man in the VIP lounge. Tom unsnapped his seatbelt and headed for the toilets in the rear. The plane continued to be buffeted by turbulence. Both toilets were occupied, and Tom heard a man's voice coming from inside one of them. He smiled. Since on-board Wi-Fi had become a thing, you could even indulge your cellphone addiction in flight. Tom couldn't understand what the man was saying, though he was talking very loudly. He was speaking Farsi, or maybe one of the Arab languages. But Tom did pick up a name: François Cloutard. After about two minutes, he heard some rattling, then someone hurriedly opened the door.

A man, in his early thirties and probably Middle Eastern, stepped out. He was visibly nervous. Sweat beaded his forehead. "Excuse me, sir," the man stammered in broken English, pushing past Tom. Tom entered the toilet and locked it behind him. He braced himself against the small washbasin and looked at himself in the mirror. He liked what he saw. He splashed water on his face to freshen up, and his mind returned once again to the man with the tattoo. When he went to dry his hands, he discovered that the paper towel dispenser was empty. He reached inside as far as could to see if there was perhaps one paper towel left over, but his fingers touched something tacky. He withdrew his hand, baffled, then proceeded to remove the cover from the dispenser. Inside he discovered a large strip of double-sided tape, to which a few remnants of plastic film still clung. Bemused, he looked around the tiny cabin and noticed that all the fresh paper towels had been stuffed in the trash.

His heart began to beat a little faster. Was this really what it looked like? Had someone planted something there in the toilet for the man before him to find? Had he blundered into the middle of one of the spate of hijackings that had happened in the last few weeks? As a Cobra, he'd spent a lot of time on planes as an air marshal and had always been bored to tears. *No one hijacks planes anymore*, he'd thought many times. But maybe he was wrong.

Slowly, he opened the door just a crack and looked down through the plane. Everything seemed normal. But he jumped when the man seated beside him abruptly jerked the door out of his hand and stood in front of him. "Other people have to use the can, too, buddy."

Tom did not return to his seat immediately, but instead strolled on into the front section of the plane, toward the cockpit. He tried to be as inconspicuous as possible, just a guy wanting to get the blood circulating in his legs. He stretched, and as he did so he looked back down the rows of seats until he located the man from the toilet in row 18. He was obviously on edge, looking around constantly and making eye contact with another man two rows behind him. Both were wearing hooded sweatshirts, and each had a fanny pack that he was fingering nervously. Nobody else seemed to notice, but Tom had been trained to spot just this kind of detail.

In the front section of the plane, Tom grabbed Denise by her arm and steered her into the kitchen, where they could talk without being seen. He held his Cobra ID up to her face.

"Look, I'm not on duty, but I'm a Cobra officer and an air marshal. In 18C and 20D there are two men who I suspect are about to try to hijack this plane. I think someone's smuggled weapons on board for them." The flight attendant looked at him, aghast. She seemed frozen. "Do you understand what I just said?"

She nodded, trembling.

"I have to speak to the captain," Tom said.

A second flight attendant stepped into the kitchen. "What's going on here?"

Tom let go of Denise, flashed his ID at the second flight attendant and raised a finger to his lips. Denise disappeared without another word and returned a moment later with the captain. All four crowded into the small kitchen space, out of sight of the passengers. Tom explained the situation, then gave precise instructions to the captain and both of the flight attendants.

"Are you out of your mind? We can't do that," the captain whispered vehemently.

"Trust me. It will work, and no one's going to get hurt," Tom said calmly, a mischievous smile on his face. It made life interesting, now and then, to sidestep standard procedure. The captain thought about it for a moment, then nodded hesitantly and returned to the cockpit. The door closed and was locked from the inside.

"Ladies and gentlemen, this is your captain speaking. Please return to your seats and fasten your seatbelts. The turbulence we've been experiencing is about to get a little worse. The flight attendants will now be collecting the trash. Please raise your tray tables and return your seats to the upright position."

"Are you sure you've got this?" Tom asked, peering intently at Denise. Without waiting for her answer, he said, "Okay. Go!"

Denise took the meal trolley and pulled it slowly toward the rear of the plane. She took up position two rows behind the dubious passengers and began collecting the trash from the seats farther back.

Tom disappeared into one of the two toilets at the front of the plane. He messed up his hair and pulled his shirt partly out of his pants. He had taken a miniature bottle of whiskey from the kitchen and now poured most of the contents over his clothes. Then he gulped down the last few drops, sat on the toilet and waited.

Not five minutes later, exactly what he had prophesied came to pass. The two men had finally worked up enough courage. They jumped to their feet and pulled their weapons.

"This is a hijacking!"

A shocked murmur ran through the passenger compartment, then screams, panic. Passengers burst into tears. Denise ducked behind the meal trolley. The terrorists waved their weapons and shouted aggressive slogans in Arabic. Tom stood, opened the toilet door, and staggered out. One of the hijackers had a large jackknife in his hand, the other a small .22-caliber pistol. Tom stumbled toward the man with the pistol, who simply stood and gaped at him, perplexed. Tom stopped one row in front of the hijacker and braced himself on the armrests left and right, playing the role of drunk in Oscar-worthy style. Then everything happened at once; the two amateurs didn't know what hit them.

Denise had released the brakes on the meal trolley. Her colleague at the front knocked on the cockpit door and a heartbeat later the nose of the plane dipped sharply. Passengers squealed in fright. The meal trolley, free to roll, slammed into the back of the knifeman, knocking him down. The jackknife flew from his hand and disappeared beneath the seats. In the same instant, Tom grabbed the hand of the man with the pistol, twisted it unnaturally and slammed him in the nose from below with the ball of his hand. The man let out a scream and dropped the gun. Tom jerked him to the floor and sent him to sleep with a strike to the head. Meanwhile, one of the passengers had jumped up and was pinning the other hijacker to the floor.

Applause, cheers and whoops of relief rang out. Tom bound the hands of the two hijackers with heavy-duty cable ties. *The things you find on planes*, he thought as he zipped them tight.

He hauled the men to the front of the plane and searched them, but found nothing of interest apart from an iPhone and two passports, obviously fake. The phone was locked, but when he went to unlock it with the thumbprint of the unconscious hijacker, he paused. The man had a tattoo on the inside of his forearm—the same as the tattoo that Tom had seen less than two hours earlier on the arm of his parents' killer.

What was going on? What had he stumbled onto? He had to find out more about the hijacker. He pressed the man's thumb to the sensor and quickly picked through the phone. At first glance, he found nothing out of the ordinary. He quickly took a photograph of the tattoo, then heard a woman's voice behind him:

"Hey, Mr. Cobra. Thanks for saving our lives." Tom decided on the spot to take the phone with him rather than hand it over to the amateurs at the airport. He dragged his eyes away from the display, slipped the phone into his pocket and turned around to Denise.

"My pleasure. Can you tell the airport police about our two patients here?" he said. Denise nodded and reached for the telephone handset.

When the plane landed, the two hijackers were first taken into custody by the airport police. Only then were the passengers allowed to disembark. As they passed, they gave Tom a nod, a handshake or a heartfelt hug of thanks. In between Denise came to him and whispered in his ear, "I'm done for the day. I'd like to say thank you myself, but in private. Do you have any other plans today?" she asked, before planting a shy kiss on Tom's cheek as unobtrusively as possible. The man who'd been sitting next to him grinned and gave him two thumbs up.

4

A dilapidated cutter chugged sedately into the freight port in Varna. It motored past the artificial headland with the luxurious Black Sea yachts, navigated between two enormous oil tankers and made for a small landing stage, almost crushed by two ocean-going behemoths. On land, the cutter was already expected. The ship tied up and the captain left the small bridge. The sun burned mercilessly overhead, and the three waiting men were glad to be able to board the cutter and find a little shade. On their way to one of the filthy cargo holds, they ran into the skipper. His body odor took their breath away. They made no claims of consistency where their own personal hygiene was concerned, but the captain was in a league of his own. A brief greeting, and one of the men handed the captain an envelope. He flipped it open, saw the wad of hundred-dollar bills, and grinned broadly, showing the gaps in his teeth.

"*Ispol'zovat' sebya*," he said, pointing to a large wooden crate, and left them to it. He had a big evening ahead of him, but first he had to decide: just drink himself sense-less, or stay sober enough to take two women for the night? Such a choice of luxuries was clearly too much for him.

Removing the nails and opening the crate, they found a flight case packed in foam, about three feet long, two wide and a foot deep. At first glance it made little impression; only upon closer inspection did it become clear that this was no normal flight case. You could drive a bull-dozer over it, go at it with a sledgehammer, or blow it up with dynamite—none of it would have much effect. The state-of-the-art fingerprint scanner was another sign that it contained something very exclusive indeed.

One of the men wiped his oil-smeared thumb on his jeans and pressed it to the sensor. He lifted the lid, looked inside for a moment, nodded, and closed it again. He took out his phone and tapped out a short message, which reached its intended recipient a few seconds later and a thousand miles away.

His two companions nailed the crate shut again, carried it off the boat, and heaved it onto the bed of an old army truck. One of them climbed up beside it and the tarpau-lins were pulled across and lashed in place. The man with the phone took his place behind the steering wheel and they drove out of Varna, heading west.

5

GLASTONBURY ABBEY, SOMERSET COUNTY, ENGLAND

Hellen de Mey felt the same thing whenever she came to Glastonbury, a peculiar energy that she could not explain. She knew all the mythical stories about Glastonbury, of course, all the tales about King Arthur, Merlin and the Knights of the Round Table. And she also knew the most fantastic story of all: that Joseph of Arimathea, who had taken the body of Jesus down from the cross and buried him, was said to have left the Holy Land some time later and visited this place. But first and foremost, she was a scientist, an anthropologist and archaeologist.

"So forget the damned fairy tales!" she suddenly said aloud to herself, and she shook her head.

Taken aback, a young couple just then standing at the site of King Arthur's tomb turned and looked at her. Hellen grimaced and raised her hands in a "sorry" gesture. *Why do you always get so impulsive here? That's not like you at all,* she thought. She walked on through the ruins of the old abbey and looked up at Glastonbury Tor, a tower crowning a small hill just outside the town. She could not explain what it was about the place. All that was left of the old abbey were a few foundations that only hinted at the former glory of the structure. A gust of wind ruffled her blond pageboy haircut. She ran her fingers through her hair, lost in thought. Completely absorbed, confused by the emotions—so unusual for her—that she felt toward a historical site, she did not even notice the woman who had already completed her third circuit of the ruins, and who seemed to be paying no attention to them at all. The woman had dark, almost ebony skin, the same color as the black pantsuit and tight-fitting black coat she wore. Her eyes never left Hellen.

The woman had already completed her most important task for the day. She knew Hellen, knew who she was and why she was there.

Although the spring sun had already gained some strength, Hellen shivered. She looked at her watch, zipped her outdoor jacket up as high as it would go, and made her way to her actual destination, the real reason she had come here: the quiet garden in St. Margret's Chapel, just a short distance from the abbey.

She strolled past the two small ponds and through Abbey Park, then turned along Magdalene Street. Something caught her eye in the window of a small antique shop called "The Startled Hare Antiques & Curiosities." It was an image of Saint George fighting the Black Knight in the abbey. That legend was why she had come to Glastonbury: could it really be true? Or was it just another of the many fairy tales and legends that swirled around

Glastonbury Abbey? She would find out the truth soon enough.

"I hope so, anyway," she heard herself say. She had spoken aloud again, and shook her head several times, annoyed to be talking to herself. She still didn't notice the woman following her a hundred yards behind.

After a short distance, she turned left into a narrow lane; a moment later she found herself in what is known as the "quiet garden." A smile crossed her face. The quiet garden was not particularly special, but she loved its cozy atmosphere. A breath of wind carried the intense perfume of the flowers to her nose, but there were no exotic plants, no artfully designed flower beds, nothing in any way out of the ordinary . . . and yet it was a peaceful place, a haven of tranquility and contemplation in the heart of the touristic hustle and bustle of Glastonbury.

Hellen looked around, seeking Father Montgomery. She had agreed to meet him there in the garden, but apart from Hellen herself, nobody was there. She glanced at her watch: 4:12 p.m. Maybe the priest was still praying inside the small chapel?

"Father Montgomery?" she said, more to herself than actually calling out to him. She stopped at the chapel door and listened. Nothing. Apart from a car passing out on Magdalene Street, there was no other sound. She waited a few seconds until the car had passed, then called out again, a little louder. "Father Montgomery?"

If he's praying in the chapel, he must have heard me, she thought. She was now standing directly at the chapel door, which was almost closed. No movement. No reply.

"Father Montgomery? It's me. Hellen de Mey, the archaeologist."

Nothing. She hesitated. Should she just barge into the chapel and disturb the priest's prayer? She wasn't religious herself, but she respected the faith of others. She knew perfectly well the kind of problems you could face if you were too much the scientist and turned up your nose at religion.

Hellen's hand pressed lightly against the door and she called out Father Montgomery's name once more. The door swung open surprisingly easily, revealing the simple, sparse interior of the chapel.

It took a few seconds for Hellen's eyes to adjust to the dim light, but when she saw Father Montgomery, her breath caught in her throat.

The priest lay on his back on the floor, his eyes wide open and a bullet hole in his chest, from which fresh blood still oozed. A truck bumped loudly down the street in front of the garden, making her jump. She jerked her head around—abruptly, she felt as if someone were standing behind her. But she was mistaken.

Hellen had seen a dead body or two in her life and thought of herself as pretty tough, generally speaking, but this was beyond anything she'd ever dealt with. Her blood pounded in her veins, and she felt her body producing an excess of adrenaline. She was breathing quickly, her face was hot and flushed, and her hands and feet were ice-cold. She stood and stared, not knowing what to do. Again and again, she looked back over her shoulder: hoping for someone who could help, terrified that the killer was still around.

Several seconds passed. Hellen remained rooted to the spot, staring at the dead priest. Then she noticed a detail she hadn't immediately seen. With his bloody finger, Father Montgomery had scrawled the word "METEOR" on the chapel floor. Tentatively, she moved closer and crouched, leaning over the priest's body to see if she could find anything else. Outside, something clattered in the garden, as if a flowerpot had fallen and smashed. The wind? Or was the killer still nearby? She was about to stand up and leave the chapel when Father Montgomery moved.

Hellen immediately reached for her mobile phone to call for help, but she didn't get that far. Without warning, Father Montgomery snatched at the amulet that had fallen free of her blouse when she leaned forward. He pulled on the pendant, drawing her closer, raising himself a little from the floor. Hellen gasped in fright, partly because she hadn't believed for a moment that the priest was still alive, let alone able to muster so much energy, and partly because she was scared for the amulet, which had been left to her by her grandmother. Wheezing, he whispered into her ear:

"You're going to n . . ." Father Montgomery coughed blood, then inhaled sharply with a whistling, gurgling sound, ". . . to need the key."

"What key, Father?"

Father Montgomery released the amulet. He sank back to the floor. She pressed both hands over the wound to try to stop the bleeding.

"Hold on, Father. Don't give up!" she said.

A tear rolled down her cheek. A moment later, a young priest suddenly entered the chapel. He jumped back with a startled cry when he saw Hellen kneeling beside the blood-covered priest with her hands pressed over the wound.

"Dr. de Mey?" he asked in shock.

The young priest was the one who had arranged the meeting with Father Montgomery. Although Hellen was afraid that the murderer might still be close by and could reappear any second, she remained calm and focused for the moment.

"Call a doctor. Father Montgomery's been shot," she shouted at the young man, who still stood frozen. "Now!" she added, louder and more emphatically.

That tore the young man out of his trance. He took out his phone and dialed 999. Hellen stayed by the priest, but after a short time she had to admit defeat. Father Montgomery was dead. She slumped back, wiping the sleeve of her jacket across her eyes. She gazed uncomprehendingly at her trembling, blood-soaked hands, and remained like that beside the corpse for a moment. Finally, she stood up and walked past the young priest, into the open air.

Hellen still failed to notice the woman, who had been leaning against the wall of a house across the street the entire time. Nor did she notice that the woman was taking pictures of her. In the distance, Hellen could hear police and ambulance sirens racing toward her. While Hellen and the young priest waited for them to arrive, the black woman turned around, looked at the ancient key in her hand, and slowly made her way back to the parking lot at Glastonbury Abbey.

6

"So you're really one of those air marshals? On just about every flight I've wondered which one of the passengers it might be, or if we even had one on board," said Denise, as Tom handed her a cup of hot coffee. She looked gorgeous: a little sleepy, her hair tousled. While he made coffee, she had borrowed one of his shirts. She looked out from the small porch of the houseboat at the quietly murmuring river.

"I'm an officer with the Cobra task force, actually. Austria's antiterror unit. Flying as air marshals is part of our job."

"And that's where you learned to foil hijackings in creative ways?" Denise held the cup in both hands and took tiny sips of her coffee.

"That wasn't exactly standard procedure last night. Not textbook, anyway." He smiled mischievously. "That was all Tom Wagner." He paused for a moment. "The job's not always as exciting as that, unfortunately. It sounds more dramatic than it really is."

"So what makes a guy decide to be an antiterror officer?" Denise looked at him with interest.

"Even as a kid, one thing was clear to me: there are too many assholes in this world."

Denise laughed. "Was that all it took?"

"My mother was a trauma surgeon and worked for Doctors Without Borders. My father was a US marine. I'm pretty sure I was conceived in a war zone; I probably absorbed all that insanity while I was still in the womb."

"You didn't grow up surrounded by bombs and body parts, I hope?" Denise narrowed her eyes, taken aback.

"Not exactly. But we traveled all over the world, and I figured out fast that it's pretty damn messed up. Especially when . . ."

His voice faltered. His eyes turned glassy, empty.

". . . especially when my parents were killed in an attack in Syria. I'd just turned seven." Tom's voice had lost its strength. Denise placed a hand on his upper arm.

"I'm sorry," she said, a little abashed.

"To this day, nobody's figured out who was behind it. It's been on my mind all these years. When I was six, I swore to myself I'd find those responsible and bring them to justice. My grandfather's still alive. He's the best. And I have an uncle in the States, too, also in the military." He inhaled deeply. "I knew very early that I wanted to do something about all the violence and injustice, and not only because I'd vowed to find out who killed my parents. I made it into the Cobras, the youngest member ever, and I thought to myself, hey, now you can make a difference."

"But you can't?"

"No," he said, his voice cold. "I spend most of my time protecting people who aren't in danger, watching buildings that don't get attacked, and showing off what I can do in stupid competitions with other special service units around the world."

"It sounds like it gets to you."

"It does," said Tom. "I go back and forth between being bored and being pissed off. There's so much going on out there, but we're so bogged down by regulations and red tape that we can hardly lift a finger against the really evil bastards."

Tom stood, stepped out onto the porch, and glanced at his watch.

"I have to go. Duty calls. Take a shower, take your time. Just close the door behind you when you leave. I don't have anything worth stealing."

He smiled and kissed her goodbye.

"Will I see you again?" She looked hopefully at him.

He turned away and gazed out over the Danube.

"I'll be honest with you. Last night was fun, but I'm not made for relationships. I've had one real relationship in my life, and all the emotional chaos that goes with it . . . well, it's not my thing. I'm good when it comes to terrorists, weapons and exploding cars. Not so much with women."

"I didn't notice that last night," she said, smiling playfully.

"You know what I mean. I'm just not good at anything long-term," Tom said.

"Now you're misunderstanding me. I fly long-distance, which means I'm only ever home for a few days, or even just a few hours. I'd settle for a little meet-up like this every now and then."

He nodded, his mind somewhere else. "I have to go. Maybe we'll find ourselves on the same plane again sometime."

Tom was almost out the door when he turned back again. He fished the hijacker's phone out of his jacket and slipped it into his pocket.

Denise watched through a small window as he climbed into his car, not turning back once. As she watched him drive away, she took out her mobile and tapped in a number. The phone was answered after one ring.

"It's me. Sorry, there was nothing I could do."

Denise listened to the reply, but cut off the person on the other end almost immediately.

"That's exactly the problem. I have no idea why he took the phone. That's why I threw myself at him and had to listen to his whole shitty, sentimental life story over coffee."

Another pause.

"That would have been nice, but we're on a mini-house-boat. If I'd grabbed the phone during the night, he'd have noticed. Now he's taken it with him and he's heading to Cobra HQ. Looks like you're going to have to get that phone back the hard way. He's driving an old red Mustang. He's just left."

7

SACHER HOTEL, VIENNA

Guerra exited the lift at the top floor and nodded to the two bodyguards stationed outside the door of the suite. He felt a little honored. He would be meeting the innermost circle for the first time. Until today, he had only ever gotten his assignments through go-betweens, and while he knew perfectly well who was pulling the strings, he'd never actually met them. It surprised him to find them all gathered in one place now. One thing was clear to him: he'd made it to the top.

He stepped into the Grand Signature suite. He'd seen a lot of hotel rooms, even high-end suites of every size, but the Hotel Sacher had a flair all its own. He couldn't say exactly what it was. The furnishings were stylish, done in white, light gray and imperial red—nothing special, but still impressive in their simple appeal. He went out onto the terrace, which offered a stunning panoramic view from St. Stephen's Cathedral to the Vienna State Opera.

He was expected.

"Sit down, Guerra."

The woman with the Russian accent who offered him a chair must have been about fifty, but she radiated the erotic allure of a twenty-five-year-old model. Her simple Chanel dress, the diamond-studded Rolex, the Hermès handbag, the Christian Louboutin shoes. None of it looked ostentatious on her. She looked born to it, as if she could not wear anything but the best of the best.

Guerra sat and looked around the gathering. From the ring road below came the sound of hoofbeats from the horses pulling the *fiaker*, the open, horse-drawn cabs that catered to the tourists. The waiter brought Guerra a cup of *Wiener Melange* and a glass of champagne. Guerra took the cup and turned to the waiter.

"Thank you. You can take this away. I don't drink alcohol."

The waiter nodded. The man in the center, wearing a three-piece Brioni suit in the exact same shade as his graying temples, opened a laptop and linked in another participant. Guerra noted the anticipation that spread among the others. Whoever the newcomer was, he seemed to be yet another level higher.

"A brief situation report, please." The voice from the laptop was neutral and yet decisive—a man used to giving orders.

Guerra straightened up a little in his seat. "As planned, most of the artifacts are now in our hands. In the last few weeks, we have been able to take possession of the Crown of Thorns from Notre Dame in Paris, the Holy Nails from Monza and Rome, Saint Wenzel's helmet from

Prague, the bones of the Three Wise Men from Cologne and the Shroud of Turin." Guerra paused momentarily and his eyes scanned those assembled. There was no sign of emotion on any of their faces. Apparently, they took such results as given. "Today and tomorrow, we will be taking possession of the last of the relics." Not for a single moment did Guerra's voice betray a hint of doubt in the flawless execution of their plans.

"They're not the last relics, as you most certainly know," piped a high-pitched voice from among those present.

To the left of the man with the graying temples sat an Asian man, whose unusually high voice did not fit at all with the rest of his body—he could have been a sumo wrestler, but he still cut a surprisingly good figure in his black suit and turtleneck sweater.

"Of course," Guerra quickly corrected himself. "However, we are confident that the problem will soon be solved, and we will discover the whereabouts of the most vital relic."

The voice from the laptop cut in. "With all due respect for your confidence, we need a Plan B in case you should fail. You know that nothing we do is done without a Plan B."

"Plan A or B aside, will we be in time to execute Project 'Cornet'? How likely is that?" the graying man asked, a typical Texas lilt in his voice, and he looked around the small gathering. "The complete 'Cornet' plan has always been our preferred alternative. It would be most advantageous if we could realize that."

The others nodded silently.

"The clues are all pointing in one direction. I therefore assume that we will be able to obtain the last of the relics in time to put 'Cornet' into operation as planned." Guerra's voice was clear and determined. He looked around, meeting every eye unflinchingly.

"Good. If that is the case, it will not be to your disadvantage," the graying man said. "We need men like you who are able to execute our plans without mistakes."

Guerra nodded and was about to reply, but he did not get the chance.

"That is all, Guerra," the second woman present said, closing the meeting. She spoke to Guerra in his native Spanish, but he could see that she was probably from the Middle East. The United Arab Emirates, he guessed.

"Guerra, radio silence from now on, until the last of the artifacts is in our hands." The words of the man from the laptop were unequivocal.

Guerra stood and departed with a nod. As he left the terrace, the last words he heard from the laptop were, "I'll make sure the media is working in the right direction. Who's sorting out our little problem here in Vienna?"

8

THE STREETS OF VIENNA

Tom dropped into the driver's seat of his 1967 Shelby Mustang GT500. He leaned his head back, closed his eyes and took a few deep breaths. Too many thoughts were swirling in his head since his talk with Denise. After a few seconds, he started the Mustang and drove off, cursing loudly at himself: "Tom! You jump out of airplanes. You rappel head first down ten-story buildings. You fight terrorists and you can fly a chopper through the tightest mountain gorges. Pull yourself together, goddammit!"

His phone rang, cutting into his thoughts. Tom, grateful for the distraction, took the call.

"Hey, Tom, where the hell are you?" asked Noah Pollock, the Cobra IT expert and Tom's best friend.

"Sorry. I got held up."

"Blond or brunette?" Noah said. "Have you got the phone?"

"Sure have."

"Why didn't you hand it over to the airport guys as evidence?"

"You know those idiots. They wouldn't even know how to unlock it. Besides, you're the only one I trust with it."

"I'm honored," said Noah. "But if you refuse to follow the rules, then you shouldn't wonder why none of the guys like you, or why the powers that be keep reading you the riot act," said Noah in a reproving tone of voice.

Tom grimaced. "Yeah, yeah. You're right, as usual. But in this case, I had no choice. Did you find out anything about the guy in those photos?"

"What does he have to do with this?" Noah asked.

"The guy . . ." Tom paused. "It's the guy who killed my parents."

There was silence at the other end of the line. Noah had to process that information. "What makes you think that?"

"I told you about the man I saw after the explosion, when I was a kid. He was in the VIP lounge in Milan with me. I recognized him by his tattoo."

"By his tattoo? Jesus, Tom, you were seven years old. Are you sure?"

"More certain than I've ever been. I can remember it like it was yesterday. No doubt whatsoever."

"Well, I haven't found out much about him yet. He's a diplomat, and he's clean as a damned whistle. Too clean.

There's practically nothing on the guy at all apart from who he is. His name's—"

The call was abruptly interrupted when Tom's Mustang was rammed from behind, almost sending him into a spin. His phone flew out of his hand and landed in the footwell on the passenger side. At the last second, he was able to switch lanes to avoid slamming into the car in front.

"Fuck!" Tom shouted. "You son-of-a-bitch!" He mentally calculated the repair costs for the Mustang. He'd inherited the beautiful beast from his father, and it was almost impossible to find parts for it in Europe. He'd be without wheels for months, all because the guy behind him couldn't watch out.

Furious, he glanced in the mirror. He was about to pull over to the right and tell the incompetent driver what he thought of him when he realized that the souped-up 1990s BMW was lining up to ram him again. He swung the wheel to the right and stepped on the gas. For the time of day, there was surprisingly little traffic on Vienna's streets. There was a charity race happening that day, and half the streets were closed. Everyone was probably using the subway, and most of those who drove had probably already made their way into the city center. He found space in the next lane and was able to squeeze past two cars that were practically crawling compared to him.

It took Tom a few seconds to fully realize that this was no normal fender bender. Someone was after him. It didn't take an Einstein to figure that out, however: in the rearview mirror he saw the passenger lean out of the window with a pistol pointed in his direction. A second later, the rear window shattered.

Tom's earlier swerve had also sent his service pistol, which he normally kept on the passenger seat, flying into the footwell. Out of reach, especially when he was weaving through the city at 100 mph. A second shot shredded part of the passenger seat.

Who the fuck are these guys? Are they totally crazy? Tom thought as he shaved the side mirrors off three cars as he roared past, fighting desperately to keep the Mustang on the street without seriously endangering anyone else. Escape opportunities were limited: on his left was the river, winding its way through the city thirty feet below street level; on his right were two lanes of traffic. Escaping into one of the narrow alleys on the right was out of the question.

In front of him, a light turned red. The intersection was still empty and Tom floored the gas pedal once again. The Mustang certainly had some years on it, but the 400+ horsepower under its hood pressed him back into his seat, putting some distance between him and the BMW.

But not for long. The BMW driver also saw that he now had a clear lane, and faster than Tom could think, he was on his bumper again. More bullets flew. Windows shattered and Tom banged his forehead on the steering wheel when he reflexively leaned forward and down as far as he could go. An idea came to him: the Ringstrasse —Vienna's grandest boulevard, on which almost all the major sights of the former imperial city stood—was closed to traffic today. At the next intersection he could swing right, against the flow of traffic, and shake off his pursuers.

A few seconds later, Tom slammed on the brakes as hard as he could, straining the Mustang's chassis to its limits. He hauled on the handbrake with his right hand while his left swung the wheel to the right. At the same time, he floored the gas pedal. The car slowed so fast that it felt to Tom almost as if he'd thrown out an anchor. For the first time, all the driver training he'd had was finally paying off.

Tires squealing and smoking on the asphalt, Tom drifted onto the Ringstrasse at nearly sixty miles an hour. Seconds later, motor howling, he raced past the Vienna stock market, the university and the Burgtheater.

He glanced in the mirror. The BMW was nowhere to be seen. Tom sighed with relief. He planned to turn into one of the side streets as quickly as possible, throwing the BMW off his tail once and for all—especially because he had no idea how far the street was closed off, or how much longer he could keep up this speed driving the wrong way on a one-way street through the heart of Vienna.

But Tom's relief did not last long. The BMW reappeared in the side mirror, and Tom was instantly certain of one thing: the BMW was far more powerful than he'd supposed. His Mustang pulled four hundred goddamned horses! What kind of beast were they driving? Because whatever it was, it was catching up way too fast.

But that was far from Tom's biggest problem. Ahead, he saw that he was racing at full speed toward the end of the closed-off section, and thousands of people were already gathered on the far side of the barriers, waiting for the charity race to start. The BMW was almost on him, and he had very few options left. Turning right was out of the question now: hundreds of spectators were already lining the street on that side. Turning left would lead him, in less than a hundred yards, to the Kärntner Strasse—Vienna's main shopping drag, a pedestrian zone swarming with tourists and Viennese alike. He was stuck between shitty and shittier.

The BMW took the choice out of his hands. The driver drew level on his right, then swung hard, ramming the Mustang and sending it skidding to the left. Tom had no choice: he roared into the pedestrian zone at high speed.

The first group that was forced to jump for their lives was a handful of tourists, who had just purchased the obligatory Sacher torte and had left the eponymous hotel not a minute earlier. The cake, presumably, did not survive their panic-stricken leap.

Tom swerved left and right, honking frantically, mowing down trash cans, street signs, advertising boards, tables, chairs and the umbrellas of sidewalk cafés. By some miracle, he managed not to injure anybody.

More shots rang out, reverberating loudly through the canyons between the buildings. Apart from the Mustang and the BMW, there were no other vehicles at all, which only amplified the howl of the engines and the sound of the gunshots. Although the bullets were whistling past Tom's head, they had one benefit: the noise of the gunshots was helping to clear the street ahead of him.

Unfortunately, Tom knew there was no way to clear the square at Stephansplatz, which lay just ahead. Every day, thousands of tourists flocked to Vienna's biggest, most impressive landmark, St. Stephen's Cathedral. The square was always jammed with people.

Tom's desperation continued to grow. He could see no way out; the BMW would force his Mustang into the crowd. He had to make a decision—and he chose to slam on the brakes. This happened to be exactly what the BMW driver hadn't counted on. Now Tom, at least for a moment, had the upper hand. Just before the BMW slammed into the rear of the Mustang again, Tom whipped the wheel around. People scattered, and the car swung around ninety degrees, crashing with its left side against the wall of a construction trailer beside the cathedral. The BMW roared past, tires screeching, just missing the Mustang.

Tom's car slid a little farther and smashed head-on into the projecting corner of the cathedral's south tower. The force of the impact turned the car clear of the edifice, and it rolled to a stop a moment later.

Tom threw his head back and took a deep breath, but he knew it wasn't over yet. He needed his pistol now, but it had slipped under the passenger seat during the chase. He unclipped his seatbelt, leaned down quickly and began feeling beneath the seat for the gun. The few seconds before his hand touched the cold metal felt like hours. Finding the pistol, he snatched it from under the seat and straightened up, just in time to see a fist coming at him. A half-second later it slammed into his left temple and everything went black.

9

In the parking lot, Ossana Ibori swung her leg over the back of her motorbike and dismounted. She was a woman with little use for sentiment, and not much in her life impressed her. But the view of the Meteora monoliths, columns of stone soaring upwards, the almost menacing drifts of fog suspended between them and the monastery complexes on their summits—this commanded respect even from her. There had been a time when the only way to reach the monasteries had been rope ladders hundreds of feet high, and many monks had paid with their lives for the path of contemplation. The monasteries had also served as a backdrop for many Hollywood productions.

The monasteries presided over the landscape with breathtaking majesty. Several buildings stood on the individual summits. Some were nothing more than ruins; others were abandoned and uninhabited. Only a handful were still intact and accessible to tourists—without the rope ladders, of course.

Ossana glanced at the key she had taken from the old priest in Glastonbury. She knew exactly what her next step was. She grabbed her backpack, which held an FN P90 machine pistol, slung it over her shoulder, and strode confidently past the crowds of tourists who had been pouring from the buses strewn across the parking lot since early in the morning. She bought a ticket and entered the monastery.

Ossana had memorized her route precisely. She quickly left the usual route that led through the monastery and exhibition rooms. She swung a leg over one of the typical museum-style rope barriers and took the stairs down to the secret monastery library, where rare and valuable books, scrolls and manuscripts had been collected since the first hermitage had been built there in the 11th century. Without hesitation, she pushed open the old wooden door that marked the entrance to the library. Its creaking caused two monks working in the library to look up in surprise.

Ossana barely broke her stride: she slid the machine pistol out of the backpack and shot down the two monks with a brief salvo. She didn't care if anyone heard the shots. By the time the Greek police arrived, she'd be miles away. She scanned the library and immediately saw what she was looking for: a shelf upon which all the books were bound in red. Two steps brought her to it, and she pushed five identical-looking books two inches back. Part of the shelf slid aside, revealing a tabernacle crafted from solid mahogany with gold inlays.

Ossana slipped the key from inside her jacket and opened the shrine, then carefully removed the book lying inside. She slid it into a large plastic bag and stowed it in her backpack, along with the machine pistol—she would not be needing it again soon, she was certain. She left the library without a backward glance, climbed the stairway and slipped in among a guided group of tourists. As the tour continued, she noticed a ripple of unrest moving through the monks. Someone had discovered her handiwork in the library. More and more monks streamed past, their agitation palpable.

The tour came to an end, and Ossana exited the monastery with the rest of the group. As she mounted her motorbike she could see the flashing blue lights of police cars down in the valley, on their way to the monastery. Just then, the fog cleared and the sun broke through. Ossana smiled, as if it were a sign from above. She started the engine and calmly rode away with the book.

10

When Tom came to, his skull was pounding.

"Holy shit, Wagner, have you completely lost your mind?" a harsh voice snarled. Tom looked around in confusion. He was lying on a gurney at the rear of an ambulance that had pulled up a few yards from his Mustang. Firefighters, paramedics, and a horde of cops surrounded him, all trying to clear the scene and reopen it to the public.

The area around St. Stephen's Cathedral had been sealed off, and most of the police officers were busy trying to explain to angry tourists from Italy and Japan that they would not be visiting the cathedral that day.

Tom recognized the cop who had just snarled at him. He'd had an unpleasant run-in with him on an earlier assignment. He was dead weight, a hack who had moved up in the department by brown-nosing his superiors his entire career; he had never seen any action "at the front". On top of that, he'd mispronounced Tom's name.

Tom sat up on the gurney and glared at the cop. "Me? Lost *my* mind? Go ask the guys who were just shooting at me!"

"Pity they missed. Then we wouldn't have this mess to clean up." The officer was getting louder.

"Sorry, did you hear what I said? Someone tried to kill me! I don't even know what those psychopaths wanted."

Tom paused and got to his feet. He stalked over to his Mustang, jerked open the door and searched through it.

"What are you doing now? What the hell are you looking for?"

Tom cursed. "They've got the iPhone. They've got the damn phone! All this for a fucking phone?"

"What are you talking about? Who's got your iPhone?"

"They totaled my Mustang for a goddamned phone!" Tom raged.

"Aw, your Mustang got a boo-boo," goaded the cop. He looked at the other officers around them, who only shook their heads. "You turn Kärntner Strasse into a war zone and crash into St. Stephen's, and all you're worried about is your damn car? Wagner, seriously, I don't know why you still have a badge."

Again, he had mispronounced Tom's name

11

"Bravo! You've outdone yourself this time, Wagner."

Tom hadn't even stepped out of the elevator, and it was already raining spite and mocking applause.

"We know you're bored, but did you really have to ram the cathedral?"

The expressions on the faces around him ranged from disbelief to scorn to downright disgust—the entire range of reactions from a team where you don't quite fit in. He looked around at the large, bleak room with its familiar desks, filing cabinets and office equipment. Air-conditioned air, ringing telephones, squeaking office chairs, the normal hustle and bustle of headquarters. He shook his head. He didn't belong here. From the beginning, Tom had been an outsider. He had no problem being a loner; it suited his temperament, and most of the time he didn't give a damn what his colleagues thought about him. But in moments like this, he realized once again just how out of place he was.

It wasn't just that he didn't get along with his colleagues; it wasn't even that they made it crystal clear to him that he didn't belong. Most of all, they didn't understand what drove him. No one seemed to understand that he genuinely wanted to make the world a slightly better place.

This had led to heated discussions more than once. Most of his colleagues saw what they did as a job, like any other. Oh, sure, they did their work with enthusiasm and idealism—they had to, considering the salary—but no one understood Tom's deeper motivation. None of them had lost their parents to war or terrorism. None of them wanted as much as he did to put their skills to work to actually change anything. And not a single one of them found the day-to-day work as tedious as Tom did. Again and again, this tedium had led to Tom to make spur-of-the-moment decisions in the field—sometimes risky, overconfident decisions—antagonizing both his colleagues and his superiors.

Tom was on the way to suit up when he spotted Noah. Every time he saw his old friend in the wheelchair, a cold chill ran down his spine. He gave Noah a pained smile.

"You okay? I just heard," Noah said.

Tom nodded. "I'm fine. The Mustang's a wreck and the phone's gone. But we got cut off just when you were about to tell me the name of the guy at the airport."

"Jacinto Guerra. Spanish. Unfortunately, that's all I know."

Tom nodded gratefully and clapped Noah on the shoulder. "Stay on it, please."

"The investigation's already in full swing anyway, but we've gotten nothing out of the hijackers from yesterday yet," said Noah, a little resignation creeping into his voice. "Any idea what that was about today?"

"The phone from the plane. After I ran into the cathedral and they knocked me out and took the phone," said Tom. "By the way, one of the hijackers had the same tattoo as Guerra."

Noah's eyes widened. "What? The same tat . . . man, Tom, what hornet's nest have you been throwing rocks at now?"

"I'm going to have a chat with those two guys personally. Maybe they know something about Guerra."

"Count yourself lucky Maierhof's not here. Your rescue 'strategy' yesterday wasn't exactly by the book. You were being impulsive and reckless again."

"But it all worked out, right? There wasn't one moment when I didn't have the situation under control," Tom said defensively.

"Yeah, right. You've got more luck than brains, you know that? You're good. Very good, even. But if you keep playing by your own rules, it isn't going to do you any good in the long run. Nobody's that good. The boss will always be on your case, and one day you're going to fall flat on your face." Noah picked up a file lying on his lap and handed it to Tom. "Here. Today's briefing."

Tom opened the file, leafed through the contents, and rolled his eyes. "Personal security. Another conference in the Hofburg. Oh, joy. Could it get any duller?" Tom could not think of a single situation in recent years in which his presence had really been necessary. He knew, of course, how important it was that politicians, industry heads and such were safe in Vienna. He even knew how threatened those people were in this day and age, but it didn't change how he felt. Walking next to some VIP and making sure they didn't stumble or get jostled or get food thrown at them was not high on his list of favorite things to do.

"When are you finally going to get it?" Noah said. "Your job here is to do a solid and very important job—one that, most days, does not make the headlines. You're not James Bond, and the job's not about breaking into fortresses or swapping bullets with terrorists every day. You're not disarming nuclear bombs like Jack Bauer. And you're not one man fighting some unknown evil, like Jason Bourne, or foiling assassination attempts on the US president or the Pope. Your initials aren't even J.B., they're T.W." Noah laughed at his little joke, but Tom wasn't impressed. "You'll have to save the world next week, Tom. All you get to do today is look after a few semi-important folks from UNESCO," he said with a smile.

Tom started at the mention of UNESCO. His thoughts began to race, and he shook his head. No, it couldn't be. The chances were slim. On any given day, countless conferences involving all kinds of UNESCO organizations took place. Fate wouldn't do this to him.

"All right. Get to it." Noah clapped Tom on the shoulder, and Tom went into the locker room. He pulled on his spare uniform, the usual dark gray, and a fresh shirt that he always kept in his locker for emergencies. As always, he wore a bulletproof vest beneath the shirt. Noah rolled in behind him.

"I'm going to pay our two hijackers a little visit." Tom narrowed his eyes.

Noah sighed audibly. "Do me a favor and stick to the rules. We're not the CIA, and this isn't Guantanamo. You can't go waterboarding them in the hospital."

Tom looked Noah in the eye as he spoke, wanting to give his words the necessary emphasis. "I got shot at today, and a lot of people had their lives put in danger. It's a miracle no one was seriously injured by a flying bullet— or a flying car. And everything, apparently, is tied to that tattoo, and to my parents' killer. I'm not going to go easy on them in there."

Noah, unimpressed, just looked at him reproachfully. Tom checked the rest of his equipment: pistol, spare magazines, ID and communications gear.

He raised his hands appeasingly. "Okay, okay. I promise I'll behave myself. I'll be nice. Scout's honor."

12

Tom stepped out of the elevator on the twenty-second floor. To the right of the elevator was a nondescript door with a sign reading "No Entry." The door led to a private wing of the hospital, to which normal patients and visitors had no access. Vienna General Hospital was located on a sixty-acre site; it was home to twenty-five different university clinics on twenty-two floors, with over 1,700 patient beds. No surprise, then, that some parts of the hospital were for patients who needed a little more than just medical attention—usually injured criminals and other offenders.

Tom strode along the sterile corridors. He felt a little ill at ease, as he always did when he visited a hospital, not least because of the unpleasantly strong smell of disinfectant filling his nose. He turned a corner and a uniformed officer came to meet him. The officer didn't look particularly happy to see him, but Tom knew the guy. That would make his job easier.

"I'm here to have a little chat with the hijackers from yesterday. A couple of their buddies tried to fill me with lead this morning. I want to rough them up a little and see if I can't get some information about who's behind this."

The officer looked at Tom and let out a loud sigh.

"Yeah, I heard what happened, Tom. But you won't be questioning the suspects today."

Tom lowered his voice. "I know it's not exactly by the book and that I'm not running the case, but I need a few minutes. Those guys—or rather some friends of theirs— have caused me a lot of trouble. I'd like to find out what it's all about." He looked hopefully at his colleague. "It won't take long, and I promise I won't harm a hair on their heads."

"You don't understand. If it were up to me, you could dangle them out the window with an IV tube to get something out of them, but it's not going to happen. They're dead."

Tom narrowed his eyes to slits. "What? No way. I mean, okay, one of them took a meal trolley in the back and a few passengers sat on him after that, and I might have broken the other guy's nose and arm. And when I dragged them to the front of the plane, maybe I put a shoulder or two out of joint, but that's it. That's not going to kill anyone," said Tom.

The cop took a deep breath. "You didn't kill them. Their injuries didn't kill them. We don't even know *how* they died—we'll have to wait for the autopsy for that. The fact is, someone got in during the night, and by the time the doctors came for morning rounds they were both dead. The shittiest part is that they also got the guy guarding the room."

"What!? They killed one of ours? Who the hell are these guys?"

Tom leaned against the wall and hammered it with the palms of his hands a few times. Cogs began to turn in his head. This whole thing was getting out of control. Guerra, the hijackers, the tattoo, the chase and the shooting that morning . . . and now more bodies. That phone must have meant a lot to someone.

"They're already working on it. You know the drill. They don't have a clear lead, though—this was done by professionals. We have no clear shot of their faces. Looks like they knew exactly where the cameras were."

"Do we know any more about the hijackers? I mean, more than that their passports were fake?" Tom asked.

"A couple of small-time crooks, a bit of smuggling and a couple of burglaries is all we've found. They were both from Tunisia, but there's no sign of a terror link. Not like with the other hijackings lately. Those were all radical Islamists."

Tom thanked the cop, took out his phone and tapped Noah in his contacts.

"Miss me already?" Noah said, clearly annoyed.

"The two hijackers I sent to the hospital yesterday are dead," Tom said evenly.

"Tom, what did I tell you not even an hour ago?"

"Oh, come on. Have a little faith. *I* didn't kill them. Someone got in during the night and beat me to it."

There was silence at the end of the line. Then Noah said, "Okay. New plan. I'll call in a favor from some friends in the US. Maybe they know something about Guerra or the hijackings."

"CIA?" said Tom.

"No. The CIA guys don't know their ass from their elbow. I prefer to talk to the grown-ups, the NSA."

"You've got contacts in the NSA? I'm impressed."

"What did you think I was doing for ten years in Mossad? Picking my nose?" Noah's sardonic undertone was unmistakable. "Now I'm interested; I'll do what I can. I suppose this stays between you and me?" Noah asked rhetorically.

"You suppose right," Tom said, and laughed. "Call me when you find out more. I've got to get to this security job at the Hofburg."

"Just be happy they didn't dump you with the neo-Nazi demonstration. Just about anyone who can stand and carry a gun is on the street. Between the UNESCO conference, the charity race, and this big demonstration, we're seriously short-staffed. They even asked me if I could go out in the field today, at least for a while."

"There'll be more going on at the demonstration than with these UNESCO bores, at least."

Tom signed off, and his mind immediately returned to the two hijackers. Shit, he hadn't sent Noah the photo of the tattoo. He quickly corrected the oversight, and on the way to his work car in the hospital's underground garage his cell phone pinged. It was a message from Noah: "I've seen that symbol before. I'll check the FBI tat database and get back to you ASAP."

13

HOTEL PARK HYATT, VIENNA

Nikolaus III, Count Palffy von Erdöd and president of Blue Shield, the UNESCO-allied organization dedicated to protecting the world's cultural heritage, sat at the luxurious hotel bar. He was taking his pipe out of its case when he remembered that smoking had now been banned essentially everywhere, and he sighed in annoyance. His idea of freedom was something different from this. He glanced at the flat-screen TV in the corner. A news broadcast was on, but there was no sound.

The world was a madhouse. Notre Dame was burning, countless aircraft had been hijacked in recent weeks, shark alarms were ringing off Malta, and a right-wing populist chancellor held the reins in Germany and wanted to ship every last Muslim out of Europe—the sooner the better. A boy had been murdered in Turin, some lunatics had used Stephansplatz as a racetrack, and last—but far from least—there was the reason he was in Vienna: the holy relics that were being stolen all over Europe. The count gazed through the elegant lobby of the five-star hotel, once a bank, and saw Hellen approaching. He was grateful for the distraction. He stood up and walked through what had formerly been the cashier's hall, now transformed into an elegant lobby with a sophisticated interplay of wood, leather, metal and copper that harked back to its banking heyday. Palffy had only gone a few steps when Hellen noticed him.

"Well, how was your vacation, my dear? Did you finally manage to get a little closer to your goal? You're putting all your spare time into that one thing. You need to take a little time for yourself, you know, and get some rest. I'm sure your parents don't like to see you so obsessed," he said. His tone was more conciliatory than accusing.

"My family . . ." Hellen drew a breath. "My mother, in particular, has been wanting to see me standing at a stove, surrounded by children, a dog and a banker husband, for years. Let's leave them out of the conversation, Nikolaus. Besides, you know perfectly well how important this is to me. And not only me. You yourself know what it means—not least for Blue Shield."

Hellen took a seat at a table near the bar and ordered a *Kaisermelange*, coffee fortified with an egg yolk and a shot of cognac. Briefly, she described to the Count what had happened at Glastonbury.

He frowned, thoughtful. "This is not a game anymore. Someone is evidently on the same track as you . . ."

". . . and whoever it is will stop at nothing," Hellen said, completing his sentence.

He was taken aback for a moment, but the scientist and art lover in him quickly returned. "Do you really think you've found a tangible clue at last?"

She sipped at her coffee and allowed the distinctive taste of the Viennese specialty to unfold. "Yes. I'm certain of it. And if I'm interpreting Father Montgomery's last message correctly, I finally know where we need to look. I want to leave as soon as possible."

Hellen shifted nervously in her chair. It was clear how much this meant to her.

Palffy seemed intrigued. "This would truly be a sensation. It would also mean Blue Shield getting a little more attention from UNESCO."

Hellen grinned. "Ah, so my flight of fancy is suddenly interesting."

"Touché. But let's put that aside for now. Our first priority has to be the issue we are currently facing, with all these stolen relics. Blue Shield's primary responsibility might be protecting cultural heritage in war zones, but that does not mean we should close our eyes to current events. The Shroud of Turin clinched it for me. I've had enough."

"What do you want to do?" Hellen was surprised. She had never seen her mentor so resolute.

"At the UNESCO conference today, we have to make it clear that we need a task force dedicated to Blue Shield. If not, we shall never see any of these artifacts and relics again."

Palffy's voice had grown louder. He was so upset that even the waiters were looking at him in surprise.

"A task force? What exactly what do you mean?"

Palffy leaned a little closer to Hellen and lowered his voice again. "I have in mind a unit perfectly equipped for the task at hand—perfect in that it will have both the necessary expertise and also the right technical equipment . . . and the right armaments."

"Armaments?" Hellen's eyes widened.

"My dear, our enemies are not exactly shy and retiring. The international grave-robbing mafia and the dealers who fence art and cultural property are well-armed themselves. These days, we find ourselves dealing with terrorists and teams of mercenaries who earn a great deal of money with treasures that do not belong to them, while we sit and watch and do nothing. We need someone from an elite unit who has been trained to fight."

"I see your point," Hellen said, nodding.

"And then we can finally tackle all those projects that no one will finance for us because they are too 'exotic.' You know what I'm talking about." Palffy was wearing his most mischievous smile now and gave her a wink.

"I certainly do. That legendary leather portfolio you have, stuffed with vanished treasures and artifacts, projects no normal politician or non-profit lobbyist would understand or endorse, let alone actually support," Hellen replied. "My Glastonbury project should probably have a place of honor in that portfolio too," she added, gazing at Palffy steadily.

"I'd be a fool to deny that now, my dear."

"But, as usual, the money is where it will probably fail. It will be very difficult to push through," said Hellen.

"We have to try, and we have to keep trying. Our chances have never been better." Palffy paused for a moment, then went on, "Perhaps I should go with you to Switzerland after all, so you're not traveling alone. You were already in danger in Glastonbury. Your family would never forgive me if something happened to you, too."

"Oh, don't worry. I'll be in no danger there. It's just an art auction, and there'll be hundreds of other people. Nothing can happen. Besides, I've been invited as an official UNESCO expert. You have enough on your plate here," said Hellen.

Palffy nodded thoughtfully. "Maybe you're right." He looked at his antique gold Patek Philippe pocket watch and waved the waiter over. "Please charge all this to my room and have my car brought around." He looked at Hellen. "Time for us to go. We should be at the Hofburg a little early to check out the lay of the land and gather our allies."

14

The boom gate swung open as the patrol car turned into the parking area on Josefsplatz, the plaza to the south of Vienna's Hofburg complex. Guerra and four other men climbed out, all wearing Vienna police uniforms. Guerra opened the trunk and the men took out their weapons. Guerra shouldered a small black sports bag.

The area around the Hofburg was swarming with police, and nobody gave them a second glance. Security had been ratcheted up to the highest level and the authorities were on high alert for the UNESCO conference. One of Guerra's men stayed with the car to make sure the gate to the parking area stayed open; the other four marched to the rear entrance of the Hofburg itself. One stopped at the entrance to the *Redoutensäle*, the Hofburg's magnificent concert and conference halls, while the other two followed Guerra to the chapel courtyard, where the entrance to the Imperial Treasury was also located.

Built over the course of seven hundred years, the complex of buildings making up Vienna's Hofburg sprawls across an area of almost fifty acres, making it the largest building ever built in Europe for non-religious purposes. Some five thousand people live or work there, and together with the adjacent park and public square at Heldenplatz, it attracts twenty million visitors every year.

There were countless ways to enter the Hofburg and even more ways to disappear from one moment to the next in its labyrinthine hallways, with their countless levels, courtyards, corridors, entrances and exits. For the Austrian police, overseeing all of it was routine, but still a major undertaking.

The conference was already underway, and Tom, bored as ever, was standing with several colleagues outside the *Grosser Redoutensaal*, the great hall where the conference was being held. He paced slowly back and forth, his mind still on Guerra and the hijacking. None of it made any sense. Stopping by one of the huge windows, he looked out over Josefsplatz and saw four uniformed police officers cross the plaza in the direction of the Hofburg chapel. It took a moment or two, then it hit him like a thunderbolt. That one looked like . . . Guerra!

Impossible, Tom thought. Three of the men disappeared into the corridor that led to the chapel. Tom snapped into mission mode, grabbing his young colleague Jakob Leitner by the arm and pulling him aside.

"Come with me. We have to check something, fast. I spotted some suspicious activity down below."

The young man looked at Tom, perplexed, but didn't dare contradict him. Tom took the lead and Leitner followed. Tom's mind was racing so quickly that he didn't think to radio in that he was leaving his post. They ran downstairs, Tom hoping desperately that he was wrong.

The man at the Imperial Treasury ticket counter looked up in surprise when three police officers entered in tactical gear, carrying machine pistols. To the left of the ticket desk was a small museum shop where a few tourists were searching for kitschy souvenirs of their visit.

"Security; we need to check the area. There's been a bomb threat against today's conference in the Hofburg," said one of the policemen.

The man behind the desk nodded indifferently and pointed the way to the Treasury. Guerra and his men took the stairs to the second floor and entered the museum area.

"Room II," said Guerra calmly. "There'll be one staff member moving through the exhibition. Unarmed, of course. There are a few cameras, but none actually at the lance."

The three men strode unerringly through the museum. The exhibition seemed almost empty; only a handful of visitors gazed into the cases, and they did not even notice the three men enter.

When Tom and Leitner reached the chapel courtyard, they were met by terrified tourists running toward them.

"Damn," said Tom. "I hate it when I'm right."

15

The sound of an explosion came from outside the conference hall, quickly followed by a second blast that rocked
the interior of the Hofburg and shook the hall violently.
Glasses fell from tables and windowpanes shattered. A
sudden dead silence followed, lasting for several seconds.
Then the main entrance opened and one of the Cobra
officers shouted into the hall.

"There's been an explosion on Josefsplatz and another at
the Imperial Treasury. We are evacuating the hall. Do not
panic. Please leave all your belongings behind and exit
calmly. There are police officers in the lobby who will
lead you safely outside."

"An explosion at the Imperial Treasury?" Hellen looked
at Palffy. "Are you thinking what I'm thinking?"

Palffy nodded. "They're after the Holy Lance. It would be
a perfect fit with the other stolen relics."

"We can't let them take it. We have to do something,"
Hellen said resolutely.

"But what, exactly? The Austrian police are here. They will take care of it," said Palffy.

"As you know, I have some familiarity with the Austrian police myself—unfortunately— and to be honest, it doesn't make me optimistic." Hellen shook her head. "They can't even look after us, let alone the Holy Lance. I have to stop this," she said, and ran downstairs.

Palffy couldn't have stopped her even if he'd wanted to, but the passage that led to the chapel courtyard was badly damaged. Smoke poured from the entrance. There was no way through. Hellen turned and ran in the direction of the plaza at Michaelerplatz, planning to reach the treasury from the Spanish Riding School side.

16

Tom hadn't been to the treasury in years and had no idea what anyone might want to steal from it, but he could vaguely recall that the exhibition had two entrances.

"Tom, we have to wait for backup. There's only two of us and we have no idea how many we're up against." Leitner, a few paces behind, was still young and had not yet been on many assignments. Tom could hear the fear in his voice.

"I counted three of them, and we're not going to sit on our asses and wait. This is what we're trained for. We have no idea what they're after in there, but it doesn't matter. Whatever it is, it's our job to stop them."

Leitner looked desperately at Tom, then summoned up his courage and moved forward to where Tom stood, just outside the exhibition entrance. Around ten yards ahead was the second door, where visitors to the exhibition would exit. A few fearful tourists ran from each door, terrified by the explosion and trying to leave the treasury as quickly as they could.

"They're not after hostages, at least," Tom noted drily.

Another explosion shook the building. This one didn't come from inside the treasury but from the courtyard. Tom narrowed his eyes. "Right. They've got multiple teams. All the more reason to find out what they're after." Tom drew his Glock and Leitner did the same.

Tom opened the door and dashed into the first of the exhibition rooms before he had even finished speaking. The windows were shuttered, darkening the interior to protect the precious garments on display in the cabinets from being bleached by sunlight. Tom stopped and listened. Leitner, behind him, was panting so loudly that Tom had to put a hand on his shoulder.

"Settle down. You're trained for this, well trained. These guys are unlikely to be any more professional than us. We've got this."

Tom, ducking low, sprinted from one exhibition room to the next. The rooms were small and numerous display cases stood on the floor or hung from the walls, each one holding treasures and relics from the Hapsburg era. Tom glanced at a diamond-studded crown.

"Okay, looks like run-of-the-mill theft is out, too. These are some valuable pieces and they didn't even look at them. What the hell are they after?"

Tom heard a sound: a boot crunching on shattered glass. More glass fell to the floor. Someone was breaking into one of the glass cases. Tom and Leitner were halfway through the exhibition rooms now. They saw a frightened museum employee cowering in a corner and pointing.

"They're at the Holy Lance. Room ii," the man whispered.

The Holy Lance. It made sense. Tom could vaguely recall that the Holy Lance, according to the legend, was the weapon the soldiers used to stab Jesus Christ in the side when he was on the cross—apparently another Catholic treasure on the thieves' list.

Tom ran into Room 10 in time to see one of the men leaving on the other side. He crept to the next entrance and cautiously looked around the corner. Nothing. He started. Was that music? His heart was suddenly pounding in his throat. He knew the piece by heart. It was burned into his brain, just as Guerra's tattoo was.

Tom crept on and was just able to duck for cover behind a free-standing exhibition cabinet. One of the men had been lying in wait for him, and a burst from the man's machine pistol poured in Tom's direction. Shards of glass and shreds of the valuable objects in the cabinet flew through the air and rained down on Tom, who returned fire from behind the cabinet.

Tom sneaked a glance around the corner and saw another man, his back to Tom, lifting the Holy Lance from the smashed cabinet and stuffing it into a backpack. When he saw the tattoo on the inside of the man's forearm, Tom had to make an effort to stop himself from breaking cover and running at him.

Apart from the tattoo, Tom was presented with a bizarre scene. Guerra stood a little to one side. In his hand he held a mobile phone that was playing the music Tom had heard just seconds earlier. Guerra had his eyes closed, and was waving his arms in the air like a conductor. Leitner had joined him now. The thieves had what they wanted and turned to go. Tom sprinted after them and threw himself on the man holding the machine pistol. They crashed together into a large display case filled with priceless robes.

Tom's opponent was back on his feet first, and while Tom was still pulling himself up, the man managed to kick the gun out of his hand.

Tom looked the man in the eye: definitely a professional. There was no trace of fear on his face. Lightning-fast, Tom stepped back to the shattered display case which had held the Holy Lance and snatched up the *Kreuzpartikel*, a fragment of the cross on which Jesus had died, now mounted in gold with a metal point at the bottom end. Tom threw it hard at his attacker, and the throw hit its mark, spearing the man's right shoulder. The man cried out, dropped his machine pistol and went down.

"You take care of him. I'll go after the others," Tom shouted to Leitner. He grabbed the gun from the floor and disappeared into the next room.

Guerra and the other guy had a good lead, but they didn't have a lot of exit options and Tom kept after them. Leaving the exhibition, he raced downstairs and looked around. The man at the ticket desk pointed anxiously toward the exit: "That way."

Tom sprinted out into the courtyard and instantly saw the damage done by the explosion they had heard earlier from the treasury. The narrow, covered passageway leading to the *Redoutensäle* and on to the courtyard at Josefsplatz was impassable, covered in rubble. Tom wheeled around and was met by a hail of bullets from yet another machine pistol. He threw himself behind one of the two columns framing the exit to the courtyard, and could only watch as Guerra and his man climbed into the patrol car in which they had arrived. The blue light came on and the car drove away. Tom bolted through the entrance to the next courtyard and saw the car moving in the direction of the Spanish Riding School, scattering crowds of tourists left and right.

Just then, another explosion roared. The archway on Tom's left, leading to Heldenplatz, now stood in flames. A wave of heat knocked him off his feet. He lay on his back, staring into the flames, and was instantly transported back three years.

He was in Jerusalem, working with Mossad to protect the Austrian chancellor. A suicide bomber had targeted the chancellor and the Israeli president. Tom could remember only fragments of the apocalyptic scenes, the screams of the injured, the inferno that followed. The chancellor and the Israeli president were saved—but Noah, who had been with him on the mission, had been less fortunate.

All because I was scared of a wall of flames! Tom mentally screamed at himself.

He gazed at the flames as if hypnotized. He felt as if he'd been turned to stone. For a few seconds he was gripped by a naked fear of the fire, then he jumped to his feet and took up the pursuit.

17

Tom ran as fast as he could after Guerra's car. The tourists who had dodged out of the path of the honking patrol car moments earlier had begun to fill the square again. "Out of the way!" Tom bellowed, barging through. He dashed through the next archway, drawing shocked and frightened looks: a man in a gray suit with a machine pistol in his hand and chasing a police car was not an everyday sight. Tom kept on, running through the enormous, domed vestibule and past the entrance to the Spanish Riding School, and a moment later found himself standing on Michaelerplatz.

He looked around quickly. In the center of the circular plaza, tourists thronged the Roman excavations. He spotted the only vehicle he could commandeer.

Not the best idea you've had, Tom thought, but it would have to do for now. With his Cobra ID in one hand and the pistol in the other, he jumped into the first of the lined-up *fiaker* carriages and shouted, "Follow that police car!" at the confused coachman.

He gestured with the gun to the northeast, toward the pedestrian street called Kohlmarkt, where the car in question was forging a path through the crowds, blue light flashing and horn blaring. The shocked *fiaker* driver hesitantly muttered a few commands in unintelligible Viennese to his horses and, with a snap of the reins, set the coach in motion.

Just then, Hellen climbed into the *fiaker* from the other side. She had spotted Tom jumping into the carriage as she ran from Josefsplatz to Michaelerplatz.

"What the . . . what are you doing here?" was all Tom could say in his amazement.

Hellen glared angrily at him. "It's nice to see you, too. Still, that's just what I'd expect, coming from you."

Tom sensed how his one-time girlfriend had managed to throw him completely off balance in a few seconds, but there was no time for that now.

"It doesn't matter," he said. "We have to follow that car." He was about to say something to the coachman, but Hellen spoke first.

"Did they take the Holy Lance?"

"Yes. Or did you think I was chasing them for kicks? Besides, this is official police business and nothing to do with you. Let me do my job."

Tom's voice was icy. He stared ahead. The car was still making its way through the Kohlmarkt, Vienna's most elegant shopping street, lined with luxury brands like Lagerfeld, Gucci, Armani, and Furla. *God, another pedestrian zone,* Tom thought.

83

"What do you mean, nothing to do with me? You know as well as I do that this is more my job than yours, and in case you hadn't noticed, they're getting away. A *fiaker* is a lousy pursuit vehicle."

The driver nodded enthusiastically.

"Then I'll just take one of the horses." Tom rose to his feet and was about to climb over the front.

Hellen pulled him back down onto the seat. "Tom, you don't know how to ride a horse. I do, and I also know that *fiaker* horses are not used to being ridden. If you get onto one of them, the poor thing will go berserk and you'll end up in a hospital. If it can gallop at all."

The driver nodded enthusiastically again.

"Do you want to ride, then? And what would you do when you caught up with them? Ask them nicely to pull over?" He put on a face. "Oh, by the way, please be so kind as to hand over the lance or my horse will drop a load of apples on your hood."

He did it every time: dragged everything down into the ridiculous. It made her angry. Still, she found herself smiling, at least a little. The coachman raised his hand to say something, but Hellen and Tom were so caught up in their argument that they ignored him completely.

"Do we *have* to discuss this now? You're not Lara Croft. You're a scientific adviser, that's all. This is my business."

The coachman raised his hand again, this time clearing his throat as well.

84

"It's just as much my business as yours. And if I think about it, it's really *more* mine than yours. At Blue Shield, our mission is to safeguard, oversee, and recover historical treasures." Hellen couldn't believe her own words. She sounded like an advertising slogan.

"Well you're not doing such a great job of safeguarding, if the news is anything to go by. Now let me get on with my job."

The coachman had had enough. "Enough! Quit yer squabblin'!" he groused in a thick Viennese dialect, turning back to them, but it still took Tom a few seconds to drag himself away from the quarrel. The driver pointed ahead and rolled his eyes. The patrol car had vanished.

"Oh, terrific. Now we've lost them, thanks to you," Tom snapped at Hellen.

"Me? If you'd jumped on that horse like you were planning to, it would *not* have followed the car. It would probably have trotted back to its stable in Prater park." Now it was Hellen's turn to roll her eyes. She looked up to the coachman. "Can you take me back to Josefsplatz?"

"Why, o' course, ma'am. That'll be 150 euros."

18

The treasury looked like a war zone. In the heat of battle, Tom hadn't noticed the destruction they were causing. He frowned. Hellen had managed to find a way through the chaos, too, and had gotten past the police barricade with her Blue Shield ID.

"Oh, nice work, Tom," Hellen said. "Really. Just your style. Do you have any idea what these masterpieces are worth? Not to mention that most of them are irreplaceable."

Tom said nothing. He went instead to Jakob Leitner, who was standing beside the body of the terrorist Tom had hit with the *Kreuzpartikel*. The terrorist lay on his back, a large shard of glass jutting from his neck.

"You didn't have to kill him. You could have just arrested him," Tom said with a dry smile.

"I didn't kill him. He did that to himself," Leitner said in his own defense.

"What?!"

"It's true. I'd love to have arrested him, but he grabbed that piece of glass and stabbed himself in the neck," Leitner said, still somewhat shocked at what he'd been through.

Tom stepped around the body. The forensics guys were already there, taking photographs and measuring the crime scene. The coroner had also arrived and was prodding at the dead man. Hellen picked her way through the room carefully, looking at the artifacts, obviously upset at the damage done. When the body was ready to be carried away, Tom noted the all-too-familiar symbol tattooed on the dead man's forearm.

On his way outside, the strident voice of his boss suddenly assaulted his ear.

"Are you out of your fucking mind, Wagner?" Captain Maierhofer's face was beet red and the veins in his neck stood out. Tom had seen this coming.

"I get that question a lot," Tom said.

Maierhofer ignored the remark. "Let me give you a quick rundown of the last twenty-four hours," the captain said. "You haven't exactly covered yourself in glory." He raised his hand, index finger extended. "First, you put the lives of hundreds of passengers on an Austrian Air flight at risk, not to mention the people on the ground." Another finger joined the first. "Second, you ignored every regulation we have, just so you could play hero. Again. Do you have any idea what would've happened if your lame-brained idea hadn't come off?"

"But—" Tom tried to interject.

But the captain was just getting started.

"Third, you took a cell phone, which is evidence that should have been handed over at the scene. And you yourself say it's just because you were curious. If you had done what you were supposed to do and handed the thing over to forensics and IT, we might well know far more than we currently do. But no, Mr. Wagner had to take it home with him."

They moved out of the treasury and down the stairway. Every Cobra, every uniformed cop, every forensics officer they passed looked at Tom with scorn, but also a little sympathy.

"And fourth, we would have been spared all this morning's shit, too. Shoot-outs and car chases belong in the movies, not on Kärntner Strasse!" He paused to draw breath. "The priest at the cathedral called the mayor, the mayor called the Chief of Police, and the Chief just tore me a new asshole. And as you can probably imagine, I don't enjoy having myself a new asshole torn at all. That's usually *my* job." He shook his head as if he couldn't believe it himself. "But we're not done yet. Oh, no. You left your post in mid-assignment without calling it in, you didn't wait for backup, and you tried yet again to tackle a situation on your own. In the process, you destroyed half the treasury and used the *Kreuzpartikel* as a fucking throwing knife! Who knows how long it will take the people from the Art History Museum to open the Treasury to the public again."

They had now arrived in the chapel courtyard. Tom had to concede that none of what the captain had mentioned would look good in his file. He'd had better days.

"And just to cap things off, you weren't even able to stop the thieves." Captain Maierhofer planted his hands on his hips and exhaled audibly. "Nice job, Wagner. Brilliant, even by your standards. Piling shit this high in twenty-four hours is an art. Do you have anything to say for yourself?"

"Yes, actually. You're still mispronouncing my name. My father was American, so my family name is pronounced in English: Wagner."

As he finished speaking, it occurred to Tom that his objection didn't do much to improve the situation. The captain seethed.

"That's your only concern? Now? We're in Vienna, and I'll call you 'Vaaahhhhgner' as long as I damn well please. You've spent the last twenty-four hours screwing up one thing after another. I've got the Interior Minister asking me if we're recruiting our Cobras from ISIS terrorist cells these days . . . give me one good reason not to suspend you until the end of the millennium." Captain Maierhofer's voice rang clear across the courtyard.

Hellen, leaving the treasury just then, looked at Tom and the captain in passing, smiled pityingly, shook her head, and exited the courtyard through the Swiss Gate. She immediately pushed any thoughts of Tom out of her mind. She had more important things to do, like pack— her flight was leaving in the morning.

"So you don't think we should follow up this lead?" Tom said. "Let me quickly sum up the facts: the dead thief up there has the same symbol tattooed on his arm as we found on the arm of one of the hijackers. Because of that hijacker's phone, someone chased me through half of Vienna, shooting all the way. The theft of the Holy Lance is connected directly to the theft of all the other holy artifacts all over Europe. Even the Blue Shield people have confirmed that."

"Wagner, *we're* not following up any leads at all! We're Cobra. We're not running around with a hot magnifying glass, investigating clues. We're not Columbo, goddamn it!"

"People are dead. Someone has to investigate."

"And that just has to be you, does it? Tom Wagner, knight in shining armor, charging in on his white horse to save the world from an international conspiracy. All at the expense of the Austrian taxpayer. Let the Italians find their own damn tablecloth! That's about as interesting to me as a wet sponge."

"But, Captain—"

But Maierhofer interrupted him instantly, raising his index finger and holding it to his lips, an unambiguous signal to shut up.

"I'm not even interested in finding out if this obscure terror organization even exists, whether they've developed a group fetish for Catholic loot to go with their matching tattoos, or what. You are taking a vacation. You are letting your bruises heal and taking the time you need to consider your future as a Cobra. I will see you again in two weeks. I've got enough on my plate with the goddamned Atlas mission in Barcelona next week without having to babysit you, too."

Tom thought for a moment about saying something but realized it would be pointless. Captain Maierhofer, drained by his extended tirade, leaned against the wall by the staircase that led to the *Hofmusikkapelle*, the Hofburg choral chapel, and searched his jacket for his cigarettes. He glowered at Tom, waiting for him to finally get out of his sight.

Tom nodded, turned on his heel, and left the courtyard. *First thing I need's a drink*, he thought. *And one probably won't be enough*. He took out his phone and dialed Noah's number.

19

"The summer wind / came blowing in / from across the sea..."

The old woman working behind the bar, mixing an old-fashioned, knew almost every song the pianist played by heart. If she were in a good mood, and if the right guests were in, she might even sing a song or two. The little bar, with its two large aquariums along the wall behind the bar and a handful of small tables, was an insider tip. Smoking was still allowed, there was no official closing time, no register for the tax office, no gadgets to electronically measure the drinks, no selfie takers or influencers, and no five-star rating on Tripadvisor. A good old bar, the kind that was regrettably hard to find these days.

The last verse of the song was very special to the elderly barkeeper. Tom always felt a shiver of excitement run down his spine in that final passage.

The old woman set his drink down beside the piano. Not many people knew that Tom played the piano there at least once a week, working through his favorites from the "Great American Songbook." He had inherited his musical talent from his mother, sitting with her at the piano from the age of four, and had developed quite a talent over the years. He was able to remember music in a few very few people could: melodies, lyrics, arrangements, tempo, rhythm, volume and everything else that mattered. Tom only had to hear a piece once and it stuck in his head, like data on a hard drive. He would spend the evening playing in the bar without once looking at a sheet of music. He loved jazz, blues and the classic American crooners—Frank Sinatra, Tony Bennett, Bobby Darin, Sammy Davis Jr., Dean Martin and Bing Crosby. His mother loved Bach, but for some reason, since her death, he could not play baroque music anymore. It had been erased from his memory, as his mother's life had been.

Tom took a swig of his favorite drink and then launched into "Fly Me to the Moon." At once, the bartender smiled and began to hum along. She only ever hummed the melody to this one out of deference to Sinatra, who had made the song world-famous. Nobody could hold a candle to Sinatra; she knew better than to try. Tom played the song at a slower tempo than usual, giving it a melancholy touch. It suited his mood today.

When the cloakroom attendant opened the door for Noah and his old friend rolled into the bar, Tom's melancholy only grew. He finished the tune, picked up his old-fashioned and went and sat with Noah.

"You still look at me so pityingly. When will you get it into your head that you're not to blame? It's not your fault

I'm in this thing." He slapped the armrests of his wheel-chair with both hands. "If you'd done anything differently back then, chances are we wouldn't be sitting here together today. You'd be a pile of ashes."

"Yeah, I know, I know. My head knows it, but my heart still has to figure it out. A guilty conscience is awfully hard to switch off. I still feel like I screwed up, and screwed over my best friend."

Noah shook his head, his lips thin with annoyance.

"You know what you need, Tom? Something that fulfills you. You need a purpose in life, a reason to get up in the morning. You go around and around in circles, but you never get anywhere. Your parents' death, the thing with Hellen, the mission we were on, your guilty conscience, your pyrophobia . . ."

"I don't have pyrophobia, for Christ's sake!" Tom had raised his voice, but none of the guests took any notice. No one turned around or took offense at his outburst of emotion. It was a real bar, and in a real bar the patrons minded their own business.

Noah raised his hands placatingly. "Okay, fine. Then let's just talk about your last twenty-four hours. Like I said, I know that symbol from somewhere, I just can't think from where. And so far, none of the databases has turned up anything useful."

"Guerra was in the treasury today. He and his men stole the lance, and probably the rest of the relics."

Noah's eyebrows knotted. "Seriously? Okay, then let's call a war council and see where we go from here. I'll dive back into the databases and look for that symbol."

"A war council won't help. For now, I'm on a leave of absence. I'm lucky Maierhofer didn't suspend me. But you're probably right. I have to change something. I'm never going to be happy with what I'm doing here. I think I need a little time to myself."

"Let's have another drink and you can get your frustrations off your chest. Nobody's waiting for you at home," said Noah.

The bartender brought fresh drinks to their table, and they lifted their glasses and drank in silence. A few minutes passed without a word passing between them. Not that they had nothing to say to each other, but they felt no need to talk all the time. They appreciated that about each other. Apparently, Tom was in no mood to get anything off his chest.

After a while he got up and sat at the piano again. Noah was surprised when Tom started to play the old Bobby Darin hit "The Good Life." The bartender instantly joined him at the piano, leaned against it coyly and began to sing.

"It's the good life ..."

Tom stopped playing instantly.

"Fuck, I completely forgot!" he exclaimed.

Noah and the barwoman looked at him in astonishment as he jumped up from the piano and almost ran back to the table. He leaned in close to Noah.

"Cloutard. François Cloutard," he said in a low voice. "The hijacker in the toilet said the name several times."

"How do you know what the hijacker said when he was on the toilet?" Noah asked. But he quickly said, "No, wait, I don't want to know."

"Does the name mean anything to you?"

"Sure. François Cloutard: international art smuggler, thief, fence and God knows what else. He runs an army of grave robbers and a global smuggling ring. There's hardly an art heist the guy hasn't had his fingers in, and he's damn good at it. There's a file on him like a telephone book, but nobody's ever been able to pin anything on him. It's like he's untouchable."

"That would fit the picture. Art thief and smuggler. In our circles, you'd call that a lead."

"I thought you were on vacation?" said Noah, irritated.

"Not if I have a chance to get my hands on Guerra. Can you find out where Cloutard is?"

"That shouldn't be too hard. But let's have another round. Tonight's my last chance to let myself go a little. Starting tomorrow, the pressure's really on."

"Oh yeah, the Atlas assignment? Maierhofer said something. That's a crazy idea, isn't it? All the European antiterror units working together. Would it work?"

Noah shook his head. "Never in a million years. We'd all be stepping on each other's toes. You're lucky you don't have to be there." Noah sipped his whiskey sour and decided it was going to be a long evening.

20

The taxi pulled up and Tom pushed a few bills into the driver's hand, not really paying attention to how much it was.

"Thankssshh," Tom slurred. His first steps outside the taxi told him he'd really had a few too many. The fresh air magnified the effect of the alcohol considerably; negotiating the gangplank to the houseboat door was a real challenge.

He fished the key from his trouser pocket, but it took him a few tries to get it into the keyhole. He smiled, not being too hard on himself.

"Winner!" he cried triumphantly when he finally managed to get the key into the lock.

But the door was not locked. He hesitated for a second, but then remembered that he'd told Denise just to close the door behind her. So much had happened that day that he'd completely forgotten about her. The pursuit with the BMW, the shooting, the crash at

Stephansplatz, Guerra and the theft of the lance, Hellen and his own near-suspension. All of it had made him forget his little tête-à-tête with the flight attendant.

The evening with Noah had rejuvenated him. He saw clearly now that he needed a change in his life. He was actually glad to be on vacation: he could use the next few days to think about where he should go from here, though he already knew he would probably go looking for Cloutard, wherever he was. He was even happier that his reunion with Hellen had been short-lived, and that she had disappeared out of his life again.

Tom stumbled inside and groped for the switch, but when the light came on, his heart skipped a beat. It took him a few seconds to properly take in, interpret and process the scene in front of him. From one moment to the next he was stone-cold sober—the torrent of adrenaline his body produced made sure of that.

Denise lay in his bed. On her back. Naked. Her arms and legs were stretched out and tied to the corners of the bed, and from her chest jutted—Tom had to blink to be sure —the Holy Lance. An enormous pool of blood had spread across the bed.

Tom stood as if rooted to the spot. Blood roared in his ears. Outside, the water splashed rhythmically against the hull of the houseboat. The sound of his cell phone ringing broke the silence. It was Noah. No sooner had Tom picked up than Noah started babbling.

"Tom, no idea what's going on, but there are patrol cars heading your way right now. Someone called in an anonymous tip, something about you, your houseboat, and a murder. Does that make any sense to you?"

"Unfortunately, yes. The flight attendant from last night is lying on my bed with the Holy Lance stuck in her chest."

"Tom, something's up. Interpol has put out a BOLO on you already, much faster than usual. They say you're a flight risk, and that you're 'armed and dangerous.' No idea who signed off on this internally, but the wheels aren't turning as slowly as usual. Someone's out to get you."

Noah sounded nervous. He didn't usually speak so rapidly.

"It's all tied to Guerra," Tom said. "Since I saw him in Milan, my whole world's been turned upside down. I'm not going to stand around and let them arrest me now. I've got to find out what's going on."

"Yeah, and you're the right guy to do it. I know where Cloutard is. He's on the guest list at an exclusive art auction tomorrow night at Waldegg Castle in Switzerland. Joan of Arc's shield is going under the hammer. Grab your go-bag and get out of there. I've just booked you a ticket on your fake passport."

Noah had switched to battle mode. This was how Tom knew and loved his old friend. He could always count on him.

"There'll be an Uber at your place in one minute to take you to the airport. Your plane to Zurich leaves in the morning, early. I've called in a couple of favors. When you land tomorrow, there'll be a bag in a locker at the airport with some gear for you. I'll send you the locker number and the code ASAP."

Tom was impressed. "Thanks, bud."

"Don't mention it. Now I want to know what's going on as much as you do. No one jerks us around. Good luck," Noah said, and hung up.

A car pulled up just then, and Tom jumped in. The police were on their way to Tom's houseboat, their blue lights flashing and sirens sounding, but they would be too late.

21

Tom was dog-tired. After several hours spent successfully avoiding a run-in with the cops at Vienna airport, he had taken the morning flight to Zurich. Once again, he had not slept for hours. The jet lag and sleep deprivation he'd been dragging behind him since Acapulco were starting to wear him down. He had to pull himself together; he couldn't afford any mistakes now. Get out of the airport as fast as possible, get to a hotel, get some sleep. In the evening, at the auction, he had to be in top form.

"Grüezi," Tom said to the visibly overweight man at the information desk.

The Swiss greeting was completely off the mark, though, and the man just gave him a friendly smile and replied in perfect, accent-free standard German, "What can I do for you?"

"Where can I find the lockers?" Tom asked.

The man at the counter quickly explained, and Tom set off in the direction the man had indicated. He crossed the arrivals hall, doing his best to avoid the countless cameras. Moving through a modern airport was like running a gauntlet. He took detours, turned away at just the right moments, and tried to use other passengers for cover. After what felt like an eternity, he arrived at the lockers. He found the message from Noah on his phone and typed in the six-digit code. The door beeped and opened with a click.

Tom withdrew a black leather travel bag and placed it on the floor. He knelt down and opened it to briefly check the contents. A Glock G19C Gen4, with laser sight, holster and spare magazines. The invitation to the auction and a USB stick with information were in the bag as well, along with the outfit he would need: a dark gray Armani pinstripe suit, complete with shirt, shoes and tie. He dug deeper and found a laptop and a disposable cell phone—he would have to get rid of his old one to prevent anyone from tracking him. As always, Noah had his best interests in mind. Tom was always amazed at what he could pull together in a few short hours, and how far his contacts stretched.

Tom didn't know what to expect that night, but he knew one thing: since the previous day, he'd been dealing with men who shot first and asked questions later. He needed to sleep as soon as he could, so that his head would be clear later on. With the rental car formalities behind him, Tom roared off in a dark-blue BMW X6 toward the town of Solothurn, where Waldegg Castle was located. Noah had reserved a room for Tom in "La Couronne," a historic, four-star boutique hotel in the old part of town.

22

Even the approach to Waldegg Castle was impressive. The edifice was illuminated by countless floodlights set into the ground, and even while driving the third of a mile along the avenue leading straight to the castle, one could almost smell the grandeur. Visitors in tuxedos, dinner jackets and one-of-a-kind couture gowns already thronged the spacious twin stone staircases that arched to the left and right beyond the wrought-iron gates, over the small baroque garden and up to the castle's main entrance. The entire event practically dripped with old-money aristocracy and the sparkle of the nouveau riche.

Tom pulled up in front of the black gates and climbed out. A young valet in a red jacket instantly jumped into the BMW, and Tom watched as the young man drove off in his car toward the back of the grounds. He slipped the ticket into his pocket and walked along the gravel path, through the perfectly symmetrical baroque garden and past six white obelisks, toward the entrance. He paused. At the door were two security guards who looked to be the equal of any US Secret Service agent. Tom immediately noted the bulges at their armpits where they carried their pistols. They wore bulletproof vests and headsets, and metal detectors had been set up at the entrance. No expense had been spared. The super-rich guests and the nearly priceless exhibits were ample justification for the security.

Trying to get inside with his handgun was out of the question. Annoyed, he found his way to the parking lot at the back of the property. With his spare key he opened the BMW, which the valet had parked between an Aston Martin DBS and a Bentley Continental GT. Tom mouthed a silent "Wow!" at the sight of the luxury autos.

Returning to the entrance, Tom risked a look through the expansive windows into the banquet hall. He heard soft music, the clinking of glasses and the incomprehensible chatter of a crowd, which always reminded him of a goose farm.

He spotted his target, François Cloutard, who was clearly enjoying himself immensely. Tom recognized him right away; Noah had placed the man's entire file on the USB stick, and Tom had studied it carefully in the hotel. Cloutard was an eccentric Frenchman, neat and dapper in a three-piece suit, a glass of cognac in his hand. On one side of Cloutard stood a short, balding man; a stunningly beautiful, dark-skinned woman clasped his elbow on the other. Both were talking to someone Tom could not see from where he stood. A waitress came, bearing a tray of champagne glasses and a bottle of cognac. Cloutard replenished his own glass first, then distributed the glasses of champagne to the group. He passed a glass to the balding man, then to his beautiful companion, and then . . . Tom couldn't believe his eyes. Cloutard handed a glass of champagne to Hellen, who was chatting brightly with him, laughing and joking.

Hellen and Cloutard? Things were getting stranger and stranger. What was Hellen doing here? Why was she talking to his target, an art smuggler and a thief? Hellen and Tom had once been very close, but had since become estranged. He had tried to forget her—or rather, he had worked hard to become indifferent to her. Not an easy task, and the sight of her still stirred the old emotions, even after all this time. He thought he knew her well: she was ambitious, and was certainly willing to go to great lengths to advance her career. But associating with a criminal? Especially one who apparently had his fingers in some very big, very dark undertakings?

Okay, Wagner, take a deep breath and stay cool. You can't afford sentimentality or misplaced emotion now.

Tom took the invitation from his jacket pocket and handed it to the woman at the entrance. She scanned the ticket, checking its authenticity. One couldn't simply walk in here just like that. She nodded and gave him a friendly smile.

"Welcome! Good luck, and I hope you enjoy the auction tonight," she said.

Tom stepped past the two beefy security guards and into the castle. An attractive waitress appeared instantly and offered him a glass of champagne. Just as well, too: he definitely needed a drink. The fizzy stuff was by no means his drink of choice, but it was better than nothing. He knocked it back in a single gulp, and set the glass back on the next waitress's tray as she scurried past. Then he noticed Cloutard and his little band departing from the hall. Tom pushed his way through the throng of guests and followed. Leaving the banquet hall, he saw the group ahead of him, entering a room at the end of the hallway. He knew hanging back and observing would not get him anywhere; he had to tackle this head on. He was already curious about how Hellen would react.

Tom walked confidently toward the room, pushed open the door and breezed inside. He scanned the room first, then the people inside. The walls were covered from floor to ceiling with bookshelves. Only a fireplace and the painting hanging above it interrupted the ranks of books. In the center of the room stood an antique billiard table. Almost everyone in the room was staring at Tom. Hellen's eyes met his. She raised her eyebrows in surprise, but quickly regained her composure.

François Cloutard had started a round of carom billiards, a form of the game that dated back to the French Revolution. The game was played with one red ball and two cue balls, white and yellow. The table had no holes at all; the aim was to hit the red ball and the other cue ball with one's own cue ball—it sounded relatively simple, but it wasn't. Cloutard was playing the more difficult three-cushion billiards, in which the player's own cue ball had to strike at least three rails before striking another ball in order to score a point.

When Tom entered the room, Cloutard's white ball was rolling to a stop. It missed the yellow ball by a hair.

Cloutard pulled a face, but remained composed. Only now did he look up and notice Tom.

"No way that was going to work," Tom said, unable to restrain himself. "The white ball had far too much spin."

Cloutard leaned his cue against the wall and went to the fireplace, where a bottle of Hennessy Louis XIII stood. He filled his cognac glass a quarter full, then swirled the glass slowly and warmed the amber liquid with his hands before lifting it slowly to his mouth. He briefly inhaled the intense aroma, took a mouthful of the $2,500-a-bottle cognac and began literally to chew on it. Anyone else would have probably made the whole process look affected and arrogant, but it suited Cloutard. The Frenchman was wearing a gray, three-piece, chalk-stripe suit by Christian Dior; his graying hair was slicked back, but did not look oily. When not holding a brandy glass, he carried a walking stick with an ivory handle. Whether ivory was politically correct or not was irrelevant to him; he also owned a few fur coats. Cloutard looked at Tom and took his time answering. Apparently, he wanted no banalities to interfere with the pleasure of the Louis XIII.

"The virtuous man is restrained in word but peerless in deed," Cloutard said coolly, and gestured invitingly to Tom. Hellen mentally rolled her eyes, but let nothing show.

Tom was already choosing a cue and taking a closer look at the table. He swept his hand over the green felt surface and tested the cushions. He studied the positions of the balls, then leaned over the table and played the yellow ball. It grazed the red, then bounced off the end cushion once and the long side cushions twice before just touching the yellow and coming to a stop in an ideal position for the next shot. Tom moved around to the end of the table. He did not think for long. His favorite shot was a backspin: he struck the white ball well below center, giving it a reverse spin. As soon as it touched one of the other balls, it spun in the reverse direction, bumped two cushions in the corner and the other long side, and finally rolled directly toward the yellow ball.

"What is a man with such talent doing at an art auction? Shouldn't you be off winning money in smoky cafés?" said Cloutard sarcastically. "With whom do I have the pleasure of playing?"

"Dr. Thomas Pfeiffer's the name. I'm a *sensal* from Vienna."

"A *sensal*?" Cloutard asked rhetorically. He knew perfectly well what a *sensal* was.

"Yes. It's an old Austrian expression for a proxy; I bid at auctions on behalf of anonymous buyers, and act as a broker between the buyer and the auction house. I've been commissioned by a collector to buy Joan of Arc's shield," said Tom, and he grinned broadly. "And I have a considerable budget to do it with."

Hellen's eyes widened and she shook her head almost imperceptibly. Once again, it became clear to her why a relationship with Tom could never work. Not only was he unpredictable, he was reckless. What was he doing here? Didn't he have enough problems to deal with in Vienna? Of all the places he might show up, why here? Was he following her? Or following a lead? She had to find out as quickly as she could.

"Then we are in the same field. I, too, deal in beautiful objects, on occasion also on behalf of a third party." Cloutard paused and glanced at his two companions. "And I assure you that you will not win the shield." He downed the last mouthful of his cognac before introducing himself: "François Cloutard, art collector." He paused momentarily and then indicated his companions one by one. "Allow me to introduce Karim Shaham, my right-hand man, Dr. Hellen de Mey, a scientific expert with UNESCO who is here to authenticate the shield, and Ossana, the love of my life." Cloutard pressed Ossana to his side and kissed her on the cheek. She giggled.

Tom nodded to each of them in turn. Hellen smiled painfully when Cloutard introduced her, then quickly turned away. Inscrutability was not her strong suit. Tom, on the other hand, was a natural.

"UNESCO? Wow. We are in very good company indeed."

Tom realized that Ossana was staring at him fixedly. Her gaze surprised him. He didn't know how to read it, although it seemed to contain a trace of lechery. Her eyes never leaving Tom, she whispered something in Cloutard's ear and tapped her Breguet watch.

"You will have to excuse me," Cloutard said. "One of the lots I am interested in will soon be going under the hammer. Alas, we don't have time for a proper game. I would gladly have challenged you, perhaps with a little wager to spice things up. It looks as if we will have to settle things in the auction room instead." Cloutard's right eyebrow twitched twice and he looked at Tom with a mischievous smile. "We're not here for our own enjoyment, after all."

Cloutard kissed Hellen's hand, nodded a farewell to Tom, took his walking stick and left the library, with Ossana at his side and Shaham trailing behind.

Hellen waited a few seconds until she was sure the others were out of earshot. Then she turned and snapped at Tom, "What the hell are you doing here?"

"I could ask you the same. Cloutard's my target. What's your interest in the guy?"

"I'm here with Blue Shield. But what does that mean, your 'target'? You're a Cobra officer. You have no business being in Switzerland," she hissed. "Why don't you just admit this is more of your unauthorized bullshit?"

"What if it is? Either way, it's nothing to do with you. But if you must know, Cloutard's name was mentioned by one of the airplane hijackers, and it's the only lead I have to clear myself of murder."

"Murder?" said Hellen, shocked.

Tom hesitated for a moment. "A woman was found dead in my bed." He considered whether that information in itself would be enough, but then went on, "A flight attendant from the plane. You know how it is."

Reluctantly, bit by bit, he told her the grim details. "She was stabbed." Hellen's eyes widened. "With the Holy Lance. I don't have the slightest idea who was behind it or what any of it has to do with me."

"What was a flight attendant doing in your bed?" But Hellen raised her hands to stop Tom before he could reply. "No. Don't tell me. I don't want to know."

Hellen was the only woman Tom had ever really been in love with. Unfortunately, conflict and passion had tipped more and more out of balance, and drama had soon gained the upper hand. They were two fundamentally different people, and there were too many ways that they simply didn't fit together. After the separation, he had sworn never again to let anyone else get as close to him as Hellen had. All this love stuff was too confusing. And now that Hellen had discovered that he had had a one-night stand with a flight attendant, the fact embarrassed him. He cursed himself for the feelings that Hellen wakened in him, time and again. From outside, they heard the voice of the auctioneer announcing the last item to go on the block.

"Where did you get the insane idea to pose as a *sensal* and say you wanted to buy the shield?"

Tom only smiled and shrugged. "I've always wanted to bid at an auction. You know, wave a paddle around and look cool while you throw a fortune out the window on useless junk." Tom gestured as if placing a bid.

Hellen looked at Tom and shook her head. She was about to say something, then thought better of it. "I have neither the time nor the nerves to continue this discussion right now," she finally said. She left Tom standing in the library and exited in the direction of the auction room.

23

Guerra kicked in the door of the old farmhouse and three men followed him inside. He looked around. An old man came down the stairs from the second floor and looked at Guerra in fright. It was as far as he got. A bullet from Guerra's Heckler & Koch killed him instantly.

"Check the rest of the house. Make sure it's clean."

One of the other three mercenaries, Scarface, ran upstairs. Another checked the ground floor. Moments later, both called back, "Clear."

"Good. You, outside," Guerra commanded the third man. "I don't want any unpleasant surprises or anyone disturbing us. If someone shows up, liquidate them."

Guerra reached into his jacket pocket and took out his Bluetooth speaker. Seconds later, Telemann's "Admiralty Music" filled the room. Guerra closed his eyes and let the music work on him. His eyes still closed, he pointed at the sniper just then opening a case and assembling the rifle parts it contained.

"You know what to do."

The other man dutifully nodded, aware that Guerra couldn't see him doing so. Guerra opened his eyes and briefly peered through the sniper's scope to see for himself the situation inside the castle for himself. And there they were: Cloutard, Ossana, Dr. de Mey and . . . the Cobra guy who'd already rained on his parade several times. How the hell did Wagner get out of Vienna?

"Our informant was right. She's really there. Still, there's one more slight change of plan." Guerra's sonorous voice sent shudders through his companions.

The overture of the "Admiralty Music" concluded, and Guerra left the house and calmly set off in the direction of the castle. Scarface and the other man accompanied him, staying a few paces behind. Telemann's music readied him for the events ahead, gave him the composure he needed. Detailed planning was important. Mistakes and inefficiency would not be tolerated.

Still, he loved it when opportunities presented themselves. The two unexpected guests made things more exciting. Adrenalin coursed through his veins as he mentally ran through the steps of the operation yet again. He had not planned on Wagner and his little girlfriend being at the auction, but it suited him perfectly, and he would reach his goal even faster than planned. His two companions were prepared, and Guerra was *always* ready.

24

Tom followed Hellen into the auction room, a spacious room off the banquet hall.

"Do you actually know who you're dealing with?"

"Of course I do," Hellen replied, cool.

"Cloutard is not just some affected Frenchman who can't play billiards. He runs probably the biggest smuggling and fencing ring for art and artifacts in the world. Officially, he's an art dealer, and he's been in business for years. But there's hardly an illicit deal in the arts and antiquities field anywhere in the world that he's not involved in. His network is huge. He's got grave robbers, professional burglars, smugglers, middlemen, and probably hundreds of museum and auction-house employees on his books. He keeps a small fleet of vehicles on land, sea and air. All kinds of organizations have been trying to put a stop to him for years, because he robs the art market of hundreds of millions of dollars every year. The guy is seriously dangerous."

Hellen stopped and glared at Tom. "Now you listen to me, Mr. Thomas Maria Wagner. I happen to be the lead archaeologist at Blue Shield. I know all that. Who the hell are you? My guardian?"

Tom hated it when she used his middle name, even more when she deliberately mispronounced "Wagner." It drove him up the wall, and she knew it.

Hellen gave up trying to have a reasonable conversation with him. "Just keep your head down for the rest of the evening. We don't need Cloutard's attention at all."

"Yes, ma'am!" Tom clicked his heels together and saluted Hellen. "Okay, I'll get a grip on myself. Maybe it's good that we've ruffled Cloutard's feathers, whatever he has to do with all this."

She hated it when he maneuvered himself and others into a perilous situation, but he was like a cat; he had nine lives. And she had to admit one thing: most of the time, his plans worked out. Most of the time, but not always.

"Let's find a seat at the back." Tom pointed to some free chairs in the second-to-last row. "The shield is up next."

Tom grabbed a glass of champagne from a waitress by the door, and they edged along the row. The room had now filled considerably, and the atmosphere was tense. Tom could literally feel the energy in the hall when the auctioneer finally called for the last exhibit to be brought out. The man peered over his reading glasses, surveying the room. *Probably checking out who's present and figuring out the commission he'll make on the sale*, Tom thought. The auctioneer smiled and straightened up a little, clearly enjoying himself.

"We now come to the highlight of the evening, a unique piece of history: the shield used by Saint Joan of Arc herself in her battles." The auctioneer let out a respectful cough. "According to legend, the shield has magical powers. It is said to have saved Joan countless times from certain death, including in the legendary Battle of Orleans against the English in the Hundred Years' War. Despite the battles it has seen, the shield is in excellent condition, and its authenticity has been confirmed by a number of scientific experts, one of whom is with us this evening: Dr. Hellen de Mey of UNESCO."

The auctioneer pointed to Hellen, who smiled mildly and half-heartedly raised her hand. There was restrained applause when two security men wearing white cloth gloves carried the shield onto the stage and placed it onto a specially prepared stand. They positioned themselves to the left and right of the shield, and the hall fell quiet. All eyes were on the auctioneer.

"We are opening the bidding at one million euros."

Cloutard was the first to raise his hand.

"We have our first bid. Thank you, Monsieur," the auctioneer said, indicating Cloutard. "Do I hear 1.2?"

"That was fast," Tom whispered.

"Yes. Strange. Cloutard is rarely at an auction to buy. He prefers to sell. First steal, then sell."

She had not yet finished the sentence when she saw Tom raise his hand.

"Thank you, we are at 1.2 million euros!"

Hellen was stunned. "Are you out of your mind?"

Tom lowered his hand and looked at Hellen placidly.

"Let's find out just how interested Monsieur Cloutard is in this shield."

Tom and Hellen saw hands go up in various rows, and the price rose quickly to two million euros. The last bid was Cloutard's. Tom's hand went up again while he looked at Hellen with a broad grin.

"There's more coming. Cloutard *has* to buy it. I don't know why, but he does. He hasn't shown any interest in any of the other items, but when he saw the shield, he instantly bid over everyone else."

"You're mad." Hellen turned demonstratively away from Tom. "There is simply no other way to describe it. You are insane. Completely mental. Bonkers. Out of your gourd."

Hellen was clearly struggling to keep her composure, but her words had drawn looks—two or three of the other guests had already turned around and glared at her reprovingly. Tom glanced ahead at Cloutard, who was looking back just then to see who had outbid him. He smiled graciously, then leaned over to Ossana, pointed in Tom's direction and whispered something in her ear. She smiled. Tom's confident grin didn't budge.

"The bidding stands at 2.5 million euros." The auctioneer paused. "Do I hear more?"

The auctioneer's gaze wandered slowly across the gathered guests. Everyone sensed that the last word had not yet been spoken. It was so quiet that the ticking of the large grandfather clock out in the foyer could be heard, even in the auction room. It sounded like a countdown, ratcheting up the tension even more. Tom was positive: Cloutard had to buy, either for himself or for a client, and Tom meant to find out one way or another. Hellen turned back to Tom and looked at him combatively. She took a deep breath. Tom knew what was coming. He knew from their past only too well where these situations went. A tirade of reproaches and accusations was building up inside Hellen, and the volcano would soon erupt. To his shame, he had to confess that most of Hellen's accusations were true and fully justified. Like today.

"You're the most irresponsible person I know," she hissed. "You're impulsive and you never think even a single step ahead. You charge in like an angry bull. You always listen to your gut, and never to your brain!"

Her words stung him. She was whispering, but her voice had an intensity and power that amazed Tom. He had never seen Hellen in such a rage.

"You know, I used to hope that one day I'd see one of your impetuous, naïve, stupid decisions backfires."

Tom sipped at his champagne and watched Hellen as she struggled for composure. Her face had flushed red and she fidgeted nervously in her seat. She couldn't help herself. She had to express her agitation with her hands and feet.

"And I guess today's the day," she seethed. "Congratulations, Tom. Great job!"

"Thank you. We are at three million euros," the auctioneer said and pointed in their direction. "Even UNESCO is interested in this exhibit, which naturally honors us very much," said the auctioneer, looking at Hellen.

Tom's heart skipped a beat. His mouth hung open. He was speechless. He stared wide-eyed at Hellen. But what he was feeling was probably nothing compared to the turmoil that must have been raging inside Hellen just then. While berating Tom, Hellen had gesticulated a little too wildly, and the auctioneer had interpreted it as a bid.

Everyone in the room held their breath. You could hear a pin drop. Or perhaps it was Hellen's heart, which had abruptly sunk into her belly. She knew the auction rules, and knew there was nothing she could do about it. Tom could only watch as her stomach clenched and tiny beads of sweat appeared on her forehead. And Cloutard seemed to have no intention of outbidding her. He knew that neither Blue Shield nor UNESCO had set aside the money to buy this exhibit, and he was reveling in the knowledge. He put aside his bidding paddle—a clear sign that he was abandoning Hellen to the consequences of her unintended gesture.

"The bid stands at three million euros. Do I hear 3.5 million for this unique piece of human history? The shield of St. Joan of Arc is a one-of-a-kind medieval Christian relic, unearthed only recently, and its authenticity has been confirmed by a number of analyses. Its value is sure to increase dramatically in coming years. And UNESCO itself is showing an interest in the exhibit."

The auctioneer intended to stretch the proceedings out as far as possible, looking to milk whatever he could from it.

"Do I hear 3.5 million euros?"

He looked across the room. No one moved. It was deathly quiet. No one dared to make a sound, or even to fidget in their seat. The entire room looked as if someone had pressed the pause button during a film. Cloutard gazed steadily back at Hellen and made no move to place another bid.

"The bid stands at three million euros," the auctioneer repeated.

Hellen's heart was pounding. Her eyes were as wide as they could get, and she could already start thinking about how she would explain this to Count Palffy and her superiors at Blue Shield and UNESCO.

"Three million going once."

There was another long pause. Tom looked at Hellen in horror. Hellen looked at Tom in horror. Cloutard's grin had transformed almost into a grimace.

"Three million going twice."

Against her will, Hellen instinctively reached for Tom's hand and squeezed it so hard it almost hurt.

"Three million euros . . ."

The auctioneer slowly raised his gavel. Hellen closed her eyes and waited for the hammer to fall, the sound that would seal her fate and end her career. But it didn't come. Instead, she and everyone else in the room heard the shattering of glass, like an explosion in the dead silence, as a windowpane at the back of the room disintegrated into a thousand pieces.

25

VLORA, ALBANIA

Their arduous fourteen-hour journey through Bulgaria, Macedonia and Albania at an end, the three men stopped a few miles outside the Albanian port city of Vlora. They got out, climbed onto the bed of the truck and began dismantling the plates that made up the floor of the cargo area. In a few minutes, the results of their efforts came into view.

An open space had appeared, into which the crate they were transporting fitted perfectly. The men lowered the box into the cavity and replaced the planks and panels. In minutes, everything was reassembled and the crate was all but undetectable, hidden beneath the bed of the truck.

They left the traffic circle marking the entrance to the city and drove on a quarter of a mile to a warehouse, where they picked up cargo to serve as camouflage and loaded it onto the truck: worthless, nondescript junk, in many different boxes with many different freight documents, meaning a lot of paperwork for customs to wade through.

More envelopes containing hundred-dollar bills had also been left for them, just in case an Italian customs officer in Brindisi decided to take his job too seriously. A ticket on the ferry from Vlora to Brindisi had been booked for them days earlier.

They arrived at the port and saw the utter chaos that would simplify their plans. With its pleasant Mediterranean climate, Vlora had been one of southern Albania's tourist centers for years. At the harbor there were already countless cars, trucks, campers and containers standing around. The ferry would be more than full, a good starting point. They drove the truck to its allotted place on the ferry and made sure that nobody came too close, then decided a little rest was called for. The crossing to Italy would take six hours.

26

The auctioneer stumbled back a step and dropped his gavel to the ground. A small, red bullet hole flared in the center of his forehead. He keeled over backward, stiff as a block of wood. For a brief moment, everyone in the room sat as if paralyzed. Then panic swept the room.

Tom looked at Hellen. "Looks like you get off with a slap on the wrist again."

His last words were drowned out by machine gun fire. The entire hall was on its feet within seconds: chairs toppled and people jumped up, screaming and pushing for the exit.

The guards at the entrance have probably been taken out already, thought Tom. He and Hellen had also left their chairs behind and found some cover. He saw Ossana exchanging a few words with Cloutard, then she jumped onto the stage and, with frightening precision, took out the two security guards flanking the shield: her true target.

"She's after the shield!" Tom shouted to Hellen, who was struggling to make her way through the chaos of people and fallen chairs.

Guerra and his two men, wearing full-face masks, had trouble making headway through the mob streaming for the exits, but with raw, ruthless violence they soon found themselves standing in the middle of the hall. Then they spotted their target.

None of the guests cared that they were pushing and trampling others in their panic to escape; everyone just wanted to get out. Guerra knew what he wanted, too.

"Get her," he ordered his men. Without a second's hesitation, his two companions stomped off, grabbed Hellen and dragged her out of the hall.

Tom, meanwhile, had reached the stage. Ossana was at the shield, turned away from him. He shoved her aside. Catlike, she exploited his thrust, using the momentum to her own advantage. Her lightning-fast reaction impressed Tom, even as she aimed a blow at his neck. At the last second, he was able to partially block it with his forearm, but he knew that if he hadn't parried, the strike would have knocked him out. Ossana looked at him and a smile appeared on her face. There it was again, that look—a mixture of hostility and admiration, even desire. Tom couldn't deal with that now, nor did he want to. He cursed all the tedious Cobra missions: now, in direct combat, he realized how rusty he'd become. This woman would beat him senseless if he didn't get his act together immediately. Tom faked a left, but Ossana didn't fall for it and saw the right hand coming. Still, he managed to throw her off balance, at least a little.

"Dr. Pfeiffer, you surprise me," Ossana said. "Did they teach you that at your *sensal* school?" Tom saw excitement in her eyes. They faced off in classic martial arts style.

"Karate summer camp and junior state champion," he countered quickly and relaxed his stance a little. *Have I blown my cover?* he thought. The "summer camp" part was true, but it had been with the IDF, the Israeli Defense Forces, and his Krav Maga trainer had given him an excellent score.

"Help!" Tom suddenly heard.

He turned to see three men dragging Hellen toward the exit. One had taken his hand off Hellen's mouth for a moment, and she had used the opportunity to cry out. He left Ossana on the stage, jumped down and ran after the three men taking Hellen.

Ossana, obviously disappointed that the exhilarating duel she had anticipated had been interrupted, turned her attention to her original goal. She grabbed the shield and, seconds later, leaped through one of the French doors that had been opened as an escape route and into the garden.

Tom's confusion was growing. What the hell was going on? What was this all about? The artifacts? Or Hellen? And if they were after Hellen, then why? All these thoughts ran through his head as he ran to pursue them. He saw the kidnapper pressing a gun to Hellen's head. She had stopped fighting back. Tom fought his way through the crowd, but he was too late. When he made it out of the castle through the main entrance, he saw a black SUV, into which Hellen had already been bundled. The SUV swung into the avenue at full throttle, spitting gravel in all directions, and Tom lost sight of the car just a few moments later.

27

Tom's mind was racing. The police would be there in a few minutes. The Interpol warrant on him was already out—he couldn't afford to be arrested here in Switzerland and shipped back to Austria. He had to get out of there fast; he could forget about going after the SUV. His BMW was parked at the back of the castle and the kidnappers had fled in the opposite direction.

He ran to the right, along the front of the castle, then turned right again, sprinting past an outbuilding and across the rear garden to the parking lot. Panic-stricken guests were scattered all around the estate. Tom ran to his car, fishing in his pocket for the key as he ran. He could see the chunky BMW from a distance—it practically towered over the Aston Martins, Lamborghinis and Ferraris. Tom jumped in. Ignoring all the other cars already causing a small traffic jam, he simply drove the X6 cross-country through the castle grounds and fields until he reached the road. As expected, the sirens of the Swiss police were already audible, coming from the southeast. They would be coming up the avenue, but Tom took the road to the north, behind the castle. After a few minutes he was sure that he wasn't being followed; his Swiss colleagues would have their hands full at the castle. He drove on a few miles and then pulled off onto a forest path in a wooded area, until the BMW was no longer visible from the road. He had to think. He called Noah to bring him up to speed.

"If I'm seeing this right, Cloutard is still your only lead," Noah said.

"I can only assume he's mixed up in this. He wanted the shield at any price, and it looks like he got himself a bargain. The shield was also the reason Hellen came to Switzerland. And yes, Cloutard is still my only lead, but now it's definitely confirmed."

"Give me a couple of minutes and I'll find out where he lives. You can pay him a personal visit," said Noah.

"By the way, his girlfriend's name is Ossana. I don't know her family name. From somewhere in Africa, I guess. Legs a mile long. Maybe you can find out something useful about her. Still nothing on that symbol?"

"Yes and no. The NSA knows *something* about the symbol, but isn't telling me what. You know the Americans and their 'national security' bullshit. Give me a minute to find out where the Frenchman is, and I'll call you back."

Noah was about to hang up, but Tom stopped him.

"Hold on. Can you dig up the number for Hellen's boss? The head of Blue Shield, Palffy. I should let him know. He and Hellen are close."

Tom was leaning against the massive hood of the BMW when a convoy of blue lights and sirens roared by out on the main road, making him flinch. He drew a deep breath. He was certain that everything that had happened in the last three days was somehow connected —and it was his job to find out how. First, he had to find Hellen; no one but he and Noah knew she had been kidnapped. No official authority—not in Austria or Switzerland, and certainly not Interpol—would believe his story, even if he weren't wanted for murder. He'd have trouble convincing a school crossing guard.

His cell phone buzzed. *Damn, he's fast*, Tom thought.

"Okay, next stop's Tunisia," Noah said. "Cloutard has a medieval fortress there that he's converted into a luxury villa. It's in a town called Tabarka. It's his official place of residence, as far as I can find out. But here's the best part: I found the name Ossana Ibori on the passenger list of a flight to Tunisia. If Cloutard is travelling with her, it's under a false name. The guys in the white-collar division of the FBI suspect he keeps all kinds of artwork stashed there. No cop from any jurisdiction has ever set foot inside his fortress, but maybe you can turn on your proverbial charm. Ossana seems like just your type."

Tom could picture Noah's smirk.

"Fantastic plan, Noah. How am I supposed to get to Tunisia from here? Interpol is after me, for Christ's sake. I can't just jump on a TUI flight from Zurich to Tunisia."

"I know. It's a problem, but I'm working on it."

Noah hung up. Tom was feeling the chill in the air: the nights here were never very warm, even in the summer.

His phone vibrated. Noah had just sent him the number for Hellen's boss. He was a little nervous and wondered how to explain to the boss of Blue Shield that his protégée had just been kidnapped, probably by the same guys who'd been stealing the artifacts. Finally, he took a deep breath and pressed the green button. When the Count picked up, he briefly outlined all that had happened.

"I know François Cloutard. Everyone in the art world does," said Palffy. "We have been trying to pin something on him for years, but he has always proved too slippery. He's one of the true masters, and unfortunately very dangerous. If he has Hellen in his hands, we must be exceptionally careful. It looks as if he is behind the theft of all the artifacts. Of course, Hellen's safety is our absolute priority, but in my capacity as president of Blue Shield, I am also required to keep my mandate from UNESCO in mind. Personally, I would like to think that we can kill two birds with one stone. If only we knew where to start."

"We have one small clue," Tom said. "Cloutard's probably headed for his fortress in Tunisia. In any case, his girlfriend has booked a flight there. But I'm in a fix and don't know how to get to Tunisia myself."

It was quiet on the other end of the line, so quiet that Tom thought the connection had been interrupted. "Count Palffy? Are you there?" he said.

"Yes. Something just occurred to me. Maybe Lady Luck is on our side after all. Not far from you is a town called Grenchen. There's a private airport there. I have an old friend, a retired Air Force pilot, who now flies Swiss bankers around for a lot of money. His name is Walter T. Skinner. I myself have frequently used his private charter planes when I have business in Geneva. I'll make some calls right away and see that he gets you to Tabarka. My diplomatic contacts will ensure that you enter the country without any problems, and your luggage and equipment will also fly under diplomatic seal. Maybe we can finally put a stop to Cloutard's game. I will have my secretary send the necessary information to your phone."

Palffy ended the call, and Tom hoped that he really would be able to enter the country "without any problems." Ending up in a Tunisian jail in his situation wasn't on his bucket list. Tom jumped into the car and tapped "Grenchen Airport" into the GPS system. A few minutes later, the confirmation from Palffy's secretary arrived. Tom hit the gas.

Tom Wagner was on an almost-official rescue mission for Blue Shield.

28

Just before the ferry docked in Brindisi, the leader's mobile phone beeped. The brief message confirmed that they would be spared any major customs searches when they entered the EU at Brindisi. A distraction had been arranged. The weather was already on their side. It was raining hard, strong winds whipped across the harbor, and no one wanted to be outside longer than absolutely necessary, including the customs officers.

And that was only the beginning. As they sailed into Brindisi, the rest became clear. From the ferry, they could make out dozens of police cars and fire engines. The port area was in an uproar. Over the ferry PA system, they heard that there had been two bomb threats at the port, and that the Italian authorities had defused one device. The second bomb had actually exploded, destroying several port buildings and also claiming human lives. But there was no need to worry. The authorities had the situation in hand, and entry into the EU would be dealt with expeditiously.

The three men shared a smile, and the entry formalities went smoothly. Their rickety old truck barely merited a glance and the officials gave their papers no more than a once-over, even less thorough given the chaos at the port and the terrible weather. Thirty minutes later they were on Strada Statale 379, heading north. The single windshield wiper did its best, and the leader studied the map.

"We're ahead of schedule. This filthy weather will slow us down, but if we drive straight through we'll be in San Marino in less than seven hours. We could even fit in a little detour to Pescara. I know a bar in the harbor there, girls you could only dream about. With the money we're getting, we could have a good time there."

The other two men grinned.

"Then step on it," one of them said with a laugh. "Don't want to keep the ladies waiting."

29

A twenty-minute taxi ride from the airport brought Tom to Tabarka. He saw the medieval fortress immediately, situated on a hill on a headland that formed one side of the harbor. Cloutard must have spent a fortune turning it into a luxury villa, and it probably wasn't the kind of place Tom could just walk into. Even Noah wouldn't be able to help him much with this one. The place was a fortress in the truest sense of the word.

Getting in from the ocean side would be difficult. Steep cliffs rose from the water's edge to the fortress walls. The only vehicle access was by a road that wound its way up the hill from the harbor. Even from a few hundred yards away, Tom could see the sentries. He suspected they would not take kindly to him stopping by.

Tom went to a café near the harbor to observe the comings and goings at Cloutard's fortress for a little while, but for an hour nothing happened.

Tabarka had become somewhat run-down in recent years after its peak as a tourist destination in the 1990s. Now there were hardly any tourists, and not even many of the locals frequented the harbor. Only a few fishing boats, surrounded by screeching seagulls, were chugging in or out.

Tom would probably have no choice but to try to enter Cloutard's stronghold at night, via the side facing the sea. He would manage it somehow, he told himself. Noah had promised to find the plans to the castle, so at least Tom wouldn't have to wander around the place in the middle of the night not knowing where he was.

During the taxi ride, Tom had noticed a sign for a golf resort directly on the water. A forty-minute walk along the beach led him to the hotel. He checked in, then bought some new clothes in the hotel boutique: jeans, two T-shirts, a linen shirt and a pair of sneakers. He was still wearing the suit that Noah had left for him in Switzerland. Tom had everything charged to his room, then went upstairs and took a long shower and a short power nap. He decided to try to break into the fortress at 2 a.m.

Refreshed, he went downstairs with his laptop, found a chair at the hotel's beach bar and ordered a whiskey sour. Noah had sent the plans through while Tom was in the shower, and he turned his attention to where to start his search in Cloutard's refuge—although he had to admit that he didn't really know what it was he was searching for. Just strolling in and asking what the hell was going on probably wouldn't work, he suspected.

As tenuous as the lead was, it could easily turn out to be a dead end. On the other hand, maybe Cloutard was behind all the raids and Tom would find not only the stolen artifacts in the fortress, but Hellen as well.

Noah had hacked into the system of the architecture firm that had rebuilt the fortress for Cloutard, and had dug up not only a map but detailed information about the alarm system. A few minutes' research on the right kind of websites provided Tom with a straightforward way to disable it. The darknet was the perfect place for a crash course. Some time earlier, Noah had shown Tom how to navigate these regions of the Internet, and Tom quickly found what he needed to bypass the alarm.

Cloutard's fortress was divided into three levels. On the ground floor were the kitchen and a few utility rooms. The second floor contained two enormous rooms—probably the living and dining rooms—with a terrace overlooking the sea, as well as a third room, perhaps a study. The top floor consisted of five spacious rooms, apparently all bedrooms, with attached baths and dressing rooms.

"Admit it, Dr. Pfeiffer. You missed me."

Tom nearly fell off his chair as a hand gently grazed his shoulder from behind. He turned his head, quickly closing the laptop as he did. His gaze wandered up a flawless ebony body in a skimpy bikini and stopped at the eyes of Ossana, Cloutard's lover.

She looked at him playfully. Then she circled him, keeping her hand on his shoulder, and pulled up another chair. She sat down, slowly crossed her slender legs, and waited for his reaction. Tom had already regained his composure and was back to his most charming.

"Dr. Pfeiffer was my father. Call me Tom. And yes, of course, after all that fuss in Switzerland, I jumped on the first plane here just to see you again," Tom answered with a wink, eyebrows raised to underline that he didn't mean a word of it.

The waiter came and Ossana ordered a white russian. Tom ordered another whiskey sour and decided to go on the offensive: "You got the shield at a very reasonable price. We were so rudely interrupted, and Dr. de Mey from UNESCO was denied the opportunity to assert her own claim to it, not to mention my client's. So I thought I should speak to Monsieur Cloutard again, face to face, and make him an offer."

He knew he was talking utter nonsense, but nothing better occurred to him just then. Ossana peered into his eyes longer than necessary, and Tom didn't know if it was the hot breeze blowing off the land or Ossana's radiance that was driving his pulse up. Her gaze wandered calmly, almost shamelessly, over his body. She liked what she saw and made no secret of the fact that she found Tom attractive.

"And you thought that Monsieur Cloutard would welcome you with open arms," she said.

There was something wicked in Ossana's voice. She spoke slowly and carefully, seeming to weigh every word; the words themselves contained something strangely melodic, almost like a hypnotic chant. Against his better judgement, Tom found himself attracted to her. He had to keep it together: he wasn't here for that. He wanted to know where Hellen was and what Cloutard was up to. Ossana was the enemy—he couldn't let himself think of her as sexy. But at the same time, he was finding it very hard to resist. She went on without waiting for Tom to reply.

"Let's find out tonight. Join us in our humble abode for dinner. You can discuss the shield with Monsieur Cloutard at your leisure. And you'll be very close to my bedroom."

She said the last sentence in an unchanged tone of voice, as if it was the most natural thing in the world. Tom didn't flinch. Self-control was one of his better attributes, and he saw that his lack of reaction left Ossana a little disappointed.

"Just because I can beat him at billiards doesn't mean we can't do business together. And I have my own bed here at the hotel."

Tom managed to put something like Ossana's indifference into own his last sentence. She smiled—she had truly found a worthy opponent in Tom. She tipped back her white russian and looked out to the helicopter just then approaching the fortress from the north, across the sea.

"Perfect timing. François is just arriving."

Apparently the fortress had its own helipad. Tom wondered if it was possible to amass so much wealth purely by criminal means. Ossana rose and took a few steps toward the water. She turned her head halfway back to Tom.

"I'm going to take a swim. I'll see you for dinner tonight at the fortress. Eight o'clock. The men at the gate will be informed. Just give them your name and you'll be granted entrance to the inner sanctum."

As he watched her step into the water, Tom wondered why her last words sounded so ambiguous. He was finding it very difficult to concentrate on his mission. Tom drained his drink as well, and went to his room to take a cold shower.

30

The road to the fort was lined with torches, and Tom wondered if it was like this every evening or if it was a special welcome just for him. He gave his name to the two guards at the entrance and, as promised, the massive gate swung open and he was allowed to pass through. The gate closed behind him and another security guard stopped Tom and searched him. Anticipating this, Tom had left his gun in the hotel room. The guard checked Tom from head to toe using a hand scanner like those used at airports. Then his money clip, keys and phone, which he had handed over before the scan, were returned to him.

Tom was impressed. From outside, the castle looked neglected, drafty and not particularly inviting. Inside, however, was another story. Tom felt he had stepped into another world; the place looked like a French baroque castle. Cloutard apparently had a predilection for Louis XIV, the Sun King, because that's exactly what the fortress looked like inside: opulent tapestries, oil paintings, stucco ceilings decorated with gold, chandeliers, an elaborate, sweeping marble staircase, wide balustrades and floral decorations. Tom, amazed, could only shake his head.

François Cloutard stood in the center of the large reception hall, master of his domain, and greeted Tom as if they were old friends.

"*Bienvenue à* Fort Tabarka. I am so glad you are joining us tonight; we so rarely entertain guests. When Ossana told me you were in town, I was overjoyed."

Cloutard seemed surprisingly hospitable toward Tom—and yet, at the same time, Tom sensed a cruelty and coldness in the man that he hadn't noticed when they had first met in Switzerland. There, he was an intellectual art collector; here, he was clearly the dictatorial lord of the manor.

"Quite an impressive house you have here. If you can still call it a house."

Tom kept looking around. One thing was clear to him: Cloutard's business—probably mostly illegal—had to be incredibly lucrative.

"I think a quick tour is in order," Cloutard said, with a little pride. "You are standing in what was once the fortress of the Lomellini, a trading dynasty from Genoa who settled here in Tunisia in the 16th century. I won't bore you with too much history, but this fort has seen many battles, and also many deaths. Thank God those times are over. The only fighting these days is for the best seat on the terrace."

On their way outside, they passed a door with a guard posted in front of it. Tom decided to start his search there that night, but exactly how and when he would do that, and how he was going to get past the guard, he didn't yet know. Cloutard led Tom to the terrace, where a table had already been set for dinner.

"The sunset from here is most impressive," Cloutard said, taking a seat on one of the thronelike chairs like the Sun King himself. Ossana was already waiting for them at the table, and stood up when they stepped onto the terrace. She was wearing almost nothing, a wisp of a beige dress that drifted around her body like a cloud. The darkness of her skin contrasted breathtakingly with the pale fabric.

"So nice you were able to make it," she said, and looked at Tom once again with that hunger in her eyes.

Tom remained unmoved, if only on the outside. Ossana slid a chair out for Tom.

"The pleasure is all mine," he said, accepting the proffered seat.

Ossana sat down too, and the appetizer was promptly served. Apparently fine dining, along with art and expensive cognac, was among François Cloutard's passions.

"I hope you like figs, Monsieur Pfeiffer. The chef has prepared fresh figs with Roquefort and a *confit de figue*, a kind of fig conserve spiced with salt, pepper and a little raspberry vinegar. As a side dish, he has baked for us some little parmesan *tuiles*, refined with poppy seed and chili, and served with a glass of Beaujolais in which the figs have been soaked for a day."

Tom's own taste in food was more down-to-earth, but he had to admit the appetizer was delicious. He took a sip of wine, gazed out to sea and forgot for a moment why he was there in the first place.

Cloutard brought him back to reality, asking, "So what brings you to Tabarka, Dr. Pfeiffer?"

"To be honest, Monsieur Cloutard: you. The auction was not concluded as it should have been. You didn't have the winning bid, but I believe the shield has come into your possession by other means. In any case, my client is still very interested."

"Excuse me, but I did not realize that you were actually serious about the shield. Truly, I thought you were more interested in beating me in a game of carom," Cloutard said, a bit cynically.

"The auction was interrupted, and I was reduced to watching"—Tom paused for a heartbeat and looked at Ossana—"as the shield came into your possession without the hammer falling. And, in fact, without payment."

"My only objective was to ensure the safety of the shield," Ossana said. "It was not clear what the assassins were after, much less who was on whose side. All that mattered to us was the shield's well-being."

Ossana smiled innocently at Tom—or as innocently as she could.

"What actually happened to Dr. de Mey?" Cloutard asked. "She seemed to have inadvertently placed a bid on the shield, although I am certain UNESCO has no budget for such extravagant purchases. You were sitting beside her, and one might be forgiven for thinking that you already knew each other."

Cloutard's tone was casual, but Tom was seething with rage inside. Did Cloutard really have the nerve to ask after Hellen, when he was obviously behind the whole thing? Tom decided not to let the son-of-a-bitch off the hook. He pulled himself together.

"She's . . . indisposed just now, I believe. But back to the reason I'm here. Allow me to say it again: I have a great interest in purchasing the shield from you," Tom said, turning his attention back to Cloutard.

"Unfortunately, that won't be possible. You see, the shield is no longer in my possession," Cloutard said with finality.

Now Tom's interest was aroused. Cloutard had already sold the shield? Maybe this was his next clue. "So you've resold an artifact that was not legally yours?"

Tom managed to stop himself from adding, "Is that how you normally operate?" He did not want to convict this man of a crime. He wanted to get as much as possible out of him, in order to find out where Hellen was.

"That was my intention from the outset. My role was that of a middleman, the same as yours."

"If you had won the auction properly, I would have no cause to complain. But . . ." Tom paused. "And who, may I ask, was your buyer? Perhaps I can make them an offer," Tom said.

"The shield is most definitely not for sale."

"I represent a very, very wealthy family. I would say it's more a question of the amount of my offer." Tom narrowed his eyes at Cloutard and put on his usual impish smile.

"No. Believe me, the amount does not matter in the slightest," Cloutard said.

The main course appeared, and Cloutard changed the topic. He raised his index finger like a professor and began to speak.

"I'm sure you are familiar with a typical *coq au vin*, a national dish in France. But our *coq* is a very special one, prepared by our chef from a Bresse chicken, a breed of chicken from the Bresse region near Lyon. Henry IV granted an '*appellation d'origine*' for these birds as early as 1601. The Bresse chicken thus has the same status as champagne, cognac or Bordeaux: it is only a real Bresse chicken if it comes from the Bresse region."

Cloutard sounded inordinately proud, as if he himself had granted the chicken its certificate of authenticity. Tom smiled. Cloutard was clearly an eccentric. If he weren't a crook, Tom would almost find him likeable.

"One last thing. Apart from the chicken itself, this is not a 'normal' *coq au vin*. It is actually *coq au riesling*, prepared with a 2008 *Brand Sélection de Grains Nobles* from the Alsace region, which is what we are also about to enjoy in the glass."

Cloutard checked the label of the bottle the waiter had just opened. He tasted the wine and nodded, satisfied. A moment later he turned the conversation back to the shield.

"It is very important to my buyer to know that the shield will remain in his possession forever." Cloutard lowered his voice considerably and added, "It is said that the shield has a special power."

"A special power? Are we talking about 'Tomb Raider' here? Do you mean your buyer is interested in the shield because it bestows some sort of special power on him?"

Tom hesitated briefly. As he spoke, he felt Ossana's foot under the table. She had taken off one shoe and was moving her bare foot up the inside of Tom's leg. Tom got a grip on himself and went on, "What does your buyer want, to start a new crusade? With a shield-bearer taking the lead? It sounds to me as if someone's been watching too many Indiana Jones movies."

"All I know is this: the shield is not for sale," Cloutard repeated. "You've come all this way for nothing."

"Oh, not at all. If I had not come, I would not have had the pleasure of your hospitality and would not have had the opportunity to visit your magnificent home. The trip has definitely not been wasted."

Against his will, Tom turned his eyes to Ossana, who smiled knowingly at him as she continued to tease him with her bare foot beneath the table.

Cloutard's right hand, Karim Shaham, came onto the terrace. François stood up. "This seems important," he said. "Please excuse me a moment."

The diminutive Arab whispered a few words to Cloutard, and Cloutard nodded and thought for a moment. "Yes. A good idea, Karim. Let's do it that way." Shaham bowed and left the terrace again.

"I would be lost without Karim. He has more talent for numbers in his little finger than I do in my whole head. We have known each other for decades. One rarely finds a person like him, unfortunately, someone you can really trust. How did you find me so quickly, by the way? My address is not exactly in the phone book."

Cloutard leaned back and took a sip of his favorite cognac.

"I have good connections," said Tom. "When I want something, I usually get it. And your house is not the most inconspicuous place to live."

"It is strange, though . . . I was unable to find out anything about a 'Dr. Thomas Pfeiffer' anywhere in the art scene. And I myself have never heard your name before."

Cloutard did not sound suspicious but rather amused, as he addressed himself to the dessert. He closed his eyes for a moment as he sampled the first spoonful.

"*Crème brûlée ménage à trois*. Three different *crème brûlées*: one with coffee, one with cocoa, and one with finely chopped pistachios. They are accompanied by a rather special dessert wine, a Château d'Yquem *Premier Cru Supérieur* Sauternes, with notes of apricot, exotic fruits, honey and flowers."

Tom sipped the wine and had to make an effort not to grimace. Calling this a "sweet wine" was a colossal understatement. He didn't care how much this swill cost, it wasn't for him. Diplomatically, he asked the waiter for a double espresso.

"But you're from Vienna, Monsieur Wagner. Wouldn't you prefer a *Verlängerter* or an *Einspänner*, or perhaps a *Kaisermelange*?" Cloutard said, smiling broadly.

"Thank you. I prefer espresso," Tom replied. "I like things simple, and not just when it comes to coffee. And I also like discretion. You know yourself that to succeed in the antiques scene, one doesn't exactly advertise on Facebook. There are less conspicuous alternatives." Tom was hoping he could bluff his way through with chatter.

"You are right to say that discretion is very important in our business. I certainly admire your enthusiasm, Dr. Pfeiffer. And your fighting spirit. Perhaps we can do business some other time."

What was this now? Tom was confused. Had Cloutard actually bought that flimsy line, or was he just trying to lure him into a trap? Tom had to watch his step. Apparently, there were forces at play here that were not to be trifled with. Finally, a little excitement. Ossana rescued Tom from his delicate situation, at least for the time being.

"It's getting late, François. Why don't you talk to Dr. Pfeiffer about other plans over breakfast? He can stay in one of our guest rooms."

"You're right, *ma chère*. Business is better discussed when one is rested, and most importantly with a clear head." He sipped his cognac again. "Dr. Pfeiffer, you will be our guest tonight. I will not take no for an answer. I'll have one of the guest rooms made up for

149

you. Someone will come to show you to your room in a few minutes."

Cloutard stood, drained the last drops of his Louis XIII, nodded to Tom and left the terrace. Ossana also wished him good night, and followed Cloutard.

Tom sat alone on the terrace, enjoying his espresso and looking out to sea, where the moonlight glittered on the water. Had it really been that simple? The lion had invited him into its den and offered him a place to stay. Tom smiled. Now he could explore the house in the night. Perhaps he would discover more about Cloutard's mysterious buyer, who might also be connected to Hellen's abduction. Tom picked up his cell phone and tapped out a message to Noah: "I'm in!"

31

Hellen's skull throbbed as if it were about to explode. She opened her eyes, straightened up and immediately fell back onto the mattress. Everything was spinning. After a few seconds, she tried again. Despite the horrendous headache, she remained sitting upright and tried to orient herself in the room. Bit by bit, her eyes adjusted to the darkness. In the pale gleam that shone beneath the door, Hellen was gradually able to make out the room around her. A bed. A window with closed shutters. A closet. A ceiling lamp. A door. The place had a specific smell to it, a smell Hellen knew very well: the familiar bouquet of old furniture, carpets, clothes and mothballs. She saw her purse on the floor next to the bed and snatched it up, knowing as she did so that the thought was foolish. Her mobile phone was gone, of course.

Memories began to return. The auction. The shot. Being dragged from the room. That was all; after that her memory was blank. She looked at her watch, which they had left with her: about four hours had passed since the auction. As her mind cleared, her emotions grew more intense. Fear of her kidnappers' plans alternated with incomprehension about why she had been taken at all.

It was not the first perilous situation she had confronted in her life. She had been in extreme danger more than once, but she had never been alone before. Now she was on her own. She had no idea who the kidnappers were or what they wanted from her. Maybe it had something to do with what she'd discovered in Glastonbury. Maybe the thieves were hunting for the same thing she was.

Hellen pressed her ear to the door of her cell and listened. The light beneath the door gave her hope that she might be able to hear something that would give her a better picture of her situation. But she heard nothing. The pounding headache was limiting her senses severely, and too many horrific scenarios were swirling in her head. She had to get her fear under control. She needed to clear her head and weigh her options.

She grasped the door handle and eased it down. It was locked, of course, but it was worth a try. Then she sneaked over to the window. It wouldn't open either. She sat down on the bed and ran through her very few options. She knew she didn't want to just wait and see what her captors intended for her, or whether she would be freed. The latter seemed unlikely, anyway. She had to find her own way out.

32

Tom planned to wait until about 3 a.m., then start his search on the ground floor. He was hoping to find a clue somewhere in the house, and wondered whether he would run into any guards during the night . . . most likely yes, he decided. He looked around the room: to describe it as opulent would be putting it mildly. Cloutard's luxurious tastes extended into the furthermost corners of the ancient structure. Tom's room alone held a four-poster canopy bed of white-enameled wood with gilded ornaments and a baroque headboard and heavy, wine-red curtains with floral patterns embroidered in gold. A gold and crystal chandelier hung suspended from the ceiling. On the mantelpiece stood a heavy gold candelabra. Sumptuous oil paintings decorated the walls, while the stuccoed ceiling and wood paneling would have done credit to Marie Antoinette. Tom knew very little about art, but he had the impression that everything he saw in there was the real thing, not some Chinese copy from Alibaba. Tom lay back on the huge bed and picked up his iPhone. To be on the safe side, he read the extensive dossiers on Cloutard and Joan of Arc's shield again, as well as the ones on Blue Shield and the other stolen artifacts. Noah was very thorough when it came to briefings of this kind, and maybe Tom would find more clues to help him locate Hellen.

Suddenly, he put down the phone and listened: footsteps sounded in the hallway outside. Tom slipped off the bed, put the phone in his pocket, and crept to the door. He listened, but heard nothing. He had the impression that the steps had stopped right outside his door. He turned out the light, grabbed a candlestick from atop a chiffonier, and positioned himself behind the door, where he could keep a close eye on the handle. Just then, it began to move slowly downward—someone was opening the door. Tom pressed himself against the wall. The intruder took a step into the room and Tom saw instantly who it was: Ossana.

He did nothing for a moment, calculating the best way to deal with the situation. What was Ossana up to? Were her intentions good? Quick as a shot, he stepped out from behind the half-open door and gave Ossana a powerful shove in the back that sent her tumbling rather awkwardly onto the bed. He closed the door and flipped on the light.

"Couldn't you knock?" he said with a roguish grin. He returned the candlestick to its place on the chiffonier.

Ossana turned over and looked at him. There was astonishment on her face, and a little anger, but also respect.

"Shouldn't you be in bed instead of lurking behind the door for burglars?" she countered.

"Maybe. But waiting for burglars in this place apparently makes sense, too."

Only now did Tom realize that, beneath her silk dressing gown, Ossana was naked. The fall onto his bed had caused her nightgown to slip a little, exposing one of her breasts. But Ossana made not the slightest move to cover herself again; it didn't seem to bother her at all to be lying so revealingly in front of him.

She got up from the bed again and sidled toward Tom. Tom was torn. On the one hand, this stunning woman standing before him, wearing next to nothing, made his pulse race—but his conscience was gnawing at him as well. He was here to track down Hellen's kidnappers and find his own parents' murderers, not to steal some French art-mafia boss's hot girlfriend.

"Well?" Ossana murmured. "What are you going to do with this burglar?" Ossana's lips were two inches from his. Her fingers slid up and over Tom's hips, and her long, coral-colored fingernails explored his torso and shoulders, coming to rest at his neck. She yanked Tom's head back by his hair and snapped at his chin with pearly teeth. "Don't you want to punish me, Dr. Pfeiffer?"

Her hands released him and slid down her own body, slowly unknotting the band around her silk gown. The delicate fabric drifted slowly down her velvety body and fell to the floor and she stood before him, utterly naked. Tom gasped audibly. It was like he was hypnotized, which turned out to be a problem. A split second later, Ossana took a step to one side and tossed him with an expert judo move. He landed on his back on the bed. Ossana jumped on top of him, straddling him, then bent down and kissed him wildly and passionately, biting a little at his neck. She grabbed his arms and pressed them firmly onto the bed, above his head. Much more firmly than expected, in fact—Tom felt as if his hands were clamped in a vice.

33

UNKNOWN LOCATION

Hellen was usually angry at herself when she wasted hours on YouTube, surfing from one video to the next. But right now, being a declared YouTube addict was reason to be grateful. Only recently, she had stumbled onto a how-to video entitled "Pick a Lock with a Hairpin" and she had tried it out. Of course, it wouldn't work with new, modern locks, but the door she was now kneeling in front of wasn't one of those.

Her hair had become completely disheveled during the struggle and abduction, and her two hairpins had vanished somewhere inside the mess atop her head. It took her a little while to find one of them and extricate it from her hair.

The principle was simple enough: use the slightly bent end of her hairpin to push the various pins up to the right position. Not an easy task, but doable. Outside, the lights had been turned off. There was complete silence. Hellen concentrated on two things: making as little noise as possible, and hearing the faint click of the pins inside the ancient lock. At home, when she had tried to apply the technique in the video to her own front door, she had succeeded in just five minutes. Horrified at how easily her apartment door could be jimmied open, she had immediately had a new security lock installed.

This lock was proving harder to crack; she had already been working at it for a good twenty minutes. She thought she had managed to push up four pins, but there was still one to go. Her neck and arms were aching, but she ignored the pain as best she could. She kept at it and was just getting the fifth pin into place when the hairpin broke. The "snap" seemed deafening in the complete silence.

Hellen froze, listening for any sound outside, mentally cursing herself. The broken section of the hairpin was still stuck in the lock; even if she managed the last pin now, she would not be able to turn the cylinder or open the door. She removed the second pin from her hair and started digging in the lock for the broken piece. With tweezers she might have been able to fish it out, but with only the tip of a hairpin to work with it proved difficult. She could feel the broken piece wedged in one of the pin slots; it would take a certain amount of force to pry it out. It would make some noise, and she risked breaking the second hairpin as well—and then any chance she had of getting out of there would be gone.

With a mixture of caution and strength, Hellen poked and prodded and finally managed to free the broken piece from the lock. One of the pins had slipped back into its original position in the process, but she was able to rectify that quickly enough. Now only one pin separated her from freedom.

Hellen's heart was beating so loudly that she was afraid whoever was outside would hear it. Her final attempt with the hairpin did the trick: the fifth pin slid into place, and Hellen began to turn the cylinder carefully. The hairpin held, and Hellen was overjoyed when she heard the low scrape of the rotating cylinder. She took a few deep breaths, relieved. Now she had to get out of there.

She grabbed her purse and returned to the door. Grasping the door handle, she turned it bit by bit. The handle made a faint squeaking sound, and Hellen could only pray that the hinges wouldn't wake the entire house when the door opened. But she had to take the risk. As gently as possible, she pushed the door. To her astonishment, it swung open silently. She found herself looking into a room faintly lit by the moon outside. Even in the dim light, she saw at once that the room was filled with art objects and artifacts of every description. Unfortunately, none of them were the artifacts she was looking for.

The next moment the room was brightly lit, and Hellen reflexively raised one hand in front of her eyes. For hours her eyes had been accustomed to the darkness, and the sudden glare hurt. She held her breath.

"Leaving so soon?"

The voice struck Hellen like a slap to the face. She stared into the eyes of her abductor. Jacinto Guerra was standing in front of her, a pistol in one hand, his other index finger raised in reproach.

34

TOM'S ROOM, FORT TABARKA, TUNISIA

There was a moment when it became clear to Tom that Ossana wasn't looking for a night of love after all: the headbutt to his face three seconds after she kissed him was fairly unambiguous. Blood spewed from his nose, and a searing pain shot through his skull.

It took him a few seconds to adjust to the new situation. Just moments before, he'd been thinking of some way to extract himself from his slippery position. Now, however, the situation had changed.

"Dr. Pfeiffer, you haven't been truthful with me," she said, putting on a scolding voice. "Or should I say Thomas Maria Wagner?" Her voice switched from childlike annoyance to ice-cold aggression.

Tom flinched. His cover was blown. But almost more annoying was that his middle name had been used—again—and that, like almost everyone, she had pronounced his family name wrong. Ossana struck again, this time with a fist aimed at Tom's face, but this time he was prepared. He managed to deflect the blow, and with a skillful twisting movement he wormed out from under Ossana, simultaneously throwing her off. He jumped up and wiped the blood from his nose with a forearm.

"Ohhhh, don't you want to play with me anymore?" Ossana pouted, standing up beside the bed and dropping, catlike, into attack position.

It was probably the most bizarre duel of his life. In front of him stood a gorgeous black woman, stark naked and blessed with a body to shame a supermodel. Highly trained in close combat, she wanted to get into his pants at any cost—but not in a pleasant way. *Concentrate*, Tom told himself. He shook his head to dislodge the blood still trickling from his nose and over his mouth. Ossana's reflexes and coordinated movements were quick and graceful. She pirouetted swiftly on her own axis, and her elbow crashed into Tom's temple. The blow made him stagger. He had never seen the technique before and, for the moment, had no desire to experience it again. He had to come up with something.

The guards, he guessed, were not only posted around the property, but also patrolled inside the fortress. His chances did not look good. He hated the idea of retreating with no new leads and with unfinished business, but he could only help Hellen if he got out of there alive.

Tom put a little distance between himself and Ossana, trying to gather himself. He had to put her out of action as quickly as possible, even if only momentarily.

He was able to dodge Ossana's next assault and got in a solid blow himself, but Ossana's next punch found its mark and Tom went down. This was exactly what he had been waiting for: he fell backward and crashed onto the floor. As he fell, he saw Ossana's confused look. But he lay still with his eyes open, staring into space.

Ossana, suspicious, moved closer, but she lost her focus for a second. That was all Tom needed to sweep his legs to the left with extreme force, and to Ossana's surprise he knocked her legs from under her. Simultaneously, he clenched both hands into a double fist and Ossana crashed forward onto it, with no way to slow her fall. Tom actually heard the air abruptly exit her lungs. She lay on the floor winded, gasping for breath. Taking advantage of the momentary lull, Tom jumped up and ran out of the room.

Ossana's piercing cry broke the silence in the fortress and brought the guards running. One came charging up the stairs three at a time, but Tom's close-combat training served him well. Faster than the man could think, Tom landed a targeted strike on his chin. The guard's head cracked hard on the stone floor and he didn't get up. In an instant, Tom relieved the man of his weapons. He pushed the pistol into the back of his waistband and hung the submachine gun over his shoulder, first checking that it was loaded and clicking off the safety— the familiar routine.

Ossana, once again in her flimsy nightgown, came running out of Tom's room. "Get him!" she ordered the two guards who came running in through the front entrance into the main hall.

Tom, in the meantime, had reached the foot of the stairs. He didn't think for long, but fired a salvo at the guards and immediately took cover behind one of the enormous columns in the hall. Bursts of machine gun fire kept him pinned there, chipping bits off the column all around him.

François Cloutard came storming out through the double doors of his room. Confused, he looked down and saw Tom where he had taken cover behind the column.

"What's going on? What do you think you're doing, shooting up the place?" Cloutard's white silk pajamas, sprinkled with Louis Vuitton logos, undermined some of his natural authority.

The guards fired another volley at Tom, who responded in kind. Ossana was standing in front of Tom's room, directly opposite Cloutard, and shouted down at the guards, "Hold your fire. I need him alive."

"What do you mean you need him alive? For what?" Cloutard yelled at her. He started to run down the stairs. "And what makes you think you can order my security people around?" Reaching the bottom of the stairs, he found himself between Tom and the guards. "Hold your goddamn fire!" he bellowed at the guards.

He looked up at Ossana expectantly, obviously waiting for an explanation. The two guards looked from Tom to Ossana to Cloutard, uncertain what to do. Tom realized that he was dealing with more than one front; Ossana was clearly playing her own game, and he had no desire to end up as collateral damage in this domestic squabble. Nevertheless, her next order took even Tom by surprise.

"You can shoot Cloutard. We don't need him anymore," she shouted down indifferently, with a dismissive wave of her hand. Her voice took on a more determined tone. "But bring me the other one. Alive."

Cloutard was a crook, but he was a man of the world, not prone to losing his composure. Still, when his lover ordered his own security men to kill him, he lost his temper completely. The guards were not quite sure who to listen to. Tom took advantage of the general confusion, firing two quick volleys at the guards at the entrance and then turning the gun upward to fire at Ossana. She stepped backward calmly, and the bullets only slammed into the solid marble railing. On the top floor, two more guards came running.

Tom yelled at Cloutard and waved him over, "If you want to get out of here alive, stick with me!"

Tom's gut told him that Cloutard had now become his only ally. He fired another volley at the guards to give Cloutard cover, and Cloutard, ducking, ran to Tom. The two guards above had started shooting, too; the hail of bullets missed Cloutard by a whisker. Now both of them were covering behind the massive column. A stream of bullets slammed into the marble next to their heads.

"You're all fired!" Cloutard yelled at his guards. "This is Lasser marble. I had it shipped specially from Vinschger Nördersberg in South Tyrol. These columns are priceless, you *bande d'abrutis*!"

Tom grinned and swapped the magazine on the machine pistol. There were two magazines, duct-taped together to allow for quick reloading. He returned fire, alternating between shooting upwards and toward the entrance, where the guards were edging closer. Then the gun ran out of ammo. Tom threw it aside, reached behind his back and pulled the pistol out of his waistband. He tugged on Cloutard's pajama sleeve.

"Where do you keep your chopper?" Tom asked in a whisper.

"In the courtyard," Cloutard replied in a tone that implied "Where else?" "Follow me!"

By now, Cloutard had also understood that Tom was the only one on his side; he ducked and ran as Tom fired two shots to cover their departure. Cloutard left the ground floor on the inland side of the fortress and ran along a corridor that led to a steep, narrow staircase. Tom kept firing over his shoulder at the pursuing guards. Moments later, he and Cloutard were standing in the fortress court-yard, where the helicopter sat waiting. The guard stationed by the machine immediately turned his attention, and his gun, toward the approaching fugitives, but lowered the weapon again when he recognized Cloutard. The news that Cloutard was now the enemy had not yet reached him. But Tom wasn't about to wait: he took the man down with a well-aimed bullet to the leg. Cloutard jumped into the cockpit to initiate the start sequence while Tom covered the entrances to the courtyard, from which several guards would come charging at any moment. Slowly the rotor blades began to turn, and Tom circled around the helicopter to climb in on the other side.

"Get us out of here, Cloutard!" Tom cried over the deafening roar of the blades.

Armed guards now appeared from all sides and opened fire on the helicopter as its skids left the ground. A whirlwind of sand enveloped the rising machine and the courtyard, leaving the guards struggling. They fired wildly, unable to aim accurately, but several shots still slammed into the body of the helicopter, and the window on Tom's side exploded into a thousand pieces. Tom returned fire.

Ossana, too, was now standing in the courtyard, bent over and holding her hand in front of her face, watching the departing helicopter. The machine rose swiftly, and Cloutard turned it out to sea. A few moments later, they were out of range.

Cloutard, furious, turned and glared at Tom. "*Merde!* What the hell is going on here—and who the hell *are* you? You're no *sensal*, that much is crystal clear."

"The name's Wagner, Tom Wagner. I'm with the Austrian task force Cobra. I don't really know the first thing about art or antiques; I'm only here to find out who kidnapped my ex-girlfriend."

With a grin, Tom held out his hand to Cloutard.

35

"An austrian antiterror unit? Ha-ha-ha..."

Cloutard began to laugh out loud and shook his head repeatedly in disbelief. It seemed like an eternity before he got himself under control again. Then he turned to Tom and narrowed his eyes to slits. Now deadly serious, he asked, "What the devil were you doing with my lover in your bedroom"?

Tom swallowed. "Honestly, I'm just glad I made it out of there alive." He dabbed at his bloody face.

Cloutard laughed again. "Well, at least I'm not the only one that bitch hurt. Sometimes she takes that whole S&M thing too far."

The two sat in silence for a few moments, until Cloutard could not keep it in any longer. "Why on earth would *cette salope* order my own guards to kill me and only take you prisoner? *Merde!*"

"You're asking the wrong guy. The first time I saw Ossana was at the auction. It was you who introduced her to me. And right now, I'm in no hurry to cross paths with her again."

"Well . . . maybe I believe you, maybe I don't. The fact is, because of you, I have been hounded out of my own house, my *former* girlfriend ordered *my* guards to kill me, and those overpaid, ungrateful *fils de putes* seemed more than happy to try. Not only that, they reduced my home to rubble." Cloutard was still stunned. "It seems more absurd every time I play it back in my mind."

Tom wondered for a moment whether he could trust Cloutard. The man was a criminal. Could he take the risk of telling him the whole story? With the exception of women, Tom was an excellent judge of character. He decided to entrust Cloutard with at least some of the story, for now.

"All right. I'll tell you what I know."

"Well, then. Out with it!"

Cloutard gestured with his right hand in a clear invitation to Tom to begin. As concisely as possible, Tom summarized the events of the last few days: the hijacking, the tattooed symbol, the theft of the Holy Lance, the murder of the stewardess, the stolen artifacts, Hellen's abduction, and his reasons for coming to Tunisia. The Frenchman listened attentively, making a face now and then, and raised his index finger questioningly when Tom concluded.

"Monsieur Wagner, this all sounds like something out of a Dan Brown thriller. But where do I fit in? I don't seem to enter your story until the end." Cloutard looked searchingly at Tom.

Tom shook his head. Cloutard, too, had managed to mispronounce his name. Although, with a French accent, it brought a smile even to Tom's face. He refrained from correcting the pronunciation.

"I first heard your name when one of the hijackers mentioned it. He was in the toilet on the plane, talking to someone on the phone."

"*Qu'est-ce qu'il y a?*" Cloutard said, turning pale. "What is going on?" But Tom thought he saw a ghost of a smile cross Cloutard's face . . . although he might have been mistaken.

"Okay, Cloutard. I've bared my soul and told you my side of the story. I still can't make much sense of what's happened in the last few days, but maybe you can shed some light on it."

Cloutard nodded. "I don't know why, Mr. Wagner, but I trust you. I like you, even if you are a policeman. Right now, you and I are in the same boat—I beg your pardon: in the same helicopter. I can only assume you are not wearing a wire, and that we don't presently have Interpol or the CIA listening in." He glanced at Tom with a smile to make it clear he was joking, then went on, "I am a thief, a smuggler, a fence, a forger, a fraud and probably everything else that one can be in the international art scene. I was approached recently, and commissioned to acquire the shield and deliver it to a certain location."

"Who approached you?" Tom's interest was aroused.

"Like you, I have an excellent network. My contacts range from the Cosa Nostra to the Vatican, from the Russian mafia to the Triads, and from pharmaceutical lobbyists to a number of political parties. And I tell you this openly: I have no idea who the client is, no idea who was really behind the people who approached me. Even *my* contacts could not help me find that out."

Tom raised an eyebrow. "Sounds mysterious. I hope you're not going to start talking about the Illuminati or some other conspiracy theory crap."

"Not at all, I assure you. These are not some devil-worshipping crazies who rip the hearts out of human sacrifices at black masses, nor are they insane billionaires planning to rule the world. And that is precisely why all sides are rather circumspect. Believe me, when the Russians and the Italians speak about a competitor with respect, then something is most certainly going on."

"You said you had to hand over the shield. Have you really done that? And if so, where?"

Cloutard turned around and opened a beautifully crafted wooden box mounted behind his pilot's seat. Inside it, Tom saw yet another bottle of cognac and two lead-crystal snifters. Cloutard removed the bottle, opened it and poured a generous amount into each glass. He handed one of the snifters to Tom, then replaced the bottle in its case.

"This is Hennessy Louis XIII, among the finest and most exquisite cognacs you will find anywhere in the world. I rarely share my cognac, you should know. But somehow I think you and I, one way or another, are going to be spending a lot of time together. For now, we should trust one another. Let us drink to that, and then I will answer your questions and even tell you one or two things that I am sure will be of interest to you."

Tom raised his eyebrows in surprise and the two men touched glasses. The chime of the elegant glasses amidst the helicopter noise and the smell of engine oil and both men's sweat gave the proceedings an absurdly formal touch. Both took a generous mouthful and let the pleasurable warmth of the golden liquid take effect.

"I love single-malt whiskies myself," Tom said. "I've never been much of a cognac man, but this isn't bad at all," he conceded appreciatively.

He looked at Cloutard, but did not urge him to go on. He respected the trust the Frenchman seemed to have in him. Cloutard was a crook, but he was a crook with dignity and style.

"Immediately after the auction, I took the shield to the agreed handover point, a villa on Lake Como." Cloutard nipped at his cognac and went on. "I did not see very much there, but I did observe two things I am sure you will be pleased to hear about."

"And they would be . . . ?"

"Madame de Mey of UNESCO was in the house. Is she the ex-girlfriend you spoke of?"

Tom gaped, unable to say a word.

"I was able to look into one of the rooms, and it was there that I recognized her. I think she was unconscious, but I believe she is well. I thought no more about it. In my trade, I have learned to mind my own business."

Tom was confused. "What do you mean?"

"It is only your story that has made me realize that Madame de Mey is being kept there against her will. It was you who told me about her abduction." Cloutard paused to weigh his next words, then asked, "Are you one hundred percent certain she is not part of this? Are you sure she was not . . . pretending . . . when you saw her in Switzerland?"

Tom and Hellen saw so many matters differently, and she had often done things that had made him furious, but the idea that she would lie to him? Impossible.

"No. No, definitely not. Not Hellen. I'd stake my life on it."

Cloutard shrugged and decided not to pursue the point.

"The other thing I noticed is that the artifacts so recently stolen are also being stored in that house. All of them. If you get Hellen, you'll also get the artifacts," Cloutard said.

"You mean the stolen relics are hidden there?" Tom's enthusiasm was palpable. "I have to get there as soon as possible."

It occurred to Tom that this could be a trap, and that Cloutard was only trying to get his own head out of the noose. He had to keep that possibility in mind, of course.

"And what will you do when you arrive?" Cloutard asked. "They have half an army there. And to my chagrin, I must confess that the men I saw there all looked far more determined and professional than my own security guards, whom you had the pleasure of meeting earlier."

Tom finished his drink. He grinned broadly. His spirits and his motivation were back. In his head he was already working on a plan to free Hellen and retrieve the artifacts for Blue Shield.

"I'll come up with something."

36

Hellen had been moved back to her room, and she was certain that guards had now been posted outside her door. She could forget about getting out of there on her own. As much as she hated it, she would have to rely on Tom. They had their differences, certainly, but he would not rest until he had found her and freed her. She was slightly disgusted at herself to admit that the thought of Tom felt good. She quickly banished the idea from her mind and blamed it on her present situation. She couldn't follow it any further anyway: the door opened and her captor entered, holding a large, ancient book in his hands. Finally, Hellen would find out why she was being held captive.

"You and me, we have a lot in common." Guerra's voice sounded neutral, almost indifferent.

"I doubt that," said Hellen, defiant.

"No, really." Guerra spoke patiently, as if to a child who doesn't understand a math problem. "For some time now, we have both been searching for something of great value." Guerra spoke very quietly now, almost whispering, and he watched Hellen closely. Suddenly, she realized what he was talking about. "We have taken some of the hard work off your hands—you can save yourself a trip to Meteora. I already have what was there to find."

Guerra tossed the old book onto the table in front of Hellen. The thick tome slammed loudly, startling her. She looked at the book. With a gesture, Guerra indicated that it was now her job.

"Take a look, be my guest."

Hellen opened the book carefully and looked at the title page in astonishment.

"The *Chronicle of the Morea*"? She glanced at the first pages. "This is a . . . an unknown version of the *Chronicle of the Morea*!"

Hellen forgot for a moment that she was facing her kidnapper and that she was his captive. Her scientist's heart somersaulted for joy.

"I see you know what we're dealing with," Guerra said. "From the information I have, the solution is in there. The book contains the clues to where it is, and you're the one to find them. Get to work."

He turned away without another word and the door closed behind him. Hellen heard the lock click and something being pushed in front of the door. She looked down at the book. Her mind was racing, as was her heart. Could it be? Could her abductor really be right, that this book held the clues she had been seeking for so long?

And another problem—how could she use this information to help herself, and prevent it from aiding her captor? *One step at a time. First, you need to find the clues,* she thought. But the book was massive. She had a lot of work ahead of her. She pulled a chair over to the table, turned the pages and began to read.

37

IN A HELICOPTER OVER THE MEDITERRANEAN SEA

"How far will this thing take us? What kind of range does it have? I need to get to Como as fast as I can." Tom was chafing at the bit.

"*Calme-toi*. The helicopter was fully fueled. If Italy is our destination, we can get as far as Rome. It is a good choice, because I have to go to Italy myself. I need to get to my safe house there and work out how I can deal with Ossana. I also have to find out how far she has infiltrated my network. Someone sent her after me and slipped her into my organization. I need to know exactly what she's up to and where she's been planting her seeds. We can land near Rome; I just have to make a couple radio calls to members of the family there."

Cloutard emphasized the word "family," and Tom understood at once what he meant. He had to squint to see the instruments in the cockpit. The bright morning sun that had risen over Sardinia an hour earlier was dazzling.

"All right. Rome is a big help. I'll take a train north and get to Como from Milan or Bergamo."

Cloutard made contact with the "family" by radio, and launched into a loud discussion in Italian with the other side. Tom decided to update Palffy. He tapped a short SMS into his phone, limiting himself to the highlights and deliberately omitting the fact that he had—at least temporarily—joined forces with an international criminal. He mentioned the lead to the artifacts, that he was on his way to Rome and would continue to Como from there. He pressed send, but the message did not go through: over the open sea, he had no phone connection. It didn't matter. He typed a second message, this one to Noah. Both messages would go out as soon as they were back on land, Tom thought, and put his cell phone away. Cloutard switched off the radio.

"It seems my network is at least partially intact," Cloutard said. "We now have coordinates for a landing site. My Italian friends will be there when we arrive and will help us. They will ensure you get to Como and that I . . . well, that I get to my safe house."

Tom nodded. Teaming up with Cloutard, and now the Mafia . . . *the end justifies the means*, he told himself. But he could never tell Hellen about it, and God forbid that Maierhofer should ever find out. Another bawling out was the last thing he wanted.

"We can land in the woods near Castel di Decima. That is about fifteen miles from Rome."

"I'm grateful for everything, Monsieur Cloutard. I'm a police officer, it's true, but I also sense you're not an evil man. You may steal works of art, but I can turn a blind eye to that. Still, I'm not sure I should be hoping that your criminal organization is still intact."

Both men laughed. They shook hands, both feeling the beginnings of a very unusual bond of friendship.

Cloutard pointed ahead and joked, "Land ho. We'll descend a little and prepare to set down."

Only now did Tom realize Cloutard was still in his pajamas. He was already imagining the looks of the hard-nosed Mafiosi when a crazy, mustachioed Frenchman climbed out of the helicopter in Louis Vuitton silk pajamas, with a cognac glass in his hand.

They crossed a narrow strip of beach and found themselves cruising over a forest. After a few minutes flying low over the treetops, Cloutard eased back on the throttle and pointed to a three-hundred-foot-wide clearing that appeared before them.

"Our landing area."

From a road a quarter of a mile away, they saw two off-road vehicles turn into the meadow and head for the field where they would land.

"The cavalry's on its way," Tom said.

He pointed to the men now getting out of the SUVs. He was impressed at how quickly the "family" worked. Cloutard had now reduced his speed to zero, and the helicopter hovered above the clearing. He had just started to descend when Tom realized that the welcoming committee was not very welcoming at all. The men had automatic weapons aimed at the helicopter.

The first shots came before Tom could even react. The helicopter was hit along one side and several shots damaged the main rotor.

"*Merde!*" cried Cloutard, already trying to regain altitude. Shots were coming from both sides, and Tom had no idea how many bullets had hit them. He was just amazed that the crate didn't explode under them.

Cloutard turned the helicopter back over the forest, veering dangerously to the right. He had no idea where he was going, but they had to get out of the line of fire fast. But the helicopter was almost impossible to control; both the tail rotor and main rotor had been hit and were badly damaged. Dense smoke spewed from the engine. They made it another five hundred yards before the helicopter went down. It fell quickly, crashing through the trees, the branches and trunks reducing it gradually to spare parts.

The fuselage slid across the ground with Cloutard and Tom inside, passing through a small stand of old pine trees and finally grinding to a halt beside a deserted country road. Quickly, they unfastened their seat belts and climbed out of the wreck. Cloutard had just enough time to rescue the cognac box from the helicopter before it exploded, and he and Tom immediately put some distance between themselves and the burning helicopter. A hundred yards away, they collapsed into the grass, both needing a few seconds to process what had just happened. Tom was back on his feet first.

"We have to get out of here. They had SUVs—they'll be here any minute. I'm not up for that right now."

Cloutard nodded. "Here's where we go our separate ways. I have to make some calls. After this attack, I have no idea how much of my organization is left."

Tom shook Cloutard's hand again, and they ran off in separate directions. Tom's phone pinged; Noah's help had come in the nick of time. The message to Palffy had also been sent.

38

Tom had been running north for about fifteen minutes before he arrived in Spinaceto, an unprepossessing district on the outskirts of Rome. He had thrown away his linen shirt; it was covered in blood from the fight with Ossana. Fortunately, the T-shirt he'd been wearing underneath had remained clean. It was still early in the morning, but the Italian sun was already making its presence felt, and the T-shirt was soaked with sweat. Tom slowed to a walk to avoid attracting unnecessary attention and made his way as casually as he could along the main street. Noah had sent him the address of a motorcycle repair shop close to Tom's location. He would be able to get himself some wheels there.

Tom looked at his phone and oriented himself. A couple of hundred yards ahead, he saw the local police station, the Carabinieri Comando Stazione Roma Tor De Cenci. He could not imagine that the Interpol search had made it this far or that his photo was hanging in every police station in Europe, but to be on the safe side he turned into a narrow street just before he reached the police building. He kept a lookout for surveillance as he went, turning away as he passed a camera-monitored entrance at the back of the station.

He crossed a few small streets and then turned into Via Livio Marchetti. He smelled motor oil, and saw the repair shop a short distance ahead. More than twenty motorbikes and scooters were standing in the driveway and on the street, ready to be picked up by their owners after being serviced or repaired. Tom walked slowly past the repair shop and saw that some of the bikes had keys in the ignition. In the driveway, two mechanics were sitting on car tires, chatting loudly and eating a typically meager Italian breakfast of espresso and biscotti. They took no notice of him at all.

Tom approached a blue Moto Guzzi V7 II Special. He quickly swung himself onto the saddle, started the engine and raced away. He turned right at the next corner and rode the wrong way along a one-way street for a block, then crossed a Carrefour supermarket parking lot diagonally and, thirty seconds later, reached the on-ramp of the Strada Statale 148 toward Rome. He twisted his right wrist down, opening the throttle. In thirty minutes, he would be at Rome's central station, Roma Termini, and from there would take the express train to Milan, about an hour away from Como.

However, hadn't noticed the security cameras installed at the motorcycle shop. The garage belonged to the regional Harley Davidson dealer, also based in Spinaceto, who had recently upgraded the repair shop with a modern security system. Five minutes after Tom had stolen the

Moto Guzzi, two *carabinieri* were looking at the security video. One of them recognized Tom as the man wanted by Interpol for murder, and minutes later an order to be on the lookout for him went out to the greater Rome area.

39

François Cloutard was far less fortunate. He had headed west through the woods, and suddenly found himself confronted by five armed *carabinieri*. Cloutard did not realize that he was on Castel Porziano, the private estate of the Italian President. The 23-square-mile nature reserve was closed to the public.

For their part, the carabinieri were astonished to see a sweaty, pajama-clad man with a wooden box under his arm emerge without warning from the forest. They wasted no time, though, and promptly arrested him. The Frenchman's protests fell on deaf ears. They bundled him into a police car and took him to the nearby Carabinieri Commando Stazione Roma Tor De Cenci, the same station Tom had passed just minutes earlier.

"I would like to call my lawyer."

Cloutard was beyond exasperated. The work of years was slipping away like sand through his fingers. He had no idea how far Ossana had infiltrated his organization in the last year, since they had become a couple. By rights, he should have been making sure his funds and the most valuable items in his possession were secure and working to regain control of his organization. Instead, he was sitting in a stuffy little Italian lockup dressed in pajamas, trying to convince the duty officer to finally let him make a phone call.

After a lengthy discussion, Cloutard was led into a small, air-conditioned room where a push-button telephone squatted on a table. The officer pointed to it, left Cloutard alone and locked the door. Cloutard punched in Karim Shaham's number and sat drumming his fingers on the table. He didn't have to wait long: after the third ring, Karim answered.

"Hello? François?" Karim said, and Cloutard knew instantly that something was wrong. Karim sounded distressed, even scared.

"You must help me!" Cloutard said. "Ossana has been screwing with us. I don't know what you have heard, but I had to fly the helicopter to Italy. Unfortunately, it looks like Ossana has gotten to our Italian friends, too, and they shot down the helicopter. I barely made it out alive. Now the carabinieri have me and I'm behind bars. I have to get out of here and get to the safe house. Can we meet there? And can you secure the money as soon as you can?"

Cloutard was speaking extremely fast. In his animated state, he did not notice that Karim was not responding. Now there was silence on the other end of the line.

"Karim? Is everything all right?" No answer. Cloutard grew suspicious.

"Karim's fine. But probably not for long."

Ossana. Cloutard had to compose himself. His equanimity and diplomatic skill stopped him from actually putting into words the ranting and raving in his head.

"What is it you want, Ossana?" he said calmly, surprising himself.

"From you, nothing. After a year at your side, I know everything I need to know. And I don't need Karim anymore."

The gunshot was so loud that the phone receiver seemed to explode. Cloutard heard a short groan, then a second and a third shot rang out.

"Karim!" Cloutard shouted into the line, but he knew it was useless.

"Stay out of my way, François. Or you'll end up like Karim."

Ossana hung up. Cloutard was stunned. He still could not fully comprehend what had happened in the last few hours. He looked around and shook his head. He had one more chance. If things went wrong again, he was finished. He picked up the receiver once more and punched in a number. Two hundred miles away, somewhere in Tuscany, an old rotary-dial phone rang.

40

Tom had abandoned the motorcycle outside the city center and had switched to a local train. As he had drawn closer to central Rome, he had noticed an increasing number of police cars; he would be able to disappear better among the overcrowded and forever-delayed trains of the Italian railway system.

He bought a ticket to Como at Marconi station. Luckily, he still had his money clip with some cash and the credit cards, as well as his fake passport. Everything else had been left behind at the hotel in Tabarka. He boarded the subway in the direction of Roma Termini, where he would change to the *Italo Treno* express to Milan. He would reach Milan about two hours later . . . if everything went smoothly.

Roma Termini, as expected, was a seething mass of people. Tom pushed his way into the large, reinforced-concrete reception hall. He moved past the remains of the Servian Wall, which dated from the 4th century B.C., proceeded through the enormous main hall and finally made it to the station shops. He bought himself a base-ball cap and an AS Roma fan scarf—not exactly the best camouflage, but better than nothing—and procured a cheap knife with a locking blade from a from a tobac-conist's shop, also better than nothing. Tom looked at the departures board and was heartened to see that a Rome-Milan express was leaving in ten minutes. The classic Italian pasta-and-pizza smell filled his nose as he melted back into the crowd, which practically carried him to his platform.

Vittoria Arcano was running late. She was furious with herself: her first day at her new job, and she already knew she wasn't going to make it on time. This was not exactly the best way to start her dream job at Interpol National Central Bureau. With a cappuccino and a copy of "La Repubblica" in her right hand and the remains of a *panino prosciutto e ruccola* in her left, she stepped off the regional train and headed for the subway. She passed a station clock: maybe she would still make it after all. With her thoughts already in the office, she collided with a man going the other way, and the hot cappuccino splashed over the new Armani costume she had bought especially for her first day at work.

"*Porca miseria*," Vittoria cursed. Could the day get any worse? She guessed not, and cursed again at the guy who had bumped into her, who was no doubt just as caught up in his thoughts as she was. The man, wearing an AS Roma scarf and baseball cap, raised his hands apologeti-cally and went quickly on his way. Vittoria was taken aback. Such a gesture was so completely untypical for an

Italian. The man had also not said a word, nor had he started to swear, as she had—very strange. Then it struck Vittoria like a thunderbolt. She fished her mobile phone out of her handbag and quickly searched her emails for the latest Interpol "wanted" mug shots.

Bingo! She knew it. She'd just bumped into an internationally wanted killer. Vittoria could still see him, the AS Roma outfit practically glowing amid the masses of commuters. *Maybe not such a bad first day after all*, Vittoria thought, as she began to pursue the man. At the same time, she called Interpol for reinforcements.

Tom had reached his platform. He threw the cappuccino-stained scarf into the trash, checked with a conductor standing by the train that he was in the right place, and climbed aboard. The Italo was one of the most modern trains in Europe, and was operated by NTV, a private train company. NTV had been founded by Luca di Montezemolo, the one-time chairman of Ferrari, which meant two things: the trains were red, and hellishly fast. On the Rome-Milan route, they would reach a maximum speed of almost 200 miles per hour, just what Tom needed. He found his seat and collapsed into it. He could use a little break. The train began to roll, and Tom was grateful when the conductor came through almost immediately to check tickets. Now he could rest, maybe even get a little shut-eye.

Vittoria had boarded one car further back, and immediately informed the train crew of the situation. She found a seat a few rows behind Tom. Interpol HQ in Rome had instructed her not to let the suspect out of her sight, and under no circumstances to act on her own. They were working on a solution; the Italian police would send a team as soon as possible.

Vittoria was not very enthusiastic about just sitting back and observing the man. She would have loved to be able to arrest him there and then, and be celebrated as a heroine on her first day on the job. But perhaps an opportunity to take the credit herself would present itself after all. Vittoria watched as the man dozed off, briefly wondering if she should try to cuff him right now. But she dismissed the idea out of hand: too many civilians. The man was said to be armed and dangerous. Injured— or, God forbid, dead—passengers would not look good on Vittoria's record. She decided to wait for the backup to arrive.

Half an hour later, the man woke up. He glanced at his watch, looked around, stood up and made his way back to the bathroom. This was Vittoria's chance. She followed him along the aisle to the end of the passenger car, where the bathroom was located. She could picture it clearly: the man would open the bathroom door and find her holding her service pistol under his nose. Snap on the handcuffs, and that was that. Vittoria grinned, already looking forward to her supervisor's praise.

She made the other passengers in the car aware of who she was, showing them her badge and gun and gesticulating frantically to tell them that she was about to arrest a suspect. Horrified, most of the passengers stood and made their way to other cars, looking for safety elsewhere. Vittoria positioned herself in front of the bathroom door, pistol at the ready. Her heart was pounding. She already loved her job.

Tom washed his hands absently. He had to check in with Noah and see if he'd been able to dig up more information about the house at Lake Como. Without Noah's help, it would probably be difficult for Tom to break in, take down the guards, and get Hellen out unharmed. But then he reprimanded himself: one thing at a time. *Focus on the current situation*, he thought. *You're not in Como yet, and a thousand things could happen before you get there.*

He took a deep breath and his mind went back to his training. He was not on a train journey, but on a mission, and was annoyed at himself for having fallen asleep. He had to be more professional, had to stay on guard. Danger could be lurking around every corner, as he had seen very clearly in the last two days. Hell, someone might even be lying in wait for him outside the bathroom door. And it was in exactly that frame of mind that he opened the door—to his great benefit, as he discovered a heartbeat later.

A pistol appeared, pointed at his nose. Tom instinctively moved his head to the right and, with his left arm, knocked the gun a few inches aside so that a shot would miss him. With his right hand he grabbed the pistol itself and twisted the attacker's arm until she screamed and let the weapon fall.

The move caused the woman to fall backward, and she hit her head against the wall. *Narrow things, trains*, Tom thought. He quickly grabbed the woman's pistol and pointed it at her head. He looked around quickly to see if he could expect any more adversaries, but the compartment was almost empty. The woman raised her hands in surrender. She looked up at Tom, her expression a mixture of astonishment, fear and anger at herself.

The train jerked slightly and seemed to slow down. Tom heard the unmistakable thrum of a helicopter and, a moment later, several dull thuds on the roof. He and the woman looked up in surprise.

No way, Tom thought. They still had to be doing a good 150 miles an hour—rappelling from a chopper to a train at that speed was suicide. Vittoria, still on the floor, took a deep breath and smiled archly at Tom. "My reinforcements are here. There's no way out."

Suddenly, Tom heard an ear-splitting whistle and two windows of the compartment shattered. Someone had used a sonic hammer, transforming the train windows into fine glass dust that was instantly sucked out of the train.

41

VILLA ON LAKE COMO

The pain in Hellen's neck was almost unbearable. She had been bent over the ancient book for hours. The *Chronicle of the Morea* was an anonymous historical text dating from the 14th century. In over nine thousand lines, it described events that took place between 1204 and 1292, following the First Crusade; some versions also included later events. Versions had been handed down in four languages: French, Greek, Italian and Aragonese; the Greek text was set in verse. Hellen was familiar with each of the different versions, which were distributed among libraries throughout Europe.

The *Chronicle* in front of Hellen was in Aragonese, but this version was unknown to her; it dealt more extensively with the Crusades and the stolen relics. More space was also devoted to the battle for Constantinople, to which Hellen paid special attention. The Aragonese version of the chronicle, she knew, covered the longest period of all the extant texts, covering events up until 1393.

Hellen combed page after page but could not begin to imagine what "clues" she was supposed to find in the book. She stood up and paced the room for a minute. Her father and grandfather had been on this same search, and from the first moment her father told her about the artifact, she had been hooked. Since then she had spent every spare minute collecting clues from around the globe. But in all that time, she had never realized that someone else might also be hunting for the same thing.

That had all changed two days before. The others on this search had clearly devoted serious resources to the job. All her doubts in recent years about whether her quest made any sense had now been swept away. Whoever was behind her abduction and the plundering of the relics was certainly committed. For Hellen, this only confirmed that the stories her grandmother had told her as a child were true. Instinctively, her fingers rose to the amulet around her neck. It was adorned with a Maltese cross, and had been left to her by her grandmother. The memory made her smile, and a small tear ran down her cheek as she recalled the many happy hours spent with her grandmother and all the exciting stories she had told. She wiped the tear away and turned her attention back to the book. It certainly meant something, if her kidnapper was right, and if the book was indeed the clue that Father Montgomery had spoken of in Glastonbury.

"For you, Grandmother," she said half-aloud as she sat back down at the table, immersing herself in the ancient language in which the book was written. She would plow through the book letter by letter if it meant that she would finally be able to unearth the clues her family had sought for so long. As she read on, she realized how indebted she was to her professor of ancient languages. Like him, she was one of around fifty thousand people in the world who could still speak Aragonese.

42

Tom ducked for cover as four men in state-of-the-art combat gear swung through the windows and rolled skillfully to their feet. Instinctively, Tom had also grabbed Vittoria by the collar and had pulled her into cover with him. It was slowly dawning on Vittoria that these guys could not be her backup. The Italian police would never board a high-speed train. Fifteen seconds after the tactical team swung inside, the train lights went out. At the same time, all the windows still intact turned black. The train was equipped with smart glass, the kind also used for offices or in the sunroofs of modern sports cars. An electrical charge could change the opacity of the glass. *Someone's hacked the train's controls*, thought Tom. He was at the end of the car with Vittoria, holed up near the exit door.

"Go! Into the next car," Tom whispered to Vittoria impatiently. She obeyed, although she had no idea which side she was on, or what was really going on. But her instinct told her she was better off with Tom than with the men in black. Ducking low, with Tom holding the pistol at the ready, they moved into the next compartment. They found the conductor huddled in a corner, screaming vainly into his radio. Tom could decipher only one word in the desperate stream of language: *Aiuto*. Help. The man was as white as a ghost and his forehead gleamed with sweat. Clearly scared to death, he kept crying into the radio for help.

Vittoria slapped the man hard in the face to break his panic. Once he had calmed down a little, she exchanged a few words with him and learned that, along with the loss of control over the train, all on-board communications had apparently been blocked. In the next car, the team was getting organized, and Tom saw them split up. He could see from their equipment that he was up against professionals: their state-of-the-art combat gear included ballistic vests, tactical helmets, night-vision goggles, grenades, Heckler & Koch assault rifles and pistols with laser sights—all the tools of the trade. Any remaining doubt about their allegiance was put to rest when one of them shot a passenger. These were the bad guys. *And they're here for me*, Tom thought. They were everywhere. Vienna, Switzerland, Tunisia, and now here. Who were they? And why did they want him so badly?

Two of the men made their way forward, toward the driver's cabin, while the other two headed straight back toward Tom and Vittoria. Once they moved away from the shattered windows, Tom could make out little more than the red shimmer of their night-vision goggles and the lasers from their pistol sights. Stunned passengers, their faces visible only as red shadows, cowered in their seats, petrified. The intruders ignored them.

The team moved with military precision. A quick look to the left, then to the right, weapons following their line of sight, making sure that the space they were entering wasn't hiding any surprises. Step by step, they moved closer to Tom and Vittoria.

Tom signed to Vittoria to move further toward the rear of the train. As they edged back through the compartment, Tom saw a camera bag on a seat beside an older passenger. Without waiting for permission, Tom opened the bag and removed a large, professional flash unit. The man looked at him angrily, but after a moment's hesitation he seemed to think better of protesting. Apparently, he had learned to distinguish the good guys from the bad very quickly. Tom gestured to the passengers, instructing them to take cover behind the seats and to stay quiet.

Tom folded down the table between two rows of seats that were facing each other and entrenched himself in the gap he'd created. On the other side of the aisle, Vittoria did the same. Then they waited.

The compartment door slid open and the two mercenaries continued their search through the dark train. Four yards, three yards, two. Vittoria clenched the flash in her trembling hands. Tom counted down with his fingers: three, two, one, go! Vittoria jumped up and tripped the flash several times. Like a stroboscope, it fired bursts of light through the dark wagon. The gunmen, blinded by the sudden brightness, swore and tore off their night-vision goggles. Simultaneously, Tom leaped from his hiding place at the nearest of the two men and rammed his knife into the man's throat. The mercenary went down gurgling, but that was the only sound he made: Tom had severed his vocal cords.

The second gunman had also been knocked down by the force of Tom's attack, but he recovered quickly and whipped his pistol into firing position. Tom was faster: his first kick sent the gun flying and it went off, firing a bullet through a window. The second kick knocked the mercenary down and he crashed to the floor between two rows of seats. As he tried to get up again, Tom, supporting himself on the opposite armrests, kicked hard at the man with both feet. The force of the kick launched him against the window; weakened by the bullet, the glass shattered under the man's weight. At 150 miles per hour the noise of the wind was deafening. It drowned out the man's scream as he was sucked out of the compartment.

A few of the passengers spontaneously jumped up and clapped, but Tom signaled to them to keep quiet and sit down. He still had the other half of the team to deal with. He bent over the dead mercenary and searched his pockets. Unsurprisingly, there were no clues to the man's identity. But he had the same, all-too-familiar tattoo on the inside of his forearm. Tom quickly removed the man's headset and attached the radio receiver to his own belt. Then he picked up the assault rifle and ran through the routine check. He looked at Vittoria, briefly considered his options, then pressed the rifle into the young Interpol agent's hands.

"Stay here and look after the passengers. There may be guys on the train that we don't know about," he said.

Vittoria was torn. On one hand, adrenaline was pumping through her veins and she felt like Lara Croft and Wonder Woman rolled into one. On the other, she was pissing herself in fear. Hesitantly at first, but then with growing confidence, she took the gun and nodded at Tom. Vittoria Arcano had grown up several years in the space of a few minutes.

Tom made his way forward with Vittoria's gun in his hand. He had to neutralize the other two men. He moved quickly through the compartments, indicating to the passengers that they should go to the rear of the train. Seeing the gun in Tom's hand, no one argued. They got up and crept toward the last compartment, where Vittoria was waiting for them.

As Tom entered the front section of the train, he heard a shot and instinctively ducked into the alcove by the bathroom for cover. Soon after, the train seemed to leap forward, picking up speed rapidly. At that moment, Tom heard one of the remaining mercenaries speak on the headset: "Have you got Wagner?"

Although Tom was not surprised to hear his name spoken—and naturally mispronounced—it was still like a punch to the gut. All this madness really *was* about him. What had he gotten himself mixed up in? Why had these guys been sticking to him since Vienna like gum to the sole of a shoe? his questions would have to wait. First, he had to neutralize these two and find out why the train was roaring through the Italian countryside at what had become a terrifying speed.

He decided to shift out of defense mode and go on the attack. Years of training were etched deeply into his brain as he switched to battle mode. He saw the two men ahead, in the next compartment.

"Sorry for the bad news, fellas, but no one's got me. One of your guys is sleeping back there. Doesn't look like he'll wake up, either. The other one had to get off the train early." He paused, then said, "By the way, you should figure out how to say the names of the guys you're supposed to kill."

While the mercenaries were still processing this new information, Tom jumped into the compartment. "Hands up and drop your weapons," he yelled, pistol in hand. The two men weren't particularly impressed by his order, and reacted more quickly than Tom had expected. They opened fire immediately.

Tom dropped behind the seats. He returned fire, hitting one of them in the knee. The man collapsed like a marionette, screaming. His partner didn't flinch and left the man where he lay.

Guns for hire, Tom thought. *No camaraderie, no loyalty.*

Tom and the last of his adversaries had both taken cover behind the seats. Stalemate. Tom had to act fast. Sneaking a glance, he saw that the man had taken cover directly beneath a fire extinguisher. He took careful aim and fired. The mercenary, trying to get clear of the chemical cloud spewing from the extinguisher, gave Tom a clear shot, and he took him down with one bullet. Suddenly, Vittoria was standing behind Tom with the assault rifle raised to her shoulder. She pulled the trigger, and the second man, whom Tom had thought out of commission moments earlier, went down for good. He had been about to shoot Tom, who had lost sight of him in the white cloud from the fire extinguisher.

Quietly, Tom said a simple "Thank you."

"*Prego*," Vittoria replied, smiling. *A good-looking guy*, she thought to herself.

Quickly, Tom opened the door to the cab. The control space in front of him looked more like something from a modern fighter jet than a train. Across one of the large touch screens lay the body of the driver, a bullet hole in the back of his head.

The lights and indicators in the cockpit were flashing like a Christmas tree. Tom didn't need to know how to drive a train to know that this was not good. He looked out of the windshield and was momentarily horrified to see the speed at which the train was slicing through the land-scape. On the map display, Tom saw a tight curve and a flashing dot moving toward it, far too quickly. At this speed, it was inevitable: the train would jump the tracks on the curve.

"Sorry, friend, but time's running out," Tom said, and he pushed the dead driver out of his seat. He tried to get an overview of the controls, found the emergency brake button and hammered on it. Nothing happened. At 230 miles an hour, the train continued its headlong rush toward the curve. If they didn't manage to stop it, there was no way they could avoid derailing.

"Any ideas?" He looked at Vittoria, who shook her head. Tom jumped up and ran back to the conductor, who was still sitting on the floor. He pulled him to his feet and dragged him forward.

"You're the only one board who can stop this train, and you're going to do it!"

"But . . . I . . ." the conductor stammered.

"Get it together! Or do you want to die here?"

Back in the driver's cab, the conductor looked around. He tapped like a madman on the touchscreen displays. "Somebody's damaged the software. I can't stop the train from here."

The curve was now alarmingly close. If they didn't come up with a solution soon, it would be too late.

"Think! There must be something!" Tom yelled at the conductor.

"All right! If sections of the train separate for any reason, it triggers an automatic brake. It's not dependent on the software that controls the train; it's a completely autonomous emergency brake."

"Then how do we separate the sections?"

"We can't. They never planned for it. It's just for emergencies."

Tom looked at the map display in alarm and then out the window.

"Are all the passengers at the rear of the train?" he asked Vittoria. She nodded.

"Okay, we do it the hard way. You two get back there, too." The conductor left at once, but Vittoria stopped for a moment.

"What . . . what about you?" she said, her voice faltering.

"Let me worry about that. Make sure the passengers are as far back as possible."

Vittoria nodded. She looked at Tom for a moment and then ran after the conductor. Tom crouched by one of the two mercenaries and took the two hand grenades clipped to his belt.

He ran to the next compartment, only then realizing that the train didn't have the usual doors at both ends of each car. In reality, it was a single long tube, with glass doors separating one compartment from the next. He yanked the pins and jammed the grenades into the joint connecting the locomotive to the car behind it. Then he released the levers on both grenades and dashed back toward where the rest of the passengers were waiting.

The grenades exploded, and the locomotive lurched and separated from the cars behind it. Just as the conductor had said, the brake system kicked in. It activated with so much force that it knocked Tom off his feet. Just ahead, at the curve, the locomotive jumped the rails and plowed into the landscape like a gigantic bullet.

Seconds later, the passenger cars ground to a stop. Tom sighed with relief, but knew he had no time to rest. Rescue teams and the police would be there very soon. He had to get away as quickly as possible and find another route to Como.

He raised one hand to Vittoria in thanks and stumbled out of the train, exhausted. Vittoria made no attempt to follow him.

43

Ready to drop, Tom stomped along a path that crossed a field, heading for the nearest road. When he reached it, he sat down on a stone mile marker at the side of the road to collect his thoughts. The midday sun burned mercilessly. He could hardly believe how many obstacles he'd had to overcome in the last few days. The enemy he was dealing with seemed to be everywhere. No matter where he went, the guys with the tattoos were there too. And they were starting to wear him down.

Once again, Tom weighed his options and thought about what to do next. He was stuck in the wilds of Italy, somewhere between Cremona and Piacenza. He had the tattoo guys and the Italian police on his tail. His phone had been smashed during the fight on the train, he was sitting on a lonely road in the middle of nowhere, and he had no idea how he was going to make it to Como. Hellen had been kidnapped about 36 hours earlier. Whatever the kidnappers were up to, he knew she didn't have much time left.

He was amazed at how quickly a life could be turned around—in fact, it was totally absurd. Out of the blue, his life was suddenly overflowing with exactly the kind of action and excitement that he'd been craving just a few days earlier. The thought made him smile. One thing was certain: if there were ever a worthy opponent in his fight to make the world just a bit safer, it was surely the tattoo gang.

The thought of making the world safer reminded him of his father. In the short time they had had together, his father had said Tom one thing that Tom had never forgotten: *"If you find something in life you believe in, never let go of it. You will never forgive yourself if you do. For the rest of your life, you'll wonder what your life could have been like if you'd only kept trying."*

So far, not much had gone his way. Every time he'd faced the tattooed guys, he'd drawn the short straw. He needed to change that dynamic, and fast. He would free Hellen, find the artifacts, hand them over to Palffy, and then hunt down his parents' murderer. As his friend Noah always said, "If there's a knife stuck in my back, it's not time to go home yet." Tom felt new energy course through him and he realized suddenly just how much Hellen mattered to him. Whether or not they ever became a couple again, her well-being meant more to him than anything else in the world.

Tom stood up from the mile marker and followed the road north, hoping to hitch a ride. At the same time, however, he realized that no sane person would pick him up—not the way he looked. He could hardly believe his eyes when he walked around a bend just after a railway underpass and saw an old but well-preserved bright red Alfa Romeo Autotutto microbus with a flat tire. Around the bus stood four nuns, looking utterly perplexed.

"*Posso aiutarti?* Can I help you?" stuttered Tom in broken Italian, and four concerned faces turned toward him.

He must have made a disconcerting picture: torn jeans, a dirty T-shirt, scratches and wounds marking his face and upper arms. For a few seconds, none of the sisters said a word. Then one of them approached Tom and asked him in English, "What happened to you? Were you on that train that just crashed? Are you all right?"

The nun's concern touched Tom.

"I'm fine, really. It's just a few scratches. And yes, I was on the train." Tom smoothed his clothes a little and ran his fingers through his hair. "I can change that tire for you real quick. It's no problem."

Tom inspected the punctured tire, grabbed the jack and the spare, and in a few minutes had swapped out the tire. The nuns were thrilled.

"Thank God for sending you to us. How can we repay you? Oh, excuse my rudeness I'm all flustered. I'm Sister Lucrezia, the Mother Superior. And these are Sisters Alfonsina, Renata and Bartolomea."

Tom had to smile: the three nuns had unconsciously lined up according to size. *Like organ pipes*, he thought. Sister Alfonsina was at least six foot three and towered noticeably over the others. Sister Bartolomea, on the other hand, was under five feet tall, with Renata and the Mother Superior somewhere in between. Tom grinned, unsure about the correct way to formally greet a nun. Shaking hands seemed inappropriate, so he nodded to the sisters one by one.

"My name's Tom, Tom Wagner. I'm with the Austrian antiterror unit, Cobra. And yes, in fact, there is something you can do for me." Tom glanced cautiously at the Mother Superior. The nuns had pricked up their ears at the sound of "antiterror."

"Should we take you to a hospital? There's a good one nearby where the nuns will take good care of you. With God's blessing, you will soon be well again."

Sister Lucrezia gazed at Tom with concern, examining his countless wounds.

"That's very kind of you, Sister, and I certainly appreciate it, but I have to get to Lake Como as quickly as I can."

The Mother Superior narrowed her eyes suspiciously.

"Why do you have to get to Como so urgently, Signore Wagner?"

Sister Lucrezia's eyes pierced Tom. He could not help himself: he had to tell her the truth.

"A good friend of mine has been kidnapped, probably by the same criminals who have been stealing the relics— the ones who set fire to Notre Dame," he said, the words pouring out in a burst.

The four nuns looked at him shock.

"You mean the bones of the Magi," said Sister Renata.

"And the Crown of Thorns," said Sister Bartolomea.

"And the Shroud," said Sister Alfonsina.

The three younger sisters looked to their Mother Superior expectantly. The diminutive Sister Bartolomea was the first to speak: "It would just be a small detour, Mother Superior. We'll still get to Barcelona on time."

"We are on our way to Barcelona for the sanctification of the *Sagrada Familia*," Sister Alfonsina added happily. "It's just been completed, you know, and the Holy Father is celebrating a mass there. We're all terribly excited. We've been looking forward to the trip for months."

"We could even pay a visit to Father Carlo in Como," added Sister Renata chattily.

Sister Lucrezia raised her hand, silencing the younger nuns. "You will have to explain everything to us along the way, Signore Wagner. But do get in. We will take you to Como. God sent you to us in our moment of need, and because I trust in God, I believe you and we will help you." She paused and squared her shoulders. "Sister Alfonsina, fetch the first aid kit from the luggage compartment. Our first priority is to treat Signore Wagner's wounds. Sister Renata, you unpack the food. Signore Wagner must regain his strength. And you, Sister Bartolomea, find blankets and pillows to make Signore Wagner comfortable. He needs to rest during the journey."

Even before the Mother Superior had finished speaking, the three nuns jumped to do her bidding.

Tom barely had a chance to thank them. "Get in, Signore Wagner. We'll be on our way in a minute."

Tom sat down on the middle row of seats and Sister Lucrezia swung behind the wheel of the vintage bus. She started the engine and floored the accelerator, pressing Tom back into the beige plastic seat. The three nuns behind him giggled. Sister Bartolomea leaned forward to Tom and whispered in his ear, "Sister Lucrezia went to high school with Michele Alboreto. Before she took her vows, he used to drive her around Milan in his Ferrari. They say he even kissed her once!"

"Enough of that nonsense, Sister Bartolomea!"

The Mother Superior's voice cut through the interior of the bus like a circular saw. Sister Bartolomea sat back meekly and held her tongue.

"So, Signore Wagner. Now tell us what's happened. And don't leave out a thing."

44

Cloutard woke with a jolt from his nap when the key clanked noisily in the lock and the cell door was jerked open, creaking loudly.

"You are free to go, Signore," said the officer stiffly. With his left hand, he ushered Cloutard out. Cloutard smiled —that had certainly been quick. He was glad to be out of the stinking cell. At the same time, however, he was overcome by a sense of uneasiness, even fear. He tried to shake it off. He was a grown man, in his fifties . . . it was completely ridiculous to be afraid of what he knew was coming. And yet, he couldn't rid himself of a queasy feeling in the pit of his stomach. He was about to get a severe dressing-down, and there was no getting around it.

The officer led him to the room where he had been relieved of the wooden cognac box and been handed his prison clothes. Someone had apparently assumed that he would be staying longer. Fortune, however, had smiled upon him. With a wry smile, the police officer handed over Cloutard's pajamas and slippers. Cloutard put them on, and the officer led him outside.

Cloutard had to blink when he stepped out into the open. The sun was blinding and there wasn't a cloud in the sky, yet a chill ran through him. He couldn't believe it. He was actually still afraid of her. He, Cloutard, who had built an international smuggling empire and had cut deals with the most villainous crooks in the world.

In his pajamas and slippers, he left the building and saw her in the parking lot. She had driven there in his own car, a 1959 Renault Caravelle convertible, and climbed out when he appeared at the station door. At her age, she was still as fit as when she had raised him. She gazed at him across the parking lot and was already shaking her head in disappointment. He walked over to her and kissed her on the forehead. "Thank you, Giuseppina. I am eternally grateful to you."

"You should be, for all the pain and trouble I've suffered for your sake. But you disappoint me, time and time again. I tried so hard to raise you well, and look what's become of you: a man I have to spring from prison."

"Your late husband ran the Mafia for all of northern Italy. You should be used to this kind of thing." Cloutard knew he'd made a mistake the instant he finished speaking. The look in Giuseppina's eyes could have frozen the Dead Sea.

"Innocento—God rest his soul—was never caught. He never brought shame on our family. He would be bitterly disappointed to that see his foster son is apparently stupid enough to get himself caught. Now stop arguing with me and get in the car. Being around so many cara-binieri is making me sick."

Cloutard refrained from any more objections. She handed him the car keys, pulled on her headscarf and sat in the passenger seat looking at him expectantly. "*Andiamo*, Francesco!"

45

TEATRO TITANO, SAN MARINO

After their brief detour to Pescara, the three men still arrived in San Marino ahead of time. The truck had made it much faster than the three men had expected from the old rattletrap. But the mountain road that led to the small republic of San Marino tested it to its limits.

San Marino is, in all likelihood, the oldest existing republic in the world, with a history that supposedly goes back to the year of its foundation by Saint Marinus in 301. It is located a few miles from the Adriatic coast, near Rimini, and is the fifth smallest country in the world, covering less than twenty-five square miles. The rocky peaks of Monte Titano—a UNESCO World Heritage Site, after which the national theater is also named—are crowned by three ancient fortresses: Guaita, Cesta and Montale. The landscape the men were driving through was a feast for the eyes.

The leader steered the truck through the narrow streets of the old town, the hairpin turns occasioning heated disputes with oncoming traffic, accompanied by the appropriate gestures, and these continued until shortly before they reached their destination. The truck turned into an avenue leading to the back of the Teatro Titano. Their orders were to deliver their package to theater director Jacopo Merelli. The rear dock of the theater, where various backdrops and other scenery were stored, often served as a kind of dead-letter office for all kinds of "deliveries."

They stopped the truck in the middle of a bend at one end of Contrada di Portanova, an old footpath that led through two early baroque arches to the Piazza Sant'A-gata, in front of the Teatro. The plaza offered a breath-taking view across San Marino and the surrounding countryside. The Sammarinese were especially fond of the intermissions and the time before and after a visit to the theater, when they could pursue their favorite pastime in the piazza: carrying on loud, animated conversations with one another.

There was little traffic at that time of day, so chaos didn't immediately erupt when the truck stopped, blocking the road completely. The men climbed out and two of them went to the back to collect the package from its hiding place. Their leader, the driver, went to a small wrought-iron gate, which, as agreed, had been left unlocked. He went down a few steps to the theater's small back entrance, which was surrounded by an old fortress wall. Although the Teatro had been built only in the 18th century, the back looked like a medieval fortress. The man knocked three times on the dark-brown door.

A few moments passed before the door opened and a small man with a bald head and an enormous belly appeared. He wore a green suit over a dark-red waistcoat; a matching tie was attached to the starched shirt he wore underneath with a pearl tiepin. He looked like a theater impresario from the days of Giuseppe Verdi. From the waistcoat hung a gold chain, on the end of which, no doubt, was an antique pocket watch. To all appearances, time in the Teatro Titano had stood still ever since it had been built.

"*Sì?*" The man's voice was croaky and typically Italian.

"We're here to drop off a package."

"You're earlier than expected," Merelli said, but he beckoned the man inside. "Who's going to collect it and when?"

The man shrugged. "When? No idea. All I know is, it's supposed to be picked up by a black woman."

Merelli showed the men the way. "Straight down the hall, then left. The sign on the door says 'scenery storage'. Turn right there and leave it by the wall."

In silence, the men carried the box onto the dock, left it as instructed, then left. Their leader raised his right hand in a departing wave, without looking back. They climbed the steps and hoisted themselves back into the truck, behind which a small traffic jam had formed. Drivers were honking furiously.

Jacopo Merelli was a little surprised: he knew all the messengers who delivered François's goods, but he had never seen these men before.

"Jacopo, the rehearsal is about to begin. We need you on stage." Merelli recognized the voice of his conductor for the evening and he turned his mind to other matters. He might call François about the box tonight, just to be sure.

46

The nuns' bus stopped just outside Milan, where the Mother Superior used Tom's fake ID and credit card to buy him a new cellphone. Now he could contact Noah again. She also surprised Tom with a fresh shirt and a hoodie—his T-shirt had suffered badly in the last few hours.

"The way you look, even the laziest *carabiniere* would pick you up," the nun only said drily when Tom tried to protest. He thanked her from the bottom of his heart.

"You only have to bring our holy relics back to where they belong, Tom. That will be thanks enough," Sister Lucrezia said and smiled at him.

Tom called Noah right away. In the meantime, he had worked out a plan for Tom to gain access to the villa where Hellen was held prisoner. He'd also given some thought to how Tom could execute a rescue. When they were finished the call, Tom turned to the nuns again.

"Well, now all we need are some explosives," he joked.

The three younger nuns looked at Tom in shock.

"*Non fare così*. These are criminals who have stolen our most sacred relics!" their Mother Superior scolded. "Tom is doing his duty, that's all. He is on a mission from God!"

The three nuns nodded diligently, and Sister Lucrezia started the van and drove on. Tom told them the address where he was to meet Noah's contact.

Como is located in the foothills of the Italian Alps, at the southwestern end of Lake Como, which splits at Menaggio into two arms, forming an inverted 'Y': the western arm is Lago di Como, and the eastern is known as Lago di Lecco. To the north, the lake is surrounded by mountains up to 10,000 feet high. On the western arm, stretching northeast from Como itself, numerous splendid villas bear witness to the wealth of Lombardy in the 18th and 19th centuries. But Lake Como attracts not only old money; it is a favored destination of Hollywood stars like George Clooney, Oprah Winfrey, Ben Stiller and Penelope Cruz. *A wealthy corner of the world*, Tom thought as they drove through the town. *And a strange place to hoard stolen artifacts.* The road along the eastern shore of the lake led them to the base of the funicular railway that led up to the mountain village of Brunate.

"This is where we part company," said Tom a little sadly. He had grown fond of his four traveling companions in their short time together. He bowed before the four nuns and shook hands with each of them, but was amazed when Sister Lucrezia embraced him and kissed him on the forehead.

"God be with you. May He protect you on your dangerous mission," she said.

Was it Tom's imagination, or were her eyes a little misty?

"I wish you a safe and pleasant drive to Barcelona. You still have a long way to go, so take care. And give my regards to your boss!"

Tom walked a few steps to the funicular station, bought a ticket, and a few minutes later was on his way to the sleepy village of Brunate. If he had had the time he would have enjoyed taking in the breathtaking panorama of Lake Como—but he didn't have the time. He had to get to Signore Pedersoli's house as soon as possible. Brunate was a small village, so it did not take him long to find out where Pedersoli lived. A few paces uphill brought him to the church, at which he turned right into a small lane. Down at the end, he could see a little man in his late sixties already waving to Tom; it looked like Noah had informed Pedersoli of his arrival. The little man greeted Tom warmly and led him down to the cellar of his house.

"I was very happy to hear from Noah again. I knew him in his Mossad days, you know. And I was on some pretty exotic missions with his father during the Cold War. There used to be a lot more going on in the intelligence world, but it's gotten pretty dull."

A few days earlier, Tom would have agreed with him. "Right now, I'm not bored at all," he said.

"So I've heard."

Pedersoli fished a heavy bunch of keys out of his overalls and unlocked the ancient cellar door. Behind the wooden door was a brand-new steel vault door, complete with a retina scanner and a coded lock. Pedersoli deactivated the security systems and slowly pulled the heavy door open. When he turned on the light, Tom could hardly believe his eyes: Cobra headquarters' armory was nothing compared to what Pedersoli had in there. Nothing but the finest. Tom's gaze swung from assault rifles to sniper rifles, machine pistols, shotguns, automatic pistols and revolvers, bulletproof vests, tactical clothing, blocks of C4, remote detonators, night-vision goggles, and much more. All the well-known manufacturers were represented, especially Glock, Heckler & Koch, and Italy's pride and joy: Beretta. There was even a classic Kalashnikov. Tom was in seventh heaven: his face shone like that of a kid in a toy store.

"Guns. Lots of guns," Tom whispered to himself, grinning.

"In the old days, my buddies used to call me 'Q', like James Bond's quartermaster." Pedersoli smiled proudly. "Life around Como ain't cheap these days. I got two granddaughters who are always after a handout, and of course I can't say no. I got to supplement my little pension somehow."

He pulled a piece of paper out of his other pocket and unfolded it carefully.

"Let's take a look at what Noah's written down."

Tom shook his head. He couldn't wipe the grin off his face. Here he was, in a small mountain village in deepest

Italy, being showered with equipment that his SAS and Delta Force counterparts would be salivating over.

Thirty minutes later, they had everything together. Pedersoli chuckled with satisfaction. "So, that's you properly set up. There's even a satellite phone so you can reach Noah anytime, anywhere."

Pedersoli handed Tom a car key. "There's a little Fiat Cinquecento down in the funicular parking lot. Take it and drive up the eastern shore to the village of Casate. It's almost exactly across the lake from the villa you're headed for. When you get to Casate, you go to the Hotel Villa Aurora and ask for Sergio."

"Sergio? From Rio? Darkish-lightish hair?" Tom said with a laugh.

Pedersoli just looked at him, clearly missing the reference. Tom waved it off. "Never mind. Dumb joke. So, Sergio," he said, growing serious again.

"Yeah. Sergio'll give you a room where you can rest a little, and also the keys to a motorboat tied up near the hotel's wakeboarding dock. From there, you can cross to the western shore at night to get into the villa. Noah's already sent you the details. Just leave the Fiat at the hotel."

Tom nodded, thanked Pedersoli, and left. When he found the Fiat, he stowed the two big black bags with all the gear in the trunk, putted up the eastern shore to the hotel, and allowed himself a few hours' sleep.

At two in the morning he left the room, retrieved everything from the Fiat, boarded the boat, and motored across to the opposite shore. Along the way, he slipped on the tactical vest with its bulletproof inserts, strapped on the thigh holster, and checked his magazines, the Glock and the rest of the equipment.

This ought to be fun, he thought.

In the dark, Tom wasn't able to make out the villa until he was fairly close to the western side. Still a few hundred yards offshore, he angled to the north, not wanting to head directly toward the villa, which lay on a peninsula on the opposite shore. Instead, he pointed the nose of the motorboat toward the woodlands on the eastern side of the peninsula. He cut the engine so that it would not be heard and drifted slowly in to the steep, rocky shore. Except for the soft lapping of the water against the hull of the boat, it was absolutely quiet.

Noah had outdone himself this time. He had hacked into a CIA satellite and streamed the satellite images directly to Tom's new satellite smartphone. The infrared gave Tom a definite strategic advantage. He could see everyone on the property and in the surrounding area. The only thing he couldn't tell with certainty from the satellite imagery was where Hellen was being kept. According to Noah's research, the former owner of the villa had been buried in a crypt on the eastern side of the property, away from the main building. From the crypt, a connecting passage led to the wine cellar of the main building. That would be his way in. But before he could free Hellen, Tom had to make a few preparations around the villa grounds.

47

Cloutard, angry, flung his phone onto his desk. He stood up and, muttering curses under his breath, prowled back and forth in his study. He'd been calling contacts for an hour or more, connections he had painstakingly built up over years, but he was running into brick walls at every turn. Everyone was telling him that plans had changed, and that from now on they would no longer be working with him. Slowly but surely, the true extent of what Ossana had been up to in the last twelve months, while pretending to be his girlfriend, dawned on him. She had undermined his complete network. All his contacts, his authority . . . his entire enterprise, in short, had turned against him.

At least he had managed to transfer the reserves from his bank accounts and put them out of harm's way, because even his private bankers were giving him the cold shoulder. Without Karim, he felt lost.

What preoccupied him most, though, was the question of who was behind it all. Ossana could not be the mastermind. If the raids on the holy relics were tied to this, and if Ossana had managed to turn his business partners—people Cloutard had been working with for years—then he had no doubt that someone else, someone wielding great power, was behind it all. On this matter, though, the usual channels were silent, or denied outright that anyone else was pulling the strings. Cloutard was at a dead end, and a dangerous one at that. He couldn't trust anybody anymore.

"*Putain de merde!*" Cloutard said, only half-aloud. Still, it was loud enough for Giuseppina to hear. She came into his study, in her hands a tray full of antipasti. Under her arm, a bottle of Chianti Classico Berardenga was pinned.

"Enough with all the cursing, Francesco. Make yourself useful and get some glasses."

Cloutard went to the old cupboard and took out two large wine glasses and a corkscrew, and they sat out on the terrace. Cloutard uncorked the wine, and they spent a few silent minutes gazing out at the Tuscan countryside: the gently rolling green hills, the cypress-lined avenues, the narrow roads that twisted like snakes through the landscape, the wafts of fog that drifted through the area morning and evening. The region never failed to calm François and clear his head.

"Maybe you can't remember it anymore, but let me remind you of something," Giuseppina said after a while. "Innocento, God rest his soul, had just picked you up from the street; he brought you here and we fed you. It was the first time in months you had something proper to eat. Back then, Innocento felt the same as you do now. All his associates and even his *consigliere* at the time had turned against him. He had escaped an assassination attempt by the merest margin. He had his back to the wall, had nothing left. Nothing but his belief, which never wavered. And you know what happened next."

Cloutard nodded. "I was still just a kid, but I remember it well. He won back the loyalty, respect and reverence of his people, every single one of them." He looked at Giuseppina sadly. "But you know I am not like that. I am not as tough and ruthless as Innocento was. I've never met a man in my life so—"

"I don't want to hear this," she snapped, cutting him off. "You have no right to talk about Innocento with such disrespect. He was a good man."

Cloutard had no desire to argue with her. His foster father had been many things, but a "good man" was not one of them. Still, Giuseppina had reminded him of something: of how hard he himself had worked to build his organization, and of the countless setbacks he had had to overcome. And most importantly of all, that he had always found some way to win respect without the need to pave his way with corpses.

"You are right, Giuseppina. I will get everything back."

He got up, knelt in front of the old woman, and kissed her hand. She placed a hand on his cheek and patted him lovingly. But only for a moment. Taking him completely by surprise, she slapped his face so hard his ears rang.

"*Avanti*, Francesco. What are you waiting for?"

Cloutard jumped to his feet, startled, partly because of the slap, partly because his phone rang just then. He looked at the screen and the name he saw surprised him.

"Jacopo Merelli! It's been a long time."

Cloutard was pleased to find that, apparently, some people were still speaking to him after all.

"*Ciao*, François. You know I rarely call, but a package has been left with me, as arranged, and it has been here longer than usual. Three men I did not know delivered it yesterday and there has been no contact since. Do you know what it's about? All they told me was that it was going to be picked up by a black woman."

All Cloutard's alarm bells began to ring. "Jacopo, if it is the woman I think it is, she is dangerous. I have no idea what is in that package, but it cannot be worth your life. Be careful. I am near Siena and I am on my way to you right now."

Cloutard hung up and looked at Giuseppina.

"You see how quickly the tide can turn," she said. "Think of Innocento and how sweet revenge always was for him."

She turned her cheek to him in farewell. He kissed her and was already on the way to his car. Yes, maybe this time revenge really would be sweeter than what he was used to . . .

48

VILLA ON LAKE COMO

Hellen had toiled through the book page by page, but without success. She found nothing in the book, nothing at all, that she recognized as any kind of clue. With every page she turned, she could only shake her head in resignation. Only a few pages remained, and she had already given up hope. Once again, her fingers rose lovingly to her amulet, and she thought of her grandmother. She turned the next page . . . and was electrified at what she found.

Something in this book was different. Very different indeed. Here was a passage that she did not know from other versions of the *Chronicle of the Morea*. She found herself reading the account of Robert de Clari, a knight during the Fourth Crusade who had left behind his own chronicle of the times; the account had obviously been incorporated into this version of the Morea text. And not without reason, Hellen hoped. Robert de Clari was one the few who had actually witnessed and documented the existence of the Shroud of Turin in medieval times, so that in itself was a direct connection to one of the stolen relics. Perhaps, she hoped, he also had a connection to the sword, the sacred weapon itself. She skimmed over the lines where Robert reported on the shroud, and abruptly held her breath. There *was* more—not only Robert's recollections of the Shroud of Turin, but about the Sword of Saint Peter.

The Sword of Peter. The sacred weapon. The very weapon she—and, apparently, her kidnappers—were searching for. The sword with which the Apostle Peter had tried to protect Jesus Christ in the garden of Gethsemane, and with which he had cut off the ear of one of the attackers, Malchus, a servant of the high priest Caiaphas.

"Put up again thy sword into his place," Jesus had said to Peter. *"For all they that take the sword shall perish with the sword."*

According to legend, Jesus Himself had even touched the sword, and mystics had attributed an incredible spiritual power to it ever since.

Hellen held her breath and translated the next lines as if transfixed. Robert de Clari reported having been given the task of taking the countless relics that had been moved from the Holy Land to Constantinople to safety. At that time, Constantinople was besieged by the Turks. The city would soon fall, and the relics could not be allowed to fall into the hands of the infidels. If they did, they would be lost forever. Following Robert's account was a detailed list of the relics and to whom they had been given. The majority of the treasures had been handed over to the Knights Templar, who were to take them by different routes and safe channels to the Pope in the Papal States. To Hellen's disappointment, the Sword of Peter was not listed among them. She read on rapidly, and soon brightened.

According to the text, Robert's brother Aleaumes de Clari was an armed monk who had been ordered by his Grand Master, Alfonse de Portugal, to bring the Sword of Peter to the Knights Hospitaller. Similar to the Knights Templar, the Knights Hospitaller were an order formed during the Crusades. A similar number of myths and legends were entwined around the power of the Knights Hospitaller, which had later become known as the Order of Malta. The diplomacy of the Grand Masters, however, meant that the Knights Hospitaller had not been crushed like the Knights Templar had been; their order still existed to the present day.

Okay. We are one step further, thought Hellen. One of the Knights Hospitaller had handed over the sword taken from Constantinople to the Grand Master of the Order. Hellen was not an expert on the Middle Ages, to say nothing of the Crusades and their associated orders, but she did know that the Order of Malta had changed its headquarters often since the Crusades—from Jerusalem to Krak des Chevaliers in Syria, then to Acre in Galilee, then on to Cyprus, Rhodes, Malta, Saint Petersburg, Messina, and finally to the holy city of Rome. The Sword of Peter could be in any of those places. Hellen hoped there were more clues, otherwise the search for the sacred weapon would continue to be like searching for the proverbial needle in a haystack.

She read on and soon reached the end of Robert de Clari's report. Nothing. She skimmed the remaining pages impatiently, but was quickly forced to admit that there was nothing else in the chronicle concerning the sword. She read through Robert's section a second time, more carefully, but she had to face the facts: there were no more clues as to where Aleaumes had taken the Sword of Peter, much less where the sacred weapon was to be found today.

Exasperated, she slammed the book shut and stood up so rapidly that the chair tipped over backward, and slammed her fist on the table. *No! This can't be a dead end*, she thought. *It has to be in here. It* has *to be.*

She opened the book once more and found the page with the list of relics and the references to the Knights Hospitaller. She read the text over and over again, but discovered nothing. She leaned back, defeated, and stared at the open double page. And then she saw it.

At the top edge of the book, close to the gutter, was a single faded word: "Meribah."

Meribah. The name given to the Sword of Peter in the myths surrounding Saint George. According to legend, Joseph of Arimathea had taken the sword to Glastonbury, where Saint George had it to defeat a black knight. The symbolism suggested that Saint George had used the Sword of Peter to defeat the devil; the monks of Glastonbury, in gratitude, gave him the sword as a gift. Saint George was also said to have used the sword in his most famous victory, when he slew the dragon in the Holy Land.

Hellen's heart was beating hard. This page did indeed contain a secret; it was no mistake that the ancient,

232

mystical name of the sacred weapon was written here. She turned the pages forward and backward, scanning the margins for other faded words, and soon found the next one: "Cesare."

"Cesare" meant emperor. The word was derived from Giulio Cesare—Julius Caesar, the first Emperor of Rome. But what did Caesar have to do with the sword? Did it mean that the sword was in Rome? Hellen doubted it. The notion was too far-fetched. But perhaps there were other words that would shed more light on the matter.

She searched on and finally found a third word, but when she read it, her heart literally skipped a beat. She read it over and over again, but simply could not begin to comprehend that this, of all words, should be printed on the page.

"Tifla," she said aloud.

"Tifla" was the nickname her grandmother had given her. As a child, she had not attached any meaning to the word, and even today she had no idea what it meant.

"Tifla" and "Cesare."

Two words that could show her the way to the long-lost sacred weapon, the Sword of Saint Peter. Two words, but she had no idea what they might mean. She needed access to the Internet. Somehow, she had to make that clear to the kidnappers. She stood and pounded on the door.

49

Tom crept through the woods to the entrance of the mausoleum, on the eastern side of the small peninsula. His phone, strapped to his forearm, showed five guards patrolling the grounds: one at the main entrance to the villa, one by the terrace, one in front of the outbuilding to the northwest of the villa, one patrolling the park on the east side of the peninsula, and one on the access road that led to the villa. He estimated he would need twenty minutes to make all his preparations without being spotted by one of the guards. Inside the villa were another five; he would have to put some of them out of action for his plan to work. The thermal imaging also showed a room with two people inside it, and he guessed that was where Hellen was being held prisoner. He hoped that the plan Noah had put together would come off, and also that the man watching Hellen would leave his post. Once he'd covered the entire area and put all his preparations in place, he was ready to go.

By rights Tom should have been on edge, but he was the picture of serenity. This was his element. Most importantly, he didn't have to put his trust in anyone else. He only had to rely on one person, and that was someone he knew well: himself. Tom crept to the mausoleum's entrance, swung the iron gate open noiselessly, and tiptoed down the stairs. Once he was deep enough into the crypt, he could safely turn on his flashlight. He oriented himself quickly. To his right was an alcove holding the vault that marked the final resting place of the villa's former owner. At first glance, it looked as if the crypt ended there, but it was an optical illusion. Just beyond the columns that framed the alcove, a narrow passage led to another door. He tried the handle, but was not particularly surprised to find the door locked. He was retrieving his lock picks when he heard a noise at the entrance. He extinguished the flashlight instantly and held his breath. Someone was coming down the stairs, probably one of the guards on his rounds. A flashlight beam illuminated the crypt. Tom pressed himself against the column. The place smelled musty and damp. His nose tingled, and he put a hand over his mouth and scrunched up his face, trying not to sneeze. He hoped fervently that the guard was not conscientious enough to check the connecting passageway as well . . . but no, the flashlight beam swept once from right to left, then disappeared. Relieved, Tom could breathe again. The guard had only given the room a quick once-over and hadn't come all the way down.

"Sector 3, all clear," Tom heard the guard report into his radio as he moved away from the tomb.

Tom waited a few more seconds, turned on his own flashlight again, and went to work on the door. With a turn of his wrist, Tom felt the cylinder rotate in the lock. He snapped the flashlight off, and the crypt was once again pitch black. Slowly, he turned the door handle and opened the old door a fraction of an inch, but no light escaped through the crack. Tom smiled: so far so good. He swung the door open, turned on his flashlight again, and moved down the long passage toward the wine cellar.

At the end was another door, where he went through the same procedure. Now he was directly beneath the villa. He looked around, the flashlight beam sweeping the room, and inhaled sharply. So here they were! Tom was standing among the relics that had been stolen in the last few weeks. All of them, and many more besides. He hadn't known exactly what had been looted, or how much of it—but he certainly hadn't counted on such a hoard of stolen treasure.

This is going make Hellen and Palffy very happy! he thought. Some of the items, he guessed, had been stolen years ago.

Hellen was tapping away furiously on the laptop. Behind her, a man stood guard, watching closely to make sure she didn't use it to contact anyone, but it didn't matter: doing so would never have occurred to Hellen just then. She had caught the scent, and soon she would know exactly where the sacred weapon she had sought for so long was hidden. How she would get out of her current precarious situation was something she would deal with later.

After a few minutes she had already shed a little more light on things. She had also begun to put together a plan to throw her kidnappers off the scent.

"Get your boss. I've found something he'll like."

The guard looked at his watch and scowled. For a moment, he weighed the abuse he was sure to provoke if he woke Guerra in the middle of the night against the obvious importance of the woman's discovery. He hand-cuffed Hellen to the armrests, left the room with the laptop, and locked the door from the outside. Then he went out to one of the outbuildings, where the men slept.

Tom had moved on, following another connecting passage to the next cellar room. He glanced at his cell phone, checking the infrared satellite feed. Directly above him should be the room where they were holding Hellen—and at that moment he saw the guard step out of the room and actually leave the house.

Easier than I thought, Tom said to himself.

Now was the time. He dashed up the stairs from the cellar and found himself in a hallway next to the main drawing room. There were a lot of art objects and relics in here, too, but Tom had no time for them now. He went to the door, knocked softly and whispered:

"Hellen? Hellen? Are you in there?"

"Tom? What are you doing here?" Hellen said, taken completely by surprise. Her heart leaped. The lock pick was in Tom's hand again, and he immediately went to work on the door.

On the other side of the door, Tom rolled his eyes and shook his head. "I was just down in Como. I dropped in to visit George Clooney and then I thought maybe I'd take a look at the villa where they filmed *Star Wars* and *Casino Royale*. What a question—I'm here to rescue you, of course. Why did you think?"

The lock clicked, he opened the door, and their eyes met. For a few seconds that felt like an eternity to them both, they just gazed at one another, neither of them knowing just how to deal with what they were feeling. Tom stepped inside and carefully closed the door again, checking to make sure no one was coming in the hallway.

"Uh, Tom . . ." Hellen began, clearing her throat. "Could you come back and save me in maybe thirty minutes?"

Tom thought he had heard wrong. "What? Are you drunk?"

"I've figured out what this is all about. It's about the Sword of Saint Peter, the sword I've been after for so long. The guys who kidnapped me are after it, too. I think I know where to find it but I have to send them off on a wild goose chase first, so your timing's a little off." She smiled mischievously. "As usual, you came a little too soon."

Tom couldn't believe it—she was actually serious. He was so put out that he didn't even notice the double entendre.

238

"A guy can't even save you normally. Is this really the time to start a debate? In the middle of your own rescue? What am I supposed to do in the meantime, go for a stroll? Maybe play a couple hands of poker with the guards until the lady's ready to be released? Forget it— this rescue is happening now!"

He knelt down in front of her and turned his attention to the handcuffs.

"Just a few minutes. The guys are on their way here anyway."

"Thanks for letting me know. I'm sure they'll be happy to see me."

In fact, Tom could hear footsteps outside, still a little way off. "Okay, you're right, they're coming. We'll postpone the rescue for now."

"Tom."

"Yes?"

"Thank you. I'm glad you're here."

Tom smiled. "See you in a few minutes. I'll get you out of here, I promise."

He went out, relocking the door, and disappeared in the opposite direction. *This isn't so bad*, he thought. *Now I can look around the house a little more.* And then Tom had an idea that made him smile.

"So you've finally got something?" Guerra said the moment he entered the room with the guard. He pressed his gun to Hellen's forehead, presumably to add a little more weight to his question, and stared down at her, his head tilted to one side.

"Yes. I've found something. I assume you're also looking for the Sword of Peter," said Hellen.

"Clever girl." Guerra took a step back and crossed his arms in front of his chest. "Talk." The guard unlocked Hellen's right handcuff.

"I found evidence in the book that a knight, one of the Knights Hospitaller, spirited the sword to safety while Constantinople was under siege." Hellen opened the book and pointed to the relevant passage. "At that time, the Knights Hospitaller, now known as the Order of Malta, were operating from a fortified complex—a castle in Syria called Krak des Chevaliers," Hellen said with as much conviction as possible.

"In Syria? Krak des Chevaliers?" Guerra's face twisted into a broad grin. "That sounds . . ."

Without warning, an explosion shook the building, taking Guerra, the guard and Hellen by surprise. Dust trickled down from the ceiling. Guerra's radio filled with chatter and he snarled into it, "Everybody shut up. I can't understand a word. What's happened?"

Silence, static. Then a voice, surprisingly timid-sounding for the situation, said, "We're under attack. They're all around us!"

"Whoever they are, find them and kill them," Guerra snapped into his radio. Then, regaining his composure, he turned back to Hellen.

"I suppose this castle in Syria is pretty big. Can you be a little more specific?"

Guerra nudged her temple with the gun again. She closed her eyes. She would have to improvise, she thought. "Well, it's difficult to say exactly . . ." she began. In the distance, bursts of machine gun fire and scattered shots and screams could be heard.

Guerra gave the guard a nod and, without warning, the man punched Hellen in the face. Her cheek felt as if it had exploded and she crashed to the floor along with the chair. The guard pulled her up again. She twisted angrily, her nose and lip bleeding. Guerra leaned uncomfortably close to her, this time pressing the gun under her chin.

"I have no time for games. Tell me," he hissed.

"Okay! Okay!"

Hellen pinched her eyes shut and forced herself to calm down, then opened them again and immediately began to speak. The words poured from her like a waterfall, and she amazed even herself at the flashes of inspiration that came to her. She was glad that Krak des Chevaliers was a UNESCO World Heritage Site, and that she knew quite a lot about it.

"In the Knight's Hall at the castle, there are several statues, including one of Saint George," she said. "Saint George possessed the Sword of Peter, and according to legend he killed a dragon with it. This part of the *Chronicle* contains the reference to Saint George."

"And this is an old Syrian word." She pointed to the faded "Tifla" in the margin. "It means 'fortress,' and it points directly to the Krak des Chevaliers. The sword is hidden inside the statue of Saint George, I'm certain of it. The Knights Hospitaller had to hide it because the castle was constantly under attack."

Hellen could not stop talking.

"The Knights' Hall in the Krak des Chevaliers was said to be comparable to King Arthur's Round Table. And another parallel: Excalibur was the sword of King Arthur, Meribah was the Sword of Saint Peter," she said, and pointed to the word in the margin. "It can only be in the statue," she said, finishing her monologue.

An icy smile crept over Guerra's face as Hellen told him the monumental lie.

"Fuck!" someone shouted on the radio. "They're everywhere. They've got us surrounded."

Two more explosions, closer this time. Screams and more shots. Hellen was trying hard not to smile. Guerra grabbed the *Chronicle* and bawled over the radio:

"We're moving out! Everybody to the speedboat. If you're not at the boat in thirty seconds, you stay here."

With one foot out the door, Guerra paused, turned back to Hellen, and pointed his gun at her.

"Thanks, by the way. You've been a big help."

Hellen eyes opened wide with fear. At that moment another explosion shook the building, but this one sounded different. It wasn't just one big bang, but a quick series of smaller explosions. Smoke, splinters and fragments of stone shot upwards from the floor in a circle around Hellen's chair. The floor trembled, then collapsed underneath her, and she and the armchair dropped straight down into the cellar. Guerra was knocked down, his shot missing Hellen by inches. In seconds, the room and the corridor filled with billowing dust. Guerra, dumbfounded, stared at the circular hole in the floor. His colleague pulled Guerra to his feet. "We gotta get out of here!"

Hellen had cried out in horror as she dropped through the floor. She coughed and spluttered. After the dust had settled, she saw Tom stepping out of the dust cloud with a grin covering his face.

"Are you crazy? You could have killed me!"

"No way," he replied. "Shaped charge. It's like an explosive scalpel." Still grinning, he showed her the remote detonator in his hand. "I wanted to make sure you'd actually come with me this time, instead of sending me away again."

When he got outside, Guerra looked around at the rising smoke and devastation, caused by the numerous explosions that had been triggered in different parts of the grounds. He ran down to the pier, followed by the last of the guards, who came running from all directions. Only four made it to the boat; the rest had either fallen victim to one of the explosions or been put out of commission by Tom. One by one, the men jumped into the speedboat as Guerra started the motor. He gunned the throttle just as the last of the survivors was pulled into the boat by his comrades. Moments later, the boat disappeared into the darkness.

Tom freed Hellen from the handcuffs still holding her to the chair and helped her to her feet. She threw her arms around his neck and held him tightly for a moment.

"Thank you for coming for me," she said. Then she stepped back and slapped his face. "And that's for almost getting me killed."

Tom lifted his hand to his stinging cheek and said, "You're welcome. By the way, the stolen artifacts are all in the wine cellar. We should tell your boss at Blue Shield."

"What? Where? I need to see this!"

She clambered over the pile of rubble and ran down the passage to the wine cellar. Tom was close behind her.

"A couple of the smarter guards let me overpower them. I've left them in cable ties for the authorities, but a few weren't so bright. They'll need to be picked up around the grounds."

Tom grinned smugly as he walked behind Hellen, who paid no attention to him whatsoever. She cried out joyfully when she entered the wine cellar, to find the stolen relics lined up neatly before her.

50

Ossana parked her Alfa Romeo Giulietta on the piazza, directly in front of the main entrance to the Teatro Titano. She never entered any building through the back entrance; that would be beneath her. The plaza was deserted. There was almost no sound at all, in fact, apart from the distant buzz of an Italian city awakening. No performances were taking place that day and only the small box office, where one could buy tickets at any time, was occupied. Ossana entered the small, musty room and leaned across the counter. On the other side sat a thin, older woman with pinned-up hair and thick glasses dangling from her neck on a gold chain.

"*Buongiorno*. Can I help you?"

Ossana saw immediately that the woman's friendliness was feigned. She had probably been selling tickets there for decades and hated her job.

"I have an appointment with Direttore Merelli."

The elderly woman's expression didn't change. She picked up the rotary phone and dialed a single-digit number. "Who shall I say is calling?" she asked Ossana without turning away from the phone.

"Just tell him I'm here for the package."

Again the woman's expression didn't change. "Direttore Merelli is in the auditorium."

"I must speak with him alone," Ossana said.

"He is alone. He likes to work on the stage or up in one of the boxes. He loves the atmosphere." The woman smiled a little wistfully, as if she admired the way the theater air could still stir Merelli's blood. The woman pointed to a door.

"Through there and left, up the stairs to the parterre. Go straight ahead and you'll come to the auditorium."

Ossana nodded and left.

François Cloutard hadn't been to San Marino in years. He was pensive and on edge, but he still smiled to himself as he steered his car up the steep, narrow mountain road. Realizing that, as usual, there would be no free parking spaces behind the Teatro, he drove around to the main entrance. He parked his old Renault and looked across the Piazza Sant'Agata. The sun was shining, and the square radiated peace and quiet. There was not another soul in sight, but there was one other car, an Alfa Giulietta parked in front of the box office. Cloutard's gut was telling him to be careful.

The woman in the ticket office looked up when he entered.

"I'd like to see Direttore Merelli," Cloutard said.

The woman narrowed her eyes. The crowds they were getting today! But she decided it was none of her business.

"You'll have to wait. He's in a meeting."

"It's important. Is he in the auditorium?"

Surprised at how well the man seemed to know the *direttore*, she simply answered, "Yes, of course. But—"

She didn't get to finish her sentence. Cloutard was already through the door and racing up the stairs.

Ossana reached the parterre and looked around. The auditorium was plain by the standards of an Italian theater: sparsely decorated, almost barren. She had never had any interest in theater or opera, and the Teatro Titano was not going to change that.

Merelli approached her from the stage, already carrying the package. Puffing a little, he placed the heavy box at Ossana's feet. "*Buongiorno*. I think this is why you're here," he said.

Cloutard reached the top of the stairs and saw the doors leading to the parterre. He paused briefly, trying to recall the way to Merelli's favorite loge, and it was then that he heard it: Cloutard was no weapons expert, but he knew what a pistol sounded like, the otherwise deafening shot muffled by a suppressor. Three more muted shots followed, and each one hurt as if Cloutard himself had been struck. Someone certainly wasn't taking any chances.

Cloutard knew at once that he was too late. He had to decide, and fast. Shootouts and hand-to-hand combat were not his style. Instead, he tiptoed to the cloakroom, crouched behind the counter, and peeked out at the main entrance to the parterre.

He ducked back and held his breath when Ossana exited with the flight case. She strolled down the stairs without haste, almost pensively, with a smile on her face as if she were enjoying herself. For a moment, Cloutard was tempted to rush to Merelli's aid, but he knew it would make no difference. His old friend Jacopo was dead. There was nothing Cloutard could do for him now. He hated himself for it, but it made more sense now to follow Ossana. He had to hurry to make sure she didn't get away, though he still had no idea what to do about her.

He hurried down the stairs, careful not to make any noise. At the bottom, he looked cautiously around the corner in time to see Ossana leaving the theater. Cloutard watched her go to the trunk of her car, put the case inside and drive off. His chances were not good. He had to wait until she left the piazza or she would see him, so she would have a solid head start. There were only a few roads from San Marino back to the valley, but Ossana would still be able to escape him quickly. He waited inside the entrance doors until her car disappeared around the corner of the building, then he ran across the piazza, jumped into his car, and went after her.

The first few hundred yards were easy, as there was nowhere a car could turn off Contrada delle Mura. The first intersection was by the Museo di Stato, but Cloutard was close enough to see Ossana's Giulietta continuing straight on. That meant she was probably taking the usual route out of San Marino, a route Cloutard knew well. The direction she took at the traffic circle at Stradale Provinciale 258, a few miles beyond the border of the tiny republic, would tell him where she was headed. Cloutard hoped he would be able to keep enough distance between them—he did not want to attract Ossana's attention.

He reached the intersection just in time to see Ossana turning north, toward the highway to Bologna. Cloutard was glad that he had filled the tank just before San Marino. He settled in for a long chase.

51

VILLA ON LAKE COMO

"Okay, tell me everything. What's the deal with this sword?"

Hellen and Tom were sitting in the living room at the villa, waiting for the Blue Shield people to arrive.

"I've been searching for the Sword of Peter for years, and my family has actually been searching for it for much longer."

"The Sword of Peter? The thing Peter used to cut off Malchus's ear when he tried to stop Jesus from getting arrested?"

Hellen was impressed. "So you've got more upstairs than guns and women after all."

"My religion teacher at school made us do drawings of every scene from the New Testament. There was blood and action in that one. That's why I remember it."

Tom smiled mischievously in a way that Hellen had always found irresistible. She caught herself rediscov-

250

ering just how attractive she found that smile, and quickly went on.

"It seems we're not alone in our search for the sword. Someone else who was looking for it murdered Father Montgomery in Glastonbury, but not before he pointed them toward a book called the *Chronicle of the Morea*. Remember that shooting at the Meteora monastery in Greece?"

Tom nodded.

"Same guys. In Meteora, they got their hands on the book —the same book in which I've just found indications that the Maltese Knights took the sword during the siege of Constantinople, after the Fourth Crusade."

"Maltese? The guys with the falcon?" Tom said, teasing. But he quickly corrected himself. "You mean the Order-of-Malta Maltese, right? The one that's a relief organization now."

"Yes, that's them—the Order of Malta. Like the Knights Templar, the Order of Malta was formed in Jerusalem in the 11th century, but quickly changed from a religious order to a chivalric order, the Knights Hospitaller. Emperor Charles V gave them the island of Malta in 1530, but they lost it to Napoleon in 1798. There are quite a few myths woven around the knights . . . and a whole lot of conspiracy theories, too. When the Knights Templar were crushed, the Order of Malta got most of the Templars' wealth. Even today, no one knows whether they ended up with the great treasure of the Knights Templar as well."

"And they still exist today? That would mean the relief agency is just a front for an ancient order of knights pulling strings in the background, an order whose power spans the entire globe? Some conspiracy theory crap like that?"

"Yes, exactly that kind of conspiracy theory crap. But let me clear that up right off the bat: there's no substance to any of it. Yes, there are definitely a couple of question marks hanging over the history of the Order of Malta, but I don't buy into the conspiracy idea at all."

"Question marks?"

Hellen pondered for a moment. "Many intelligence officers were part of the Order: Hitler's chief of intelligence, Reinhard Gehlen, was a Knight of Malta. So were William Casey, the CIA chief during the Iran-Contra affair, and Alexandre de Marenches, head of the French secret service. And they're just the ones we know about."

"That doesn't sound all that dubious." Tom shrugged.

"That's right, it's not. But Licio Gelli, Roberto Calvi and Michele Sindona were also members."

"Never heard of 'em. Pizza guys?" said Tom.

"They led an organization called Propaganda Due, an Italian Masonic lodge set up in the 1970s as a front for a secret political organization. Propaganda Due was a conspiratorial network created by leaders of the police, military, business, politics, the Mafia and the secret services. They had plans for a *coup d'état* that was linked to the staged terrorist attacks of the 1970s; it was all confirmed later in judicial inquiries. Propaganda Due was disbanded and banned outright in 1982."

"You mean they committed terrorist acts and tried to pin the blame on someone else?" Tom asked.

"Yes. But it was just a handful of black sheep. The Knights of Malta aren't out to run the world. Today, they really are a humanitarian institution; they've put those old stories behind them. Even Otto von Habsburg was a Knight of Malta, and no one can accuse him of anything underhanded. I'm just surprised that they're supposed to be in possession of the sword, or at least were."

"I see. So exactly what clues do we have now?", asked Tom.

"Like I said, I found indications hidden in the *Chronicle of the Morea*. There were three words written in the margins that might help us: 'Meribah,' 'Tifla,' and 'Cesare.'"

Tom looked at her in anticipation. "Don't keep me in suspense. What do they mean?"

"Well, 'Meribah' is a clear reference to the Sword of Saint Peter. That's what it was called in the legend of Saint George."

Tom nodded.

"With 'Tifla' it's a little different. My grandmother used to call me Tifla."

Tom looked up. "What does your grandmother have to do with all this?"

"I'm not sure, but I do know one thing. 'Tifla' is more than just a cute name. It has many meanings, including 'little girl' in the Maltese language."

"So another reference to the Maltese?" Tom wanted to know.

"No doubt. The third word makes it interesting. 'Cesare' has a historical link to the word 'emperor.' But I believe it has nothing to do with that, because there's also a second connection. The Maltese surname, Cassar, derives from 'Cesare.' And Cassar was an important name in the history of the Order of Malta. Girolamo Cassar was the most famous Maltese architect of the 16th century. He built a number of important buildings in the capital, Valletta—the Grand Master's Palace, St. John's Co-Cathedral, and quite a number of palaces. He was the favorite architect of the Order of Malta's Grand Masters."

Tom was warming up to Hellen's story. "So we have to go to Valletta?"

"We?" Hellen looked at Tom in surprise. "You want to help me find the sword?"

"Sure. The Guerra who kidnapped you is the same guy who killed my parents. If he's after the sword, then I'm after the sword. Have you found out anything else?"

"Okay," Hellen began. "The short version: Aleaumes de Clari was entrusted with keeping the Sword of Peter safe on behalf of the Order of Malta. The faded 'Meribah' was a clear reference to the sword, 'Tifla' points us to Malta and 'Cesare,' or Cassar, narrows the search even more. It may be that the sword is hidden in the Grand Master's Palace in Malta."

"It *may* be?" asked Tom.

"I'm convinced the trail leads to Malta. But the Order has a long history, and it has also moved around a lot. There are actually two Grand Master's Palaces; there's one in Rhodes, too. So there are several possibilities. The Order also spent quite a long time in Syria, which is where I sent Guerra on a wild goose chase." Hellen proudly folded her arms over her chest. "Your timing was great, by the way. Your fireworks spectacle went off right after I lied to Guerra about Syria. He had no time to get anything else out of me, so he's probably on a plane to Syria right now. But he's not going to find anything there —at least, I hope he isn't."

"While we go find the sacred weapon in Valletta," they suddenly heard Count Palffy cut in. He'd apparently been hovering behind them for some time, listening to Hellen's explanation. "Although I must say, I don't believe we will find the sword in the Grand Master's Palace."

Hellen jumped up and hugged her mentor.

"Thank you for bringing my Hellen back safely," Palffy said, shaking Tom's hand warmly. "And for retrieving the lost artifacts, of course."

Palffy had brought company. A team from the Italian Blue Shield unit had arrived with him. He instructed them to catalog all the recovered artifacts and return them to their rightful owners as soon as possible.

Together they went into the basement, where Palffy could hardly contain himself. "Good Lord!" he cried, inspecting a painting that was leaning against a wall. "This is 'The Storm of the Sea of Galilee' by

Rembrandt. It was stolen in Boston in 1990. They had this, too?"

"I doubt it will be the last valuable work of art you find," said Hellen. "There are countless boxes here. It's going to take a long time to go through everything."

The Blue Shield team had already started loading the artifacts onto the trucks parked outside the villa.

Hellen remembered what Palffy had said earlier: "You said you didn't think the sword was in Valletta. Why? Did I send those guys to the right location by mistake after all? Or should we be looking at Rhodes, instead?"

"I did not say the sword wasn't in Valletta, my dear. I only said that I do not believe it is in the Grand Master's Palace," Count Palffy corrected her.

Hellen looked perplexed. "Yes, but where else could it be?"

"I believe your theory is correct, Hellen. But the whole of Valletta is basically a monument to the Order of Malta. The entire city is a UNESCO World Heritage site, as you know. There are many, many places where the sword could be. I do believe, however, that I can help you find it."

"Do you know Valletta? Do you have some idea where we ought to start?" Hellen was only a little surprised—Palffy always had a surprise or two up his sleeve.

"I happen to be a member of Sovereign Military Hospitaller Order of Saint John of Jerusalem, of Rhodes and of Malta, as we are officially called. In other words, I am a Knight of Malta myself. In fact, my family has been asso-

256

ciated with the Order for centuries. I have never flaunted it, of course; we Knights don't like to make a big deal out of these things. But my inside knowledge of the Order can probably help. I think we should start our search at St. John's Co-Cathedral. Gerolamo Cassar built that one, too. And the Cathedral is an important place for the Order of Malta; almost all of our Grand Masters have been laid to rest there."

Palffy took out his cell phone and tapped in a number. He lifted the phone to his ear, and when the call went through, he instantly slipped into his command tone.

"I need the private jet again, Milan airport to Malta, ASAP. How long before we can take off?"

Palffy waited a few seconds, then nodded, satisfied, and ended the call. With a gleam in his eye, he looked at Hellen and Tom.

"Better pack your things. We fly to Valletta in two hours. We must hurry, lest someone interfere. The Sword of Saint Peter is waiting to be found."

52

ST. JOHN'S CO-CATHEDRAL, VALLETTA, MALTA

Tom, Hellen and Count Palffy were standing in front of St. John's Co-Cathedral in the center of the Maltese capital, Valletta. The city is situated on the northeast coast of the island, on the headland of Monte Sciberras, which is surrounded by the two largest natural harbors in the Mediterranean: Grand Harbor and Marsamxett Harbor. Valletta is surrounded by a ring of bastions and was historically considered one of the most secure cities in the world. The southern entrance through the former city gate is flanked by two cavaliers, named for Saint James and Saint John. From the entrance, clockwise, follows a series of outward-facing bastions, most named after saints: Michael, Andrew, Salvatore, Sebastian, Gregory, Elmo, Lazarus, Barbara and Anthony. At the time of the Knights Hospitallers' rule, each of the bastions was defended by a different so-called "Tongue" of the Order of Malta. The Order of Malta officially named the city *Humilissima Civitas Vallettae* ("Most Humble City of Valletta") after Jean Parisot de la Valette, the Grand Master of the Order at that time. A place of indestructible bastions, baroque edifices and the splendor of the later Grand Masters, Valletta earned a reputation as the most splendid of all European cities; it has been a UNESCO World Heritage Site since 1980.

Hellen, Tom and Palffy entered the cathedral. Inside, the walls were covered by magnificent gold reliefs stretching from the floor to the very top of the arches that formed the entrances to the chapels, a good thirty feet or more. The floor of the church consisted entirely of a series of tombs, the slabs forming a kind of medieval "Walk of Fame." The richly decorated tombstones told the stories of the 375 Grand Masters of the chivalric order who were buried there. The cathedral ceiling was decorated with a succession of glorious paintings; while perhaps not quite as magnificent as the ceiling of the Sistine Chapel, it was still a breathtaking sight.

"If I remember correctly, you said the version of the *Chronicle of the Morea* you read was in Aragonese, didn't you?"

Palffy's question took Hellen by surprise. "Yes. Will that help us find a clue about the sword here?" she asked excitedly.

"St. John's is unusually constructed for a cathedral. Instead of the side aisles you find in many cathedrals, there are eight ornately decorated chapels, each one allocated to one of the 'tongues' of the order and dedicated to its patron saint."

"Tongues?" Tom asked.

"The headquarters of the order was moved to Rhodes in the 14th century, and ever since, the order has been divided regionally into eight branches, which we call 'tongues,'" Palffy explained. "And one of those eight chapels is the Chapel of the *Langue* of Aragon."

Hellen could hardly contain her excitement. "Which one is it?"

The three visitors made their way through the nave, about a hundred and fifty feet long, until they found the Chapel of Aragon, the third one on the right side. When Hellen entered the chapel, she burst out, "Oh my God! Saint George!"

At the far end, flanked by four red marble columns, hung a painting by Mattia Preti depicting the myth of Saint George's victory over the dragon. "Saint George is connected directly to the Sword of Peter," Hellen said. "According to legend, he had the sacred weapon in his possession for a time, when he slew the dragon. We're in the right place."

Hellen's cheeks were flushed with excitement. Tom grinned. He found her enthusiasm endearing. Palffy was also clearly excited. Beneath the painting was a small tabernacle, on top of which stood six candlesticks and a black metal cross about two feet high. Three solid marble steps led up to the tabernacle. Hellen stepped over the red cord prohibiting access to the altar area; she wanted a closer look at the painting. Palffy followed.

"Stay here and make sure nobody comes," Hellen said to Tom in a surprisingly imperious tone.

Tom shrugged. He posted himself at the chapel entrance and stood lookout. It was late in the day, and the church was not very crowded at that time anyway. Hellen inspected the painting more closely, but found nothing to help them.

"In the *Chronicle*, I saw the clues only when I looked a third time. They aren't supposed to be easy to find."

She ascended the three stairs and examined everything carefully: the six candlesticks, the golden frame of the tabernacle, the portrait of a monk and an angel that graced the tabernacle door. In her enthusiasm, she got carried away—she picked up the candlesticks one by one, yanked on the tabernacle door and examined each decorative element for clues. Nothing. In ten minutes Hellen and Palffy had scrutinized the entire chapel and studied all the marble panels, but had found nothing useful at all.

"Perhaps the cross holds a clue?" Hellen already sounded a little disheartened. She stretched as far as she could and grasped the cross that stood atop the tabernacle. She lifted it, but nothing happened. It didn't make much difference what she did with the cross now, so she took it down and turned it this way and that. Both she and Palffy inspected the front and back and the base plate, looking for any possible moving parts.

"Maybe we shouldn't be so fixated on this particular chapel," Hellen said. "Maybe we should take a closer look at the others, as well."

Tom glanced at the time. "We probably won't get to it today. They'll be closing soon. And to be honest, it's probably best if no one catches us tearing their church apart."

"You're right. Maybe we ought to do some more research overnight and come back tomorrow. I'll put the cross back," said Hellen.

Palffy nodded and retreated to the other side of the rope barrier. Hellen stretched to return the cross to its place, but only when she went to set the cross down did she notice the recess in the marble for the base. Standing on tiptoe and stretching as far as she could to fit the cross into the recess, she lost her balance for a moment. Harder than she had intended, the cross dropped back into place. A soft "clack" sounded, and the door of the tabernacle sprang open a crack.

An excited squeal escaped Hellen, a sound that Tom knew well. Palffy spun around and opened his eyes wide. He was back at her side in a moment.

Together, Hellen and Palffy peered into the space inside the tabernacle. Inside was a black marble sphere, with a Maltese cross carved into the side facing them. Inspecting it more closely, they saw that it was topped by another Maltese cross, this one made of black metal. On one side was a cavity, about the right size to fit a small candle. The object reminded Hellen of the *globus cruciger* on display with the Holy Lance in Vienna. Hellen and Palffy looked at each other in delight. As thrilled as a schoolgirl, Hellen reached into the tabernacle and lifted out the heavy sphere.

"Damn it, Hellen, what are you doing?" Tom said. He looked around to see that no one was watching her. At the cathedral entrance, he saw a priest who had just started to inform the few remaining visitors that the church would soon be closing. "Someone's coming," he hissed. "Hurry!"

Hellen, meanwhile, was taking a closer look at the artfully worked object. She discovered that the cross on top was a kind of lid. She removed it, revealing a small, circular recess underneath. She could see that the recess was connected to the candle-sized niche on the side. Hellen saw four small hollows carved into the marble around the circular recess; if connected, they would form another Maltese cross. She started, drawing in a breath sharply.

"Oh my God," she cried.

Her hand moved to her chest and she began almost to hyperventilate. Palffy looked at her with concern. "Are you all right?"

Hellen had turned chalk-white. Her hand seemed to be cramped around the amulet under her blouse.

"A little quicker, please," Tom hissed again. "We'll have a visitor any second."

He looked anxiously toward the approaching priest, but Hellen and Palffy ignored him. Hellen voice was almost inaudible: "I think I know now why my grandmother used that Maltese word as my pet name, and why she left me this amulet."

Hellen fished the pendant out from under her blouse. Her memory flashed back to Father Montgomery, who had seized it at the moment of his death and had said something about a "key." Palffy stared at the amulet.

"That's—", his voice faltered. He seemed to have trouble believing what he was seeing. "The amulet is a Maltese cross."

Hellen took the pendant from around her neck, removed it from its chain, and slid the amulet into the recess atop the black ball. There was a soft click. The amulet fitted perfectly into the recess on the sphere, and the ball was now complete.

"'Cherish it always. One day, in a dark hour, the light will lead your way,'" Hellen whispered to herself. "Those were my grandmother's last words. When she closed her eyes forever, she pressed the amulet into my hands." Hellen had a lump in her throat. She found it difficult to speak, and a hot tear ran down her cheek. "I had no idea what she meant back then. I always assumed they were just the confused last words of my dying grandmother. Forgive me, *Grootmoeder,*" she said, the last words murmured to herself.

Tom couldn't wait any longer. The priest had almost reached at the Chapel of Aragon. He had to act. Tom strode toward the priest and struck up a conversation with him. The man was already alarmingly close—a few more steps and they would have been discovered. Tom put on a look of despair. "Father, I'm afraid I'm in trouble. I need to confess my sins." Tom took the priest by the sleeve and pulled him away toward the confessional.

Palffy, meanwhile, calmly took the orb in his hands and looked at it more closely. He noticed that the bottom had been flattened; two small, parallel indentations seemed to suggest that the ball could be attached to something—

and he already knew to what. There was only one place in the church where the sphere was meant to rest.

He pointed to a tiny coat of arms between the indentations. "I know where the orb belongs, my dear. This is the coat of arms of Grand Master Jean de la Cassière. I never thought I would see the day . . . Historically, Jean de la Cassière was one of the most controversial of the Order's Grand Masters. He fell out with the Order, and they went so far as to depose him and imprison him at Fort St. Angelo. For a while, in fact, there were two Grand Masters, not unlike the time when there were two popes. In the end, Pope Gregory XIII settled the dispute and officially reinstated Jean de la Cassière as Grand Master."

Palffy looked as if he was about to launch into an even more in-depth history of the Grand Masters, but Hellen headed him off.

"Tom's distracting the priest. If we want to get anything else done today, we don't have much time. Where do we have to go, Nikolaus ?"

Palffy nodded. Taking the ball and the small cross, he indicated to Hellen to follow him. Hellen closed the tabernacle door, and they left the chapel and hurried off toward the crypt, which housed the sarcophagi of several important grandmasters. Tom was just leaving the confessional, slipping a few cable ties back into his pocket and leaving the priest securely bound and gagged behind him. Hellen, speechless, could only gape. Tom put on his most innocent face, shrugged, and hurried after Hellen. Palffy was already descending a stairway ahead.

"It was a boring conversation anyway," he said.

When Tom reached the crypt, Hellen and Palffy were already standing next to one of the sarcophagi. The crypt was a surprisingly welcoming place, with light-colored marble floors, white walls with baroque-era decorations in gold and a simple altar on the left, decorated with the crucifixion scene and the obligatory Maltese cross. The most important Grand Masters of the chivalric order had been laid to rest here, each in his own white, elaborately decorated marble coffin. On the right, in a niche directly opposite the altar, was the coffin of Grand Master Jean de la Cassière. Small notches had been chiseled into the center of the marble slab that formed the top of the coffin; they looked to be the exact counterparts of the indentations in the sphere. Palffy set the orb onto the guides and slowly pushed it backward. Again, a soft click sounded.

"We need a candle," Palffy said.

"I left the Christmas decorations at home, but maybe this would do the job?" said Tom, handing Hellen the small tactical flashlight he kept in a belt clip at his waist. Hellen rolled her eyes, then clicked the button and aimed the beam into the opening in the side of the sphere.

"Wow!" all three said at once.

Small apertures in Hellen's amulet allowed light to escape at the top and an image was projected onto the arch of the niche where the sarcophagus stood. The projection showed the coat of arms of the Grand Master Jean de la Cassière—the same coat of arms emblazoned at knee level on the side of the sarcophagus, and which also adorned the bottom of the sphere.

But something was different. In the center of the projection was an area that did not exist in the real coat of arms. Hellen knelt and took a closer look at the version on the side of the sarcophagus. Tom, beginning to chafe at being relegated to the role of mere muscle, bent down behind Hellen and peered over her shoulder. Hellen ran her fingers over the surface of the black coat of arms, about two feet high.

"There's a little edge here!" she cried.

Hellen and Palffy looked at each other and smiled. Tom had already taken out his knife; he drove it into the narrow slot. A small stone plate opened up in a cloud of dust, revealing a cross-shaped incision. Palffy knew immediately what to do. He took the cross that had previously served as a lid on top of the sphere and pressed it into the incision. It clicked into place seamlessly. Slowly, Palffy turned it counterclockwise. This time there was no soft click. Instead, they were startled to hear a loud scratching and scraping, as of enormously heavy stone slabs sliding over each other. Behind the sarcophagus, a small passage opened.

53

Despite his bad mood, François Cloutard was feeling a little proud of himself. If he could have, he'd have patted himself on the back. He had managed to track Ossana from San Marino across half of Italy to the Côte d'Azur in Nice without arousing her suspicions. Throughout the long journey he had racked his brains, trying to work out some way to use Ossana to regain his lost control. But until he knew what was really going on, and who Ossana was truly working for, he was helpless. She hadn't personally collected a package and murdered the theater director for no reason; he needed to find out where she was headed. Cloutard would stick to her heels until he figured out her plan, then he would think of a way to avenge himself and reassert power over his organization.

They had left San Remo, driven through Menton—for Cloutard the most beautiful and underrated city on the French Riviera—then taken the scenic Grande Corniche through Monte Carlo toward Nice. Cloutard recalled the old Cary Grant films he had seen as a child, which had been shot along the Côte d'Azur. He had always loved these mountainous coastal roads. Unfortunately, he wasn't able to enjoy the spectacular views along the coastal route quite as much as he might have otherwise.

Just before Nice, Ossana turned off the Grande Corniche and onto a narrow road that wound its way up into the mountains. Cloutard had to be careful. He dropped back a little, putting more distance between them. He hadn't come this far only to be spotted right at the end of Ossana's little jaunt.

The road climbed steeply for a while, then ran parallel to the coastal road before turning downhill again. From above, Cloutard could now see the winding road below easily, and could follow Ossana's path with little risk of being seen by her. Finally, she stopped at an old farmhouse a couple of hundred yards off the road and got out. A small, Arabic-looking man emerged from the farmhouse. They shook hands and he pointed to a small, white van. Apparently, the van had been freshly painted —the paint buckets and tarpaulins around it suggested as much. The two exchanged a few words and went to Ossana's car. They lifted the flight case out of the Alfa Romeo, carried it to the van, carefully placed it in the back and covered it with a tarpaulin.

Ossana and the man spoke briefly again, and the man returned to the house. Ossana climbed into the van and drove back to the main road.

Cloutard quickly evaluated the situation: he had a perfect view of the road from where he was. There were no turn-offs at all on the route back to the sea, which meant she was heading back to the coastal road. He had a little time. He could afford the risk of searching the car that Ossana had left behind.

He stopped at the farm and rushed across to Ossana's car. It was locked. Without stopping to think, Cloutard picked up a large rock lying on the edge of the road. Then he took an old piece of tarpaulin lying by the paint buckets. Holding it in front of the window to muffle the noise, he smashed the side window of the car with the rock. He reached inside, unlocked the door and began feverishly searched the interior. Back seat, trunk, passenger seat, footwell, glove compartment. Nothing. Frustrated and discouraged, he decided not to waste any more time and to renew his pursuit of Ossana. He was in the driver's seat, still leaning across toward the glove box, and when he sat upright again he saw a small piece of paper that had slipped between the seats. The few seconds it took to tease the piece of paper out of the narrow space felt like hours, but when he had it in his fingers, he saw that it was a rectangular slip of thermal paper—a ticket of some sort—with a turquoise logo near the bottom edge. A closer look at the cheap printing yielded the following:

Area Barcelona
Autoritat del Transport Metropolità
Linea 2

Cloutard had no idea how Barcelona's public transport system was involved, but he shoved the ticket into his pocket.

54

THE CATACOMBS OF VALLETTA

Hellen, Tom and Count Palffy exchanged excited smiles and peered back into the newly revealed passage that had opened in the wall.

"Ladies first," said Palffy, extending an open hand toward the opening. "You have waited a long time for this moment, my dear."

Hellen was about to accept his offer, but she paused for a moment and retrieved her amulet from the black sphere. It had accompanied her all her life, and she did not want to leave it behind. But Tom sensed that this was not the only reason for her hesitation.

"I'll go first. God knows what's waiting for us down there." Tom turned on his flashlight and slipped past the sarcophagus and into the opening in the wall. Hellen followed, with Palffy close behind. Immediately before them, a steep and extremely narrow wooden staircase spiraled into the depths. Despite the powerful beam of light from Tom's SureFire flashlight, the bottom of the staircase lay hidden in the darkness somewhere below. Slowly, step by step, they made their way down the ancient, creaking stairs, Tom leading, Hellen behind, and Count Palffy bringing up the rear. With every step, the stairs groaned frighteningly.

How many years has it been since someone last used these stairs? Hellen thought. Just a few seconds later, she heard a crack behind her. Palffy had lost his balance. He toppled backward, falling back onto the stairs and then sliding down, crashing hard into Hellen in the process. The tread under Hellen gave way, and she lost her footing as well. Palffy and Hellen began a bumpy slide together, one stair after another breaking under their combined weight. Tom, about ten steps ahead, was already bracing for a hard impact when his foot touched solid ground. He had reached the bottom of the staircase. Hellen and Palffy followed seconds later, sliding onto the floor behind him.

"Everybody in one piece?" Tom asked.

Hellen was the first one back on her feet. "I'm fine," she said.

She was just giving Palffy, also uninjured, a helping hand when Tom suddenly sprang forward and pushed both of them away from the staircase. He was the first to hear the groan of the wood overhead—the staircase was about to collapse. Moments later the wooden frame came crashing down. If Tom hadn't pushed Hellen and Palffy out of the way, they would have been buried beneath it. It was some time before they could breathe easily again, or even see their own hand in front of their face, but when the dust finally settled Tom shone his flashlight around, lighting up a circular chamber some sixty feet in diameter.

"Let's hope there's another way out. We're not going back up there." Tom peered back up the shaft, but the remains of the staircase dangled a hundred feet overhead. He turned back to the chamber. The smell of salt water was strong down here, and there were passages leading off in all four directions. Tom shone the flashlight down each of the four corridors in turn, and they all peered after the light as far as they could. One passage—the one on the south side—had caved in after a few yards and was impassable. That left three, all filled with dense black-ness. They examined the walls for clues, but found nothing.

"Useless," said Tom. "We'll have to check each passage. Any ideas, Count?"

"Valletta has a vast network of catacombs, many of them only discovered a few years ago. Some of the passages are a major tourist attraction today, but to my knowledge only a small part of the tunnel system has been explored." Palffy waved his hand in a circle. "We seem to have the dubious honor of having stumbled upon an unexplored section."

Two of the tunnels, he suggested, probably led more or less directly to opposite sides of the peninsula on which Valletta's city center was situated.

"The passages to the north and south may be a kind of escape route, or a connecting tunnel between the cathe-dral and the Grand Master's Palace or other buildings. Perhaps in earlier times they enabled the high officers of the Order to come and go in secret. I consider myself quite knowledgeable in the history of the Order, but this is all unknown territory to me, I'm afraid." Palffy snapped a few pictures with his phone camera.

"The western passage leads down much more steeply than the eastern one," Hellen observed. She was taking a closer look at the texture of the walls. "Looking at the condition of the collapsed staircase and the stonework, I think we can assume that this chamber and the passages sometimes get flooded during high tides or storms," she said.

"And me without my Speedo," said Tom.

"Ha ha," said Hellen humorlessly. "We might be under water here soon, so we'd better hurry up and explore the passages. It'll be faster if we split up."

"I'm not keen on splitting up," Tom said. "The staircase just showed us how quickly things can go to hell."

"Then we'll just have to be more careful," said Palffy, who had switched on the light on his phone and was already disappearing into one of the passages.

Hellen, a little disconcerted, looked at Tom. "Looks like the boss has made up his mind." She went off in another direction, also using her cell phone to light the way.

Tom had to admit defeat, and took the third corridor. "Meet back here in ten minutes," he shouted after them before they disappeared completely in the darkness.

Tom had taken the passage to the west. It dropped steeply and, after a short distance, began to twist back and forth with increasing frequency, becoming almost serpentine. Sometimes it swung to the left, sometimes to the right, and here and there were little niches in the walls. Just in time, Tom grabbed hold of a small ledge— in front of him, the tunnel floor abruptly vanished, interrupted by a gaping hole. He looked around, realizing that the water must have worn away the rock; it looked as if part of the tunnel had collapsed into the sea at some point in the past, and he could hear the sound of water surging down below. On the other side of the chasm, the passage continued, but it would mean a jump of maybe ten feet: not an easy leap at all. He decided to turn back.

He was the first to return to the circular chamber. A few minutes later Palffy appeared.

"The passage runs for a few hundred yards and stops. It is a dead end, I'm afraid," Palffy reported, disappointed.

"Where's Hellen?" Tom asked, concerned.

"Her passage leads north, so she could be directly beneath the Grand Master's Palace. Maybe she found something and lost track of time in her excitement. You know what she's like. Who could blame her, after all?" Palffy said, and he waved Tom into the northern corridor.

"I'm sure she could use reinforcement," Tom muttered.

After a couple of minutes they saw light ahead, and the passage widened considerably.

"Hellen?" Tom called.

"I've found something," she called back enthusiastically.

Hellen was standing in a large chamber about thirty feet square, its walls covered with faded frescoes. On the floor of the chamber was a huge Maltese cross. Between each of the arms of the cross was a marble pillar about eight feet high topped by a brazier, apparently used to light the chamber in earlier days. In the center of the cross was a circular opening about ten feet across, bordered with blocks of red marble. One of the blocks, also marked with a Maltese cross, protruded a little.

Palffy approached the frescoes and clapped his hands in delight. "These are by Mattia Preti! Probably no one has seen them for centuries." Palffy walked eagerly from wall to wall, taking pictures of everything. "The technique is fascinating. It seems he's used some sort of special preparation here to protect the frescoes from humidity."

Hellen saw Tom's face and had to smile. "Mattia Preti is the same artist who painted the picture of Saint George we saw up in the cathedral," she explained. "He worked in the tradition of Caravaggio; he's one of the most important artists of the entire Renaissance." Hellen went from one wall to the next, and Tom followed. "The frescoes depict the capture of Jesus on the Mount of Olives. Here's the scene where Peter takes his sword and defends Jesus against Malchus. We must be in the right place."

Hellen walked carefully to the opening in the center of the cross and looked down into the darkness.

"Just a hole in the ground? That's all?" Hellen seemed disappointed.

Tom knelt at the edge of the opening and shone his flashlight down into it. "It looks like some kind of well leading down to the sea. Look, you can the surface of the water.

But the walls are completely smooth. Climbing up or down would be impossible," he said.

"It must be down there," Hellen said.

Palffy pointed to the lower right corner of the fresco with the scene on the Mount of Olives. "That is strange. There is a kind of snail painted there that doesn't seem to have any connection with the rest of the picture."

Hellen took a closer look at the symbol. "That's not a snail. It looks to me like a spiral staircase seen from above."

"But there's no staircase here," Tom said. "There's only this well, and it seems to drop straight into the sea." He shone his light into the well again, and his eyes locked onto the uneven marble block with the Maltese cross.

"Look. There's a notch here, too, like the one on the sphere in the chapel."

Hellen hurried to Tom. "You're right," she said. She quickly took off her amulet and pressed it into the small recess. Once again, they heard heavy blocks of stone grinding against each other. But this time the sound lasted longer and gradually grew fainter. It came from inside the well. Tom shone his light into the shaft and all three looked down curiously in time to see individual stone slabs sliding out of the wall, each offset about eighteen inches to the side and down, gradually forming a staircase spiraling down inside the shaft.

"I'd say that's a clear sign of where we're supposed to go from here," Tom said dryly.

"But the staircase is flooded," Hellen said as she hung the amulet around her neck again. "We can't just walk into the water. It can't be the right way,"

Palffy spoke up. "Yes, Hellen, it can. The catacombs of Valletta were only opened to tourists a few years ago. Presumably, special paths have been built for tourists to visit the catacombs and also to allow boats to pass through them. It is quite possible that the water levels within the entire system have changed as a result, and you can add to that the rise in sea level since the 14th century. And unless I am mistaken, it's a full moon right now, which would also have an impact," Palffy said. "Maybe the spring tide has already started, and that is why the water is so high," he added.

"Well we can't wait for the moon to change before we continue our search for the sword," Hellen said impatiently. "I've never been this close to my goal before."

"I'm going to take a closer look," Tom said, already removing his shoes.

"What are you doing?" Hellen asked.

"I'd love a foot massage, would you mind? It's the perfect time for it." He grinned at her. "I'm going to go down and take a closer look."

"What, just climb down and dive the rest? Are you insane? You have no idea what to expect down there!" Hellen said.

"What's to expect? The little mermaid? A great white shark? Aquaman? Come on, I'm just going to check it out."

"There *are* great whites in the Mediterranean, you know," Hellen said. "I heard it on the news just the other day."

But Tom wasn't listening. He took his waterproof flashlight and descended several steps until he reached the water. Palffy and Hellen stood on the edge, looking down at him hopefully.

"See you soon!"

Tom mock-saluted and dived into the water, which was surprisingly warm and clear. He used his flashlight to light the way and was surprised at how swiftly he was able to progress. The space between the stone steps was wide enough and he kept going deeper and deeper until, about fifteen feet down, he reached the bottom. He saw two shafts leading off horizontally, to the southeast and the northwest. If his orientation was right, one of them had to lead to the sea and the other back under the center of Valletta.

Tom chose the northwest passage and swam onward. It rapidly became narrower and narrower until he had to squeeze through, and he was glad that claustrophobia had never been an issue for him. Then it widened again, and just as he was thinking of turning back, he saw a reflection above him, caused by the flashlight. He knew what it was: an air pocket that had formed in the passageway. He surfaced and gulped a few breaths of air. Unable to see how far the passage continued, he decided to turn back. Once again, he had to pass through the narrow stretch, but from this side it seemed more difficult than the first time through. His trousers caught and he scraped his thigh. Parts of the wall broke off as he went through.

I hope it doesn't all come down on top of me, Tom thought as he pushed clear of the narrow point.

The salt water burned his grazed thigh like fire and if he wasn't mistaken, the water had taken on a pink tinge as well. He thought of Hellen's shark story, but knew there was no chance of that in the flooded corridors. He decided to surface and report back to Hellen and Palffy.

"There are two passages down there," he called up breathlessly. "Both are flooded. I swam into one of them, but I couldn't see how far it went and don't think I could have got much further without scuba gear. I'm going to take a look at the other one."

Tom breathed deeply in and out a few times. Then, without waiting for a response from Palffy and Hellen, he swam down again. This time he took the other passage, which was much wider than the first. He swam a few yards straight ahead and was surprised to see steps coming down into the water from above, all the way to the floor of the passage. It looked as if a stairway here also led up to a room that was not completely flooded. He followed the stairs upward and emerged in a small, circular chamber with a column—again made of red marble—at its center. The column was about three feet in height and topped by a stone slab on which a black chest lay, its sides decorated with rubies in the shape of a Maltese cross.

Tom grabbed the chest and swam with it back to the original shaft. It had been several months since his last dive training. He was out of practice, and hauling the chest slowed him down. He felt the pressure building in his lungs, his need for air. His lungs began to burn as he swam up through the spiral staircase. When he finally broke the surface, he felt like he'd been punched in the gut—not because he'd run out of air, but at the sight of Guerra and two other men holding their automatic weapons to Hellen and Palffy's heads.

55

"Thank you for doing the dirty work for us, Señor Wagner." Guerra's arrogant laughter echoed across the chamber, but at least he had pronounced Tom's name correctly.

Tom briefly thought about diving again, but knew there was no way out. He wouldn't be able to escape, and Hellen and Palffy would still be in Guerra's hands. Slowly, he ascended the steps. One of Guerra's men took the chest from him and pushed him over to join Hellen and Palffy. The second man kept the three of them covered with his machine pistol, while Guerra trained his on Tom's head. Guerra seemed to be enjoying himself, standing there like a gangster out of Grand Theft Auto.

Guerra turned away from Tom and began to examine the chest.

"It looks brand-new," Tom whispered to Hellen.

"I know. That puzzles me, too."

Impatiently, Guerra tried everything he could to get it open, even bashing it with the butt of his pistol. Hellen couldn't suppress a smile. Palffy pointed to the place where the chest would normally have a lock. But there was no lock, just another one of the now-familiar recesses.

"Hellen, your amulet," Palffy said nervously and pointed to the notch, a twin of the one on the black marble orb.

Hellen, aghast, could only glare at Palffy. She could not believe he had opened his mouth and blurted out the words. Palffy slapped his hand over his mouth in mortification, but it was too late: Guerra grinned and nodded his thanks. He walked toward Hellen.

"An amulet?" he asked. "Where have you hidden that?"

He jabbed his gun into her temple and with the other hand began to unbutton her blouse. The amulet appeared, but Guerra seemed to like what he was doing, because he opened Hellen's blouse further than necessary. He stroked the amulet, at the same time caressing Hellen's naked skin under the blouse. He grinned diabolically.

"Get your filthy hands off of her!" Tom snarled. He tensed, ready to throw himself at Guerra. But the guns pointed at him kept him in check. Guerra slowly moved his hand under the amulet, hefted it briefly in his hand, then snatched it from Hellen's neck, breaking the chain. His eyes moved from the amulet in his hand to the chest. Hellen took a quick backward step, closed her blouse again angrily, and folded her arms.

Guerra ignored her. He was still staring at the amulet, and gradually realized what Palffy had meant. He placed the amulet into the notch on the chest. Click. Guerra turned the amulet first clockwise, then counterclockwise. There was the sound of a bolt sliding in a lock. Everyone held their breath. Slowly, Guerra lifted the lid. Everyone peered into the chest, which was lined with red velvet. Inside gleamed a magnificent short sword. Like the chest itself, it was in immaculate condition. Hellen looked at the Preti fresco. The sword in the chest looked exactly like the sword that Saint Peter held in the painting.

"The Sword of Saint Peter. The sacred weapon touched by Jesus Christ himself, and which has been said ever since to carry indescribable power," Count Palffy murmured, his voice trancelike as he slowly approached the chest. He gazed down into it and lifted out the sword. Neither Guerra nor either of his men moved to stop him. They kept Tom and Hellen in their sights. The fact that Palffy held the sword in his hand, staring at it with a look somewhere between rapture and delirium, didn't seem to bother them in the slightest. Palffy looked up from the sword and smiled.

"Good work, Guerra," Palffy said, patting him on the back.

It took a few seconds for Tom and Hellen to realize what was going on. Tom was the first to recover himself.

"You son of a bitch. You're all in this together?"

It took Hellen a little longer. She wanted to scream at Palffy, shout "Why?", claw his eyes out all at once. But she could do none of it. She stood as if frozen in place, realizing that her mentor had been playing her for a fool for years. Not just her, but Blue Shield and UNESCO as well.

"Don't look at me like that, Hellen." Palffy handed the sword to Guerra, who put it back in the chest and locked it away again. He passed the amulet to Palffy.

"I will look after this for you, and honor it," Palffy said to Hellen as he slipped the amulet into his jacket pocket.

Hellen finally found her voice again. "But why, Nikolaus? Why?"

"My dear, it would take too long to explain everything to you now, and you wouldn't understand it anyway. This is just one piece of a very, very big puzzle. It is not about the sword or the other relics."

"Then what is it about?" Hellen snapped.

"It is about putting some things in our world back in their rightful place. It is about saving our culture." Palffy looked away.

"Saving our culture?" Tom said. "By hiring mercenaries to steal artifacts and create chaos? By sowing fear and insecurity across Europe?"

"You have hit the proverbial nail on the head, Tom. You see how easily fear is brought into the world? How easily people today are manipulated? All one has to do is fly a couple of planes into the Twin Towers, or steal a few Christian artifacts, manipulate the media a little, and wait until the idiot mob on social media joins in. The panic follows naturally."

Palffy's voice sounded cold.

Hellen shook her head. "I have no idea what you're talking about, Nikolaus."

"We are fighting a new Crusade. If we continue the way we are, European culture will perish. In a few years, Europe will have more mosques than churches, and nobody is doing anything to stop it. Our democratic system is broken. Europe is divided. And all we do is sit back and watch as Islam infiltrates us."

"Is that what this is about? You staged all this to pin it on Muslims? You're a sick man." Tom was stunned.

"No. I am the only one *not* sick. Europe simply needs a strong hand to put a stop to it, someone who will ensure that our culture is preserved, that we do not degenerate into one gigantic kebab joint."

"And you want to be that strong hand?" Hellen laughed contemptuously.

"Not alone, of course . . . see, I knew you would not understand. And honestly, I do not have the time, or the inclination, to explain it to you." Palffy looked at his watch and turned to Guerra. "We have more important things to take care of now."

"Project Cornet," Guerra said quietly.

Palffy nodded and looked at Guerra eagerly. "The final realization of our plan. Get started. You do not have much time. By noon tomorrow, the world will look very different."

Suddenly, a rumble sounded from the opening in the middle of the chamber. Frighteningly powerful, it resounded throughout the room. Palffy tapped his watch.

"Time for us to leave. The spring tide is rising. Soon everything here will be under water." He looked first at Guerra and then at the other two men. "You know what to do."

Palffy turned to leave, paying no more attention to Hellen or Tom. Tom could only watch as one of Guerra's men attached explosive charges at the entrance to the chamber. Guerra took two pairs of handcuffs from his bag. He forced Tom and Hellen over to one of the four marble columns and had them face each other on opposite sides of it. He cuffed Tom's left hand to Hellen's right and did the same on the other side. Tom looked up at the pillar. He could see immediately that there was no escape. Guerra laughed.

"No need to check the column, Wagner. You won't get out of here alive."

Guerra looked over the handcuffs one last time, then at the man with the explosives.

"All set?"

The man nodded and set the timer.

"They say there is no crueler way to die than drowning." Guerra's tone was chillingly casual. "No form of torture comes even remotely close to the despair people experience when they drown. The only downside is that I can't stay to watch."

Guerra and his henchmen left the chamber.

56

Hellen looked at Tom, blank despair etched on her face.

"We're going to die here, Tom," she said, trembling.

"I was about to say 'over my dead body,' but I can see how that would be inappropriate."

"How can you crack jokes now? How the hell do we get out of here?"

Just then the chamber was shaken by the detonation of the explosive charges. Tom was impressed: the guys were certainly good at their job. The blast had brought down the exit but had left the rest of the chamber undamaged. As far as he could judge from where he was, it would be impossible to clear the rubble to get to higher ground.

"Oh God, Tom, the room is starting to fill with water. The spring tide . . ."

Water shot upwards into the chamber from the opening in its center. In a few seconds the floor was covered, and moments later Tom and Hellen were already ankle-deep.

"Okay, here's the plan," Tom said. "We wait for the room to fill with water, which will float us up. When we're high enough, we can lift our hands over the top of the column and we're free."

"Free? My God, Tom, we won't be free!" Hellen was starting to sound panicked. "We'll still be trapped in a room that's filling with water. We'll drown!"

"No we won't. We're going to dive down. The chest with the sword was in a chamber that wasn't flooded, and I don't think the tide had ever filled it. It must be higher than this one. It was dry as dust, and nothing suggested that it had ever been under water."

By now, the tide had reached their hips. Hellen tried to stay calm, but fear was overwhelming her.

"'You think?' But what if you're wrong, what if it does get flooded? What do we do then? We're handcuffed together. We'll never get out of here alive. God, Tom, I don't want to die."

"Slow your breathing, Hellen. We take this one step at a time. We solve one problem and then we focus on the next. If we try to solve everything at once, it's not going to work. I know it's not easy, but you need to stay calm now. Step one is to tread water and to get high enough to get our hands over the top of this column. Step two, we dive down the well and swim to the chamber where the chest was. We rest there and plan our next step."

Hellen was not enthusiastic, but she had no choice. She admired Tom's stubborn composure. It gave her the faintest glimmer of hope that they could make it, though the water was literally up to their necks by now.

"Come on, Hellen. From now on we tread water until we get to the top."

The column was actually wider at the top because of the brazier set on top of it. Tom hoped that the brazier was not firmly attached, otherwise they would have a very difficult time of it.

"We have to try to push the brazier off. On three, we lift it up and tilt it to the left."

Hellen lifted her right hand and, although their situation was deadly serious, Tom had to laugh. "That whole left-right thing is still hard for you, isn't it?"

"Shut up, smart guy, and let's get on with it," Hellen yelped back.

"Okay, on three: one, two, three." They both pushed up as hard as they could. With a dull crunch, the heavy bowl detached from the column, tilted to the side, and instantly sank into the clear water.

Their joy was short-lived, however. They were coughing and swallowing too much water. Little waves were forming in the chamber, forcing Tom and Hellen to gasp for breath before they were even ready to dive. Hellen's legs were already starting to burn from treading water, and she hoped she would be able to hold out. The water pushed them higher, and they were soon able to lift their hands over the top of the column and free themselves.

"Okay, first problem solved." Tom pressed himself closer to Hellen.

"What are you doing? This is no time to get romantic."

"Believe me, that's the last thing on my mind, but we have to stay close and coordinate our movements or we're not going to get anywhere. I'll set the rhythm." He took a short break. "Remember when we waltzed at the Opera Ball? That worked out fine."

Hellen nodded.

"Three deep breaths, and then we dive." Tom shouted to make himself understood over the rush of water. "Down the spiral staircase as quick as we can, then to the right. It's only a few yards until the passage leads up again. But before that, there's one more thing. I've got two glow sticks in the right pocket of my cargo pants. We'll need them to help us find our bearings."

Their hands moved down and found the glow sticks, and together they cracked them. A pale glow appeared, and each of them took a stick.

"Ready?" Tom said.

Hellen nodded, although she felt anything but ready. They dove. Once inside the shaft, they were able to pull themselves quickly down the projecting stone steps; when they reached the bottom, they took the passage to the right and swam on. It took them a few strokes to find a rhythm, but they made faster progress than Tom had expected. The light sticks helped immensely, and after a few yards Tom could already see the steps in front of him. He prayed that he was right about the chamber being dry. They swam up the stairs. Tom's head appeared first, and Hellen's followed. Gasping for breath, they hoisted themselves up the last few stairs and dropped to the floor, exhausted.

"You see? That wasn't so hard," Tom said calmly, wiping the water off his face.

He gave Hellen a few moments to recover as he watched the water level. They were lucky: the water was not rising here at all.

"Okay. What's next?" Though they were far from safe, Hellen's sense of achievement had given her new strength.

"First, we have to get out of these handcuffs. To do that, you have to get to the fly of my pants," Tom said as if it were obvious.

"I have to *what*?" Hellen said, thinking she had heard wrong.

"Relax. I broke the tag on the zipper, and replaced it with a paper clip," he said with a grin.

"And we can use the paper clip to open the handcuffs," Hellen said, brightening.

"That's the idea. So go on—you ought to remember where it is."

Hellen smiled and shook her head, but their lives were still in danger, and she hesitated only for a second. She reached down, found the zipper and began unthreading the paper clip. Her hands trembled.

"You never used to be this nervous," Tom said. He couldn't help himself.

"You are such an idiot," Hellen scolded. A few seconds later she held the paper clip triumphantly in her hand.

Tom took the paper clip and in two minutes had opened the locks on both pairs of handcuffs. He stowed them in his cargo pants; you never knew when a pair of cuffs might come in handy. He eyed the glow sticks, which were slowly starting to dim. Hellen leaned against the wall and closed her eyes for a few seconds to recover her strength.

"Shall we go on? If we don't, we'll be sitting in the dark soon," said Tom. Hellen looked at the glow sticks and got back on her feet.

"Okay, what do we do now?"

"Bad news, I'm afraid. I don't know where the other corridor leads. I swam in a short way and found an air pocket, but then I turned back. I saw light coming from somewhere, but I don't know if we can get out that way. And there's a narrow spot in the passage, too." He showed her his torn trouser leg and the raw skin below it. "You have to be careful. I suggest we get to the air pocket and decide what to do from there."

Hellen nodded. She trusted him and had regained a little of her confidence—after all, everything had gone smoothly up till now. But her fear was still strong.

"Don't worry, we can always come back here," Tom said, trying to allay her fears. "You swim behind me, but I'll be looking back to make sure you're doing all right."

They went down the stairs and back into the water, took a deep breath and dived. In a few seconds, they passed the spiral staircase and swam into the passage that led to the northwest. For Tom, getting to the point where the passage narrowed seemed to take much longer than the first time; his exhaustion was slowly but surely taking its toll. He looked around and saw Hellen right behind him. He squeezed through the narrow spot, and Hellen also made it through quickly. Above and to one side, he saw the reflection of the water's surface at the air pocket, and he swam up. Hellen followed. The space was too narrow for the two of them, though, and they had to hold onto each other tightly to avoid banging their heads against the walls in the tiny hollow. Hellen spat out the mouthful of salty water that she had taken when she surfaced. She struggled, gulping at the air in the air pocket, and Tom could see that she would not be able to hold out much longer.

"From here, I have no idea what to do," he said. "I suggest I swim ahead and check things out. Then I'll come back and we'll decide on our best course."

"I'd rather come with you right now. Waiting here alone would scare me even more."

She hated showing any sign of weakness in front of him, but she couldn't help herself. Tom didn't reply. He wedged himself with one arm and pulled her close with the other.

"We can do this," he whispered.

And though Hellen was trembling all over, for a few seconds she felt warm and safe.

"No time like the present," she whispered back.

"You sure about this?" Tom asked.

"Come on, our lights are fading. Mine's down to a night-light. I want to get out of here."

Tom wasn't sure if this was newfound courage or plain desperation, but the message was clear. They took another deep breath and dove again. Tom swam ahead. After a few yards, he realized the passage was narrowing again. Dangerously, too, it looked like. He swam ahead strongly and squeezed himself between the walls. The masonry scraped against his shoulders and he felt the wall partially begin to loosen. Hellen was close behind him and, like him, pushed through the narrow spot. Without warning, part of the wall came loose, pinning Hellen against the opposite side. Panic instantly overcame her. More of the masonry broke away; she was in danger of being buried underneath it. Tom saw her eyes widen in horror as she frantically tried to break free. She almost made it, but her right leg was still stuck fast. She began to tug desperately at her calf, but her leg didn't move an inch.

Tom tried frantically to help Hellen free herself. And gradually, he began to notice the pressure in his chest. His lungs started to burn, and he realized that there was no way they could make it back to the small hollow with the air pocket. He felt the fear rising inside him, too. But he also knew that fear was the surest way to die down here. He pulled himself together, kicked some rocks clear, and between them they were able to pull Hellen's leg free. He grabbed her by the hand, and they swam on. His lungs burned like fire; he could hardly imagine how Hellen had held out this far. He felt her grip slacken in his hand, and then her strength vanished completely. Her hand slipped from his, and she hung motionless in the water.

57

Cloutard sighed with relief when he saw that Ossana had stopped. He had been trailing Ossana for more than 24 hours and had felt himself nodding off at the wheel time after time; he wouldn't have lasted much longer. Now she had stopped at a gas station on the outskirts of Barcelona. Next to the gas station was a car wash which, like the station itself, was open around the clock. Cloutard had pulled over on the opposite corner and watched her drive into the car wash.

He frowned. *Why would she bother washing the van now?* he wondered. *She drives through half of Europe from San Marino to Barcelona and the first thing she does is wash her car?*

Cloutard could feel himself starting to doze again when he saw her emerge from the car wash. And all of a sudden, he was wide awake again. The van had been plain white when Ossana drove into the car wash, but it had come out bearing the same logo and text on its sides as on the ticket he'd found in her car just outside Nice. In turquoise letters it said "Area Barcelona – Autoritat del Transport Metropolità."

What was Ossana up to? What was she planning with Barcelona's public transport? And what was in the van?

Cloutard had no time to dig into these questions; the next surprise was not long in coming. Ossana parked the van in a small parking lot next to the gas station. She got out and looked at her watch, obviously waiting for something or someone. She got coffee from the gas station shop, leaned against her van and waited.

I could use some of that right now, Cloutard thought, rubbing his eyes.

Before long, an old blue Seat Ibiza arrived and pulled up next to the van.

Cloutard couldn't make out who was in the Ibiza, into which Ossana now climbed on the passenger side. Ossana and the man kissed fiercely, falling on one another like hungry wolves attacking a flock of sheep. When their passion had subsided a little, it gave way to a no-less-heated discussion. After about fifteen minutes, Ossana got out of the car and returned to her van.

When the blue Seat left the parking lot again, Cloutard was finally able to catch a glimpse of the driver.

Cloutard knew him only too well. *So these were the people Ossana was in league with.* Cloutard was furious that he had let the woman fool him.

Ossana drove off too, and Cloutard resumed his pursuit. In his present situation there was only one person he could think of to ask for help, but first he had to find a way to contact him.

58

THE CATACOMBS OF VALLETTA

Not like this! cried his inner voice. *We will not die here!*

Adrenaline pumped madly through his body. He fought down his panic, fought his empty lungs. If he wasn't hallucinating, that reflection above him suggested air. With his last ounce of strength he swam toward it.

Just before his lungs exploded, his head broke through the surface and he sucked in air. He could not remember the last time he felt a release like this, as fresh oxygen flooded his lungs and reenergized his body. It was not just an air pocket, it was the end of the flooded passage. He was in a chamber like the one where he had found the chest, with stairs leading up from the water ten yards ahead of him.

He hauled Hellen's lifeless body out of the water, laid her on her back and started to try to resuscitate her. He placed his fingers at her neck: no pulse. Gently, he placed his hand under her neck, puller her chin down and turned her head to the side. He put the heels of his hands on her chest and began chest compressions. Water gushed from her mouth. After thirty compressions, he stopped, held her nose closed, raised her chin, pressed his lips to hers, and blew. Two breaths. His strength almost gone, depleted air from his lungs passing into hers. He checked her pulse again—still nothing—and started over.

He repeated the procedure several times. His hope was fading when Hellen suddenly reared up and coughed her soul out. Tom pulled her close.

"Don't ever do that again," he whispered, endlessly relieved.

It took both of them some minutes to recover from the shock. Tom was back on his feet first. "We have to go," he said. "We're almost out of light." Tom's glow stick was no more than a faint glimmer. Ahead of them was a long, straight passage. The walls looked sturdy, and best of all, they were dry. There was no sign that they had ever been under water.

"I just want to get out of here," Hellen said as Tom helped her up.

He kept his arm around her, supporting her a little, and they walked straight ahead for a few minutes. Gradually, the path rose.

"What do you think Guerra meant by 'Project Cornet'?" Hellen's spirits seemed to be returning. Tom was impressed at how quickly she was recovering from her ordeal.

"We're not even out of here, and you're already thinking about that?"

"Apparently they need the sword for this 'Project Cornet,' whatever it is." She stopped. "Cornet. Cornet . . . I have no idea what it means."

The passage continued to rise. When Tom looked up, he saw small openings along the ceiling. *Probably air vents*, he thought, but the moonlight entering through the openings also lit the passage a little.

"Look. We'll be out in a few minutes." Tom directed Hellen's gaze up to the holes, and she smiled tiredly and hugged him. She laid her head on his shoulder and closed her eyes for a moment.

Then, without warning, she pushed away from him.

"Oh my God!"

"Was the hug that bad? It can't be my BO—you smell just as bad as I do," Tom said, a little offended.

"What are you talking about? No, not that." She waved dismissively. "It's Project Cornet. I know what Nikolaus is up to. And we have to hurry."

59

Tom tipped the iron grate out of the way and they clambered out of the shaft. Tom was the first to surface. In front of him was the sea and behind him a high wall, like the wall of a castle. They were alone and in no immediate danger. The starry night and the full moon offered enough light for them to orientate themselves. Tom took a deep, relieved breath and helped Hellen out of the shaft.

"So Antoni Gaudí i Cornet was Gaudí's full name," Tom said, repeating Hellen's theory.

"Yes. And it *cannot* be a coincidence that they named the project after the lesser known part of Gaudí's name and that tomorrow marks the official completion of the Sagrada Familia, Gaudí's greatest work of art, in Barcelona."

Tom's eyes widened. "Woah! The Pope will be there in person to celebrate mass. The nuns who drove me to Como told me."

"The opening of the Sagrada Familia, the Pope, and the Sword of Peter in the hands of psychopaths. And the whole world will be tuning in tomorrow morning." Hellen looked at Tom in horror. They were making their way around the side of the construction, moving away from the sea. "My God. They're planning to murder the Pope with the Sword of St Peter and broadcast it live to the whole world."

"It would be a catastrophe for the Catholic church and the faithful all over the world. It would be Europe's 9/11," said Tom in dismay.

"All that nonsense Nikolaus was spouting . . . they'll blame Islamists for the whole thing. We have to try to stop them!"

"Noah's in Barcelona," Tom said as if it were obvious.

Hellen looked at him in surprise. "Why would Noah be in Barcelona?"

"Maierhofer mumbled something about an 'Atlas mission' when he so kindly gave me this little vacay. It must be for the Sagrada Familia event. The Cobra are working there with other antiterror units. Noah has to be there."

"Then it's up to us to warn them about what Nikolaus is up to," said Hellen.

"That won't be so easy. What are we supposed to tell them? That a murderer wanted by Interpol and his ex-girlfriend, who is an archaeologist, think that the boss of Blue Shield wants to destabilize the political situation in Europe, so he's hired a few insane killers and has been swiping Catholic artifacts all over Europe? And now he's found the Sword of Saint Peter and wants to kill the Pope with it? Even if they listened to us for that long, they'd think we were batshit crazy—to put it mildly."

Hellen was not about to give up easily. "But we have to try, at least," she said despairingly.

"I know how these things work," Tom said. "Every time there's an event like this, you get an endless stream of threats. They won't take ours any more seriously than anyone else's. Less, probably, since our version sounds *really* loony. They'll tell us they've got the highest level of security in place and they're already on top of it. And if I go to my boss, he'll tell me to go to hell and won't do a thing."

Tom's eyes scanned the large, open square ahead, just to make sure there wasn't someone at the next corner waiting to kill them. "Where are we, anyway?" he asked.

Hellen looked around. "Ah, Manoel Island. On the west side of the fort, by the looks of it. She pointed to the northwest. "In that direction is the Carmelite Church and back there is the Grand Master's palace."

"If I have the map right in my head, we must be close to the marina. I have an idea, but we need a phone. Noah can help us," said Tom.

They started running toward the marina. The last few hours had taken a lot out of them, but their strength returned quickly. This was no time to be tired. They had things to do, and the sooner the better.

The marina lay before them, peaceful in the moonlight. Countless luxurious yachts of every size and price range bobbed at their moorings. Only the moon and the sparse lighting on the jetties gave them a little light. It was quiet except for the gentle wash of the water and the creak of mooring ropes.

"This looks like the harbormaster's office." Hellen stopped in front of an ancient, light-blue house that, in another city, would probably have been a landmark. Here in Valletta, however, it was nothing special. Tom went to the door and tried it.

"Locked. Go figure."

He took a few steps back, then threw himself against the door with all the force he could muster. The old door gave way more easily than expected and he stumbled into the office. Hellen followed; she was getting used to not doing things by the book. You make an omelet, you break a few eggs. But more importantly: the clock was ticking. In a few hours the Pope would be sanctifying the Sagrada Familia.

Seven hundred and fifty miles northwest of Malta a telephone rang. It rang twice, then Noah picked up.

"What the hell are you doing in *Malta*?" said Noah before an astonished Tom could say a word.

"How did you know . . . ? Look, never mind. I don't have time to tell you the whole story right now. In about twelve hours, there's going to be an assassination attempt on the Pope in Barcelona. The killers are planning to use the Sword of Saint Peter to kill him, on camera. I'm with

Hellen in Valletta. We found the sword, and Hellen's boss and some other bad guys—"

Noah interrupted him. "I thought you didn't want to tell me the whole story. What do you need?"

Tom took a breath. "You're in Barcelona, right? I don't think explaining all this to Maierhofer would help."

"Yes, I'm here. And yes, no one's going to listen to the crazy story you just babbled. We're going to have do this our own way," Noah said, already thinking.

Tom smiled. His old friend had gone over to "we" straight away. He was on board without even knowing all the details. "We are," he said. "The question is, how do I get from Valletta to Barcelona as fast as possible?"

Tom could already hear Noah typing frantically on his computer.

"Well, you can forget the regular flights. You'll never make it. Boats, no way. The fastest yacht in the world would be too slow."

Tom shook his head at what Noah could learn in seconds. He hadn't even finished the thought when he heard Noah say, "Hold on, this could work! Where are you exactly?"

"The marina on Manoel Island."

"Perfect. Harbour Air Malta is just around the corner."

"Harbour Air Malta?" Tom shook his head, not understanding. Hellen, who had her ear pressed to the back of the phone receiver, was just as confused.

"Harbour Air Malta. They offer sightseeing flights over Malta and Gozo, the island next door." Noah paused for effect. "With seaplanes."

"Woah, woah . . . a seaplane? I have to get to Barcelona. I don't want to go sightseeing."

"No problem, they've got a Cessna 172 Cutlass there, amphibious version. That baby will get you almost 1200 miles. Barcelona's about 750 miles from Valletta. You'll be here in a few hours.

"Noah, it's almost 11:00. No one's going to . . ."

Tom stopped talking and smiled. He could see where Noah was headed.

Hellen had overheard and already suspected the worst. She looked at Tom. "So now we're going to steal a plane?"

Tom nodded and put on his biggest smile. "Hey, anyone can just *charter* a plane. And stealing is such an ugly word—we're just borrowing it."

"The alarm system shouldn't be a problem," said Noah. "Just get in, get the keys and go. According to the online logbook, the Cessna's fueled up and Barcelona-ready. All you have to do is turn off the transponder. Then no one will see you until you're close, at least. I'll stay in touch on the radio."

Tom didn't stop to think about how Noah was once again pulling him out of a hole. He asked for directions to the Harbour Air Malta office, hung up, and they ran off. Hellen had given up trying to stop Tom from doing dumb things. As she ran after him, she called out, "When was the last time you flew anything? It must have been years ago. Can you even fly a seaplane?"

"Fly, yes," Tom answered confidently.

Hellen was not content with that, however. Why did she sense there was a catch?

"Land, no," he added, as he kicked in the door of the Harbour Air Malta office. Hellen decided not to ask any more questions. She had no choice now, anyway. Tom searched the small office, found the key box, and took all the keys in it. One of them would fit. Then they ran back to the harbor where the planes were moored. Tom grinned when he saw the Cessna. He tried a few keys, found the right one, and climbed into the plane. Hellen hesitantly unfastened the Cessna's mooring ropes and climbed into the copilot's seat beside Tom, who was studying the countless lights, buttons and levers in the cockpit. Hellen looked at him doubtfully.

"Don't worry. It's like riding a bike," Tom said as he started the engine. The plane began to move.

60

Tom looked at the GPS and then at his watch. "Two hours to Barcelona."

Hellen was about to say something, but an incoming radio call interrupted her.

"It must be Noah. Maybe he's gotten somewhere with Atlas."

"There's that word again: Atlas. What is it?" Hellen asked.

"Atlas is a union of all 38 European counterterrorism units. The Barcelona operation is the first joint exercise by the Atlas states. It's a stupid idea, actually. The teams aren't working together very well, at least not yet—but it doesn't matter. Maybe Noah was able to get the big boys to at least consider our warnings."

"Cloutard's in Barcelona, too!" was the first thing Noah said. "He called me and told me he'd trailed Ossana across half of Europe. She's here, here in Barcelona, and she met with Guerra here, your very special friend."

Noah brought Tom and Hellen up to speed and told them what Cloutard had observed.

"I figured as much after the bitch tried to kill Cloutard and me," Tom fumed. "So they're all in bed together, and Count Asshole's in charge of the whole outfit." Suddenly, another radio message cut their conversation short.

"Unidentified aircraft heading two-niner-five, this is USS Ronald Reagan. Identify yourself. Over." The radio message was repeated immediately with slightly more urgency. Then the voice said, "You are in a military training area. Alter your course immediately. Over."

Hellen, startled, turned and looked at Tom.

"And now this," he sighed.

"This is Niner Hotel Mike Charlie Romeo Foxtrot, Lieutenant Thomas Wagner speaking, Austrian Special Forces Cobra, part of Atlas Command. We are en route to Barcelona to prevent an assassination attempt on the Pope. Over."

Tom released the talk button and turned to Hellen. "They're never going to believe us."

Radar Specialist Carlson on the aircraft carrier below raised an eyebrow, but he was not particularly impressed.

"I repeat, you are in the military training zone of USS Ronald Reagan. Turn to heading zero-six-zero immediately. Over."

Radar Specialist Carlson turned to his commanding officer.

"Sir, I have an unidentified aircraft on heading two-niner-five. The aircraft's transponder is offline, and the pilot said something about a terrorist attack on the Pope in Barcelona. I can't find a filed flight plan, either."

"Who's this lunatic?" the CO muttered, bending over the large radar display. He donned a headset and said, "Identify yourself, pilot. Over."

Tom repeated his original statement and added, "Also, we do not have enough fuel to change course. Over."

The commanding officer snapped his fingers and Private Carlson typed Tom's information into a computer terminal. Seconds later, Tom's photo and bio appeared on the screen—alongside the Interpol BOLO.

"Pilot, are you trying to tell me you want to prevent an assassination attempt on the Pope? My information suggests that you're the terrorist here. Well, son, either you change course immediately or you're going to learn all about the firepower of the United States Navy. Over."

The CO turned to his radar operator. "Who's in the air right now?"

"Lock and Dookie, Shorty and Butcher," Carlson said instantly.

The CO nodded. With a concise radio message, he redirected the two F/A-18s onto an intercept course, and a minute later they were flanking the Cessna. One of them moved in front of Tom's plane and waggled its wings—the internationally accepted sign to follow him.

The voice of one of the pilots crackled on the radio. "Change course, pilot. You are in a military training area. If you do not comply, we are authorized to take you out."

Hellen, helpless, stared fearfully at Tom, who was a little rattled now himself.

"Noah, can you call somebody for me and patch him through to the radio?"

The F/A-18s' request was repeated. Then the lead jet dropped back to its flanking position, and the two jets drifted dangerously close to the Cessna.

"Who do you need to speak to so urgently?" Noah asked.

"The admiral," was all Tom said.

The line went quiet for a second before Noah came back on.

"You sure?"

"Yes. And hurry, we're running out of time."

"Last resort, you can try to divert a missile with the flare gun. They're heat-seeking," Noah joked, already dialing the admiral's number.

"My God, Tom, they're going to blow us out of the sky!" Hellen peered fearfully left and right out of the window of the Cessna. Six thousand miles away, Admiral Scott Wagner's cell phone rang at the US Naval Base San Diego. He picked up.

"Uncle Scott, hi, it's Tom. Long time no hear—how are you? Look, I've run into a patch of trouble here and I figured maybe you could help. I'm in a light plane over the Mediterranean, and I'm currently flanked by two Navy F/A-18s. Looks like they're going to blow me out of the sky at any moment."

Admiral Wagner was famous for his poker face; it had won him the base poker tournament years before. But even he could not hide his astonishment now.

"Tom? What the fuck have you landed yourself in this time?"

"I'll explain later. I just need you to get in touch with the USS Ronald Reagan right now. Get them to call off their guys, or we're going to be a little pile of ash any minute."

Admiral Wagner was not a man of many words. "I trust you, Tom. Consider it done." He hung up and bellowed from his office into the anteroom, where his assistant sat.

"Connect me with the commanding officer of the USS Ronald Reagan, fast."

Naval aviator Lieutenant Daniel "Shorty" Lane had only recently transferred to the USS Ronald Reagan. Today's mission was one of his first and he was feeling nervous, which annoyed the hell out of him.

How do you ever expect to make it as an elite pilot if you have to change your shorts after escorting a seaplane? he thought. His hands trembled and he clenched the control stick of the 250-million-dollar fighter. It was less the fear of his own death that bothered him, however, than the fear of disappointing his old man. In his family, service to God and country came first—no ifs, ands or buts, and no failure tolerated. He had completed his education, as tradition demanded, quickly and with distinction. Being a naval aviator, however, was not his calling. For him it was only a job, and one he'd prefer to give up sooner rather than later. The thought that one day he'd get an order that might force him to take the lives of thousands of people—or even just one—was unbearable to him. A new order dragged him out of his morbid thoughts.

"Turn onto heading one-six-five. Prepare warning fire," the CO ordered the two pilots.

Here we go, Lieutenant Lane thought. Tense, his adrenalin level rising, he and his far-more-experienced wingman Butcher did as they were told. The two F/A-18s broke off their flanking positions and turned off to port and starboard, curving away and coming around into firing position.

"Not good . . . They're going on the attack. They really plan to shoot us down!"

"I hope your uncle didn't think you were telling him a bad joke," Hellen said. "It's what I'd expect in your family. Let's hope he really has the influence you think he has."

The next moment, one of the planes opened fire. Tom, his heart in his mouth, swung the wheel hard, but the twenty-millimeter cannon fire flew right past them anyway. Just a warning shot.

"Heyyyyyyy!" Tom shouted in surprise, and Hellen screamed. Tom quickly pulled the plane back on course and they flew onward.

"Abort! Abort!" Lieutenant Lane heard the CO say. He would not have been able to pull the trigger anyway. His wingman, however, had obeyed the order without hesitation.

"Return to the carrier. Over." The radar specialist was on the line again. *Someone's in trouble*, he thought. *But thank God this mission's over.*

"My apologies, sir," the CO said, on the radio now to Tom. "Admiral Wagner's just filled me in. Your flight path is clear. We're in touch with the Spanish authorities. You shouldn't encounter any more problems. Good luck, soldier."

The radio fell silent and Tom looked at Hellen with a cheeky grin. Hellen was speechless, but obviously relieved.

"Still there, Tom?" they heard Noah ask.

"Yep. Uncle Scott came through," Tom answered.

"You better get your ass here fast. Meet me in about forty minutes at the public viewing area, at La Monumental. Can you do that?" Noah asked.

"No problem. See you there."

As they approached the coast, Hellen asked, "How are we going to get to downtown Barcelona in forty minutes? We'll never manage that. And where exactly do you plan to land? There are small boats everywhere. Probably people swimming, too."

"No sweat. We'll take a short cut," Tom said.

Oh God, she thought. She clutched her harness and sank back as deeply as she could into her co-pilot's seat.

"What are you doing?" she asked as Tom turned north and the plane swung into a wide curve, heading straight for the city.

"Like I said, a short cut," Tom replied. "There must be a few blocks closed to traffic around the Sagrada Familia and the public viewing area."

"Yes . . . and you're telling me this why?" Hellen said, already suspecting the worst. "You're not planning to land in the middle of Barcelona, are you? There'll be hundreds of people down there. Thousands!"

"They'll move when they see us coming," Tom said with conviction.

He turned the plane back to the west and lined up to land on the Avinguda Diagonal, one of Barcelona's main arteries. He dipped the nose of the Cessna a little too quickly and Hellen let out a sharp cry.

"Tom, please don't! You're putting hundreds of lives in danger just to avoid running a few blocks."

She looked out the window and froze. Trees. As far as she could see. They lined the street, which was several miles long and about 150 feet wide, sometimes in rows of three or four. Tom was so low he was buzzing the topmost branches. From the cockpit it almost looked as if they were floating on the treetops, and every now and then the floats crashed through small branches. To the left and right, buildings whipped past. Hellen could literally see into people's apartments. Tom had slowed the Cessna to just above stalling speed.

Naturally, the people below began to take notice of the plane—it was about forty feet overhead, flying through a ravine of buildings. They stopped walking, and some started filming on their smartphones.

"Tom, you're out of your mind." Hellen gripped her harness even harder.

"Trust me," said Tom, his voice calm and even. "The Cessna 172 is the most forgiving, most robust plane in the world. In the eighties, a guy landed one on Red Square right outside the Kremlin. And he was only eighteen years old, fresh out of flight school."

"I'm not talking about the plane. I'm talking about those!" Hellen pointed frantically at the trees.

Tom remained a picture of calm. "You've heard of Kai Tak Airport in Hong Kong, haven't you? It closed in the late nineties." The plane grazed another few branches again. Tom went on, unmoved: "One of the most dangerous airports in the world, they said. Well, this is like that, only easier." Tom smiled. Hellen looked at him scathingly. Suddenly, he shouted, "Hold on!" and at the same moment abruptly dipped the nose of the plane. The rows of trees came to a sudden end and a clear stretch of road about 300 yards long opened in front of them. Frightened people, phones in their hands, scattered screaming, some running, others leaping over hoods of cars to get to safety as quickly as they could.

Tom put the machine down hard and immediately slammed on the brakes. The plane abruptly slowed, but the next row of trees still loomed inexorably. Hellen squeezed her eyes closed, as if that could prevent the worst. Two seconds later, she opened them momentarily only to see the trees getting frighteningly close. The plane finally trundled to a halt, six inches short of a parked car.

"Didn't I tell you? Scattered like zebras on the plains of Africa."

Tom unbuckled his harness.+

61

Tom leaned back and took a deep breath. Hellen still had a vice-like grip on her harness. She seemed not to have realized yet that they had actually landed and that the plane wasn't moving.

"We'd better get out of here or this is going to be a very short visit. We get arrested and it's all over with saving the Pope," said Tom.

Tom helped Hellen to unfasten her harness, then both jumped out of the plane and headed for the side of the street, watched by dumbstruck, still-frightened passers-by. Some had their phones in their hands, taking pictures or filming.

"Cool airport you've got here in Barcelona," Tom shouted in his rocky Spanish to a passer-by. "Very central. But man, we're hungry. Who makes the best tapas round here?" The young man had apparently just posted their photos on his Instagram. Tom took Hellen by the arm.

"Come on, we need to get off the main street."

They dashed into a side street and threw themselves into the throng moving in the direction of the Sagrada Familia and the public viewing area. All around were police, barriers, security.

"We have to get to the Sagrada Familia as fast as we can. I have no idea yet how we're going to get inside, but we have to try," said Tom. "And we need to find out what Ossana is doing here."

The chaos in the streets of Barcelona was indescribable. The city, lively and tourist-packed even on a normal day, was verging on chaos. Crowds filled the streets, along with a convoluted mess of roadblocks, traffic jams, police cars, security guards, and cordoned-off zones. Tom did not envy his colleagues their responsible to maintain security, especially since they had no idea an assassination was planned. He had been racking his brain ever since they'd left Valletta, turning over all the possible ways you could assassinate a Pope with a sword during a mass. He'd thought it all through countless times and had come up with nothing. The Pope's security detail would stop any attempt before it got started. Nobody would even be able to get close to the Pope with a sword. Which meant one thing: for the assassination to succeed, Count Palffy and Guerra must have something much bigger in mind. And that had Tom worried.

Hellen spotted Cloutard: with his hat and walking stick, he stood out from the crowd. A smile appeared on Cloutard's face as he saw them approach, and he and Tom embraced warmly. Cloutard greeted Hellen with a kiss on the hand.

"*Enchanté*, Mademoiselle de Mey."

"Thank you for telling Tom where to come and find me," said Hellen gratefully, but she remained a little suspicious. Unlike Tom, she still saw Cloutard more as an art-smuggler than an ally. But for now they had no choice; they needed all the help they could get. Everything else could be sorted out once this was over. Cloutard gave them a brief account of what had happened since his and Tom's escape from the burning helicopter, and everything he'd observed Ossana doing.

"I was just thinking that Guerra and Palffy must have a bigger plan," said Tom. "They can't stage an assassination in the Sagrada Familia any other way; it's just not feasible. We have to find out what they're really up to as soon as we can."

"Unfortunately, I've lost Ossana's trail," Cloutard said.

All of a sudden, Tom heard a familiar voice call his name.

"Signore Tom? Is that you?"

Tom turned around and saw the group immediately. The sight of four nuns arranged side by side like organ pipes and grinning at him broadly was hard to overlook. All four of them rushed over to him.

"What are you doing here? Have you found the Shroud yet? Did you save your girlfriend?"

Hellen raised an eyebrow. "Girlfriend?"

Tom shrugged evasively and quickly introduced the nuns to Hellen and Cloutard. "And yes," he said. "We managed to recover all of the relics. But now we have a whole new problem. Someone's going to try to assassinate the pope with the Sword of Saint Peter."

"*Madonna mia!*" The nuns' eyes widened. Speechless, they could only stare at Tom.

"I think we can use your help," Tom continued. "Somehow, we have to get past the barricades and into the Sagrada Familia. You told me you'd been invited to the mass. We have to get in there."

Sister Lucrezia frowned.

"I could give my habit and access card to Hellen," said Sister Renata, looking Hellen up and down appraisingly. They were about the same height and build. She nodded. "Yes, it ought to fit her. She could get in easily."

"And we're here with Father Giacomo." Sister Lucrezia pointed to a priest standing a few steps away. She pulled him over by his sleeve. "We borrow his cassock and *voilà!* Tom's a priest."

Taken unawares, Father Giacomo could only stare at the Mother Superior, but he did not dare to contradict her. He merely nodded.

"There's just one problem," Hellen piped up. "Tom, they'll recognize you in there. It's like Noah said: this whole event has been planned by Atlas, and there are Cobra guys in there, too. If they see you in the church, it's all over. Even Noah said you have to keep your head down."

"Then I will wear the cassock, and you and I will just have to do it on our own," Cloutard said to her grimly.

Sister Lucrezia did not look particularly convinced, but she looked at the group around her and finally came around. "They say that the end justifies the means. Our bus is only a block from here. You can change there."

Just then, Cloutard's phone rang. It was Noah on the line. Cloutard handed the phone to Tom.

"Tom, I've found a way to get you inside the restricted area. Meet me at the corner of Carrer de Mallorca and Carrer de Lepant in ten minutes. I can leave my post for a moment. I have extra earpieces, too, so we can stay in touch."

"Okay," Tom said. He hung up and turned to the others. "We split up here. I'll find Noah and get the equipment. You get changed. I'll meet you inside and bring earpieces for you."

Hellen and Cloutard went with the nuns while Tom made his way to the corner where he'd arranged to meet with Noah. He crossed Avinguda Diagonal, a little surprised to see that the Cessna was still standing where he'd left it. A few helpless-looking policemen were standing around, but they obviously had more important things to do just then than babysit an abandoned seaplane. The road was closed anyway, so arranging to have it towed away was not so simple.

Tom smiled when he spotted Noah at the corner of Carrer de Valencia. He went to his friend and hugged him. "Thanks for all the times you've dug me out of the shit in the last few days," Tom said.

"You know what you really need, Tom? A angel to sit on your shoulder and tell you what not to do. I think we can forget about you ever actually growing up. They send you on vacation and in the blink of an eye you turn it into an

assassination attempt on the Pope. Nice work, buddy."
Still in their embrace, he patted Tom on the shoulder.
They looked at each other in silence for a short moment.

"Okay, enough mushy stuff," said Noah, breaking the
silence. "Here's your pass. You won't have full access, but
that will at least get you through security. There are a few
Cobra people inside, like I said, especially in the basilica
itself, so make sure no one sees you. You're still a wanted
man."

Tom nodded, took the pass and lanyard, and slung it
round his neck.

"There's a guy from the counter-terrorism center in
Hungary next to me in the ops center. I stole his jacket.
It'll help you move around more freely."

Tom put on the jacket. "TEK/CTC" was printed on the
back, the abbreviation for the Hungarian anti-terrorism
unit.

"The Hungarians are a mess. They're the least likely to
notice if an unfamiliar face is running around in one of
their jackets," Noah said dryly as he opened a small flight
case. "Last but not least, the earpieces." Inside the case
were several earpieces embedded in styrofoam. He put
one of the earplugs in his ear and handed the case to
Tom, who did the same. Then he tapped a few buttons
on his tablet. and looked at Tom.

"Say a few words," Noah told him.

"A few words," Tom said with a grin.

"Oh, you're hilarious," said Noah. "Okay, we're good to go,
you're online. Give the others to Hellen and Cloutard,"

said Noah. "Let's get going. I'll give you the standard kit inside, once you're through the checkpoint. You never know."

In the meantime, Hellen and Cloutard had visited the nuns' van with the hapless Father Giacomo and had exchanged clothes.

"Father Giacomo, that suit, hat and walking stick really suit you," Sister Lucrezia said. Father Giacomo smiled benignly. Hellen, wearing Sister Renata's habit, headed for the security checkpoint with the cassocked Cloutard and the nuns.

"What do we do while we're waiting?" Father Giacomo called after them.

"Don't attract any attention," Sister Lucrezia called back, and set off with the others.

Two blocks away, they reached the security checkpoint, which they passed without a hitch. Hellen passed through the metal detector and spotted Tom in the crowd on the other side.

"We should split up. It's the best chance we've got." Tom gave Hellen and Cloutard an earpiece each.

"None for us?" complained Sister Bartolomea.

Sister Lucrezia narrowed her eyes at her young charge. "We have done enough already. We are servants of the Lord, not secret agents."

Tom agreed with her. "I already owe you more than I can repay. We have to leave now. I'm going to meet Noah for a minute to get another pistol."

The nuns were shocked. "Tom, this is a sacred place!" Sister Lucrezia said. "You're not going to start blasting away in here, I hope?"

"Not if I can help it. But we're here to stop an assassin from murdering the Holy Father."

Sister Lucrezia nodded. Then Tom went in search of Noah, and the rest of the group headed for the main entrance of the Sagrada Familia.

62

"Oh my God! There's Count Palffy!"

Hellen tapped Cloutard on the shoulder and pointed urgently toward the main entrance, where a small stage with a lectern had been set up on the stairs, intended for the Pope's blessing after mass. It was surrounded by security guards and crowded with cardinals and other personages. The Pope himself was standing at the back of the stage. Palffy approached the lectern, where a microphone had been installed. He held something in his hand, but from where Hellen was, she could not see it clearly.

"My God, François," Hellen cried. "What if Palffy plans to carry out the assassination right here and doesn't even wait for the mass? We have to get to the stage!" She was already pushing her way through the crowd when Palffy began to speak.

"Holy Father, it is my very great honor to be able to announce that we at Blue Shield and UNESCO have been able to recover all of the sacred relics stolen in recent weeks."

Spontaneous applause and cheering interrupted Palffy, and he waited a few seconds for the clamor to subside. He was obviously enjoying the moment.

"I have the honor to present to Your Holiness the Shroud of Turin, as symbolic of all the precious relics. The other treasures are safe and will be returned to their respective homes within the next few days."

The Pope nodded gratefully and accepted the leather roll that apparently contained the Shroud of Turin from Palffy. He took a step toward Palffy and leaned close to say a few personal words of thanks.

"My God! Palffy's only inches away from him," Hellen hissed to Cloutard. "Now's his chance!" She was now standing directly in front of the stage, where a line of security men blocked her way. "He's going to try to kill the pope, right now!" she shouted at one of the security men, but the man did not even flinch. He looked as if he hadn't even heard what she said, because the cheering at the handing over of the Shroud drowned out Hellen's voice. Cloutard was now standing behind her.

"Hellen, I do not think Palffy has any intention of murdering the Pope himself."

Cloutard pointed up at the stage. Palffy was just taking his leave of the Holy Father, and now turned toward the Sagrada Familia. The Pope handed the Shroud to one of his aides and also retired to the basilica to prepare himself for the mass. Hellen furrowed her brow. She looked at Cloutard in confusion.

"That would have been the perfect opportunity. What are they planning?" Hellen said.

Cloutard shook his head. "I have no idea. I can only hope that we have been entirely mistaken about an assassination attempt. We had better find seats inside." Cloutard activated his earpiece. "Tom, we are going inside. We've just seen Palffy and the Pope in front of the basilica," he said. He updated Tom on what they had seen.

"All right," Tom replied. "Make sure you keep an eye on Palffy."

The church began to fill. Nine thousand people fit into the Sagrada Familia, and every last seat would be filled that day. People streamed in through the side entrances as well. Everything was orderly, though there was no particular seating arrangement apart from a few rows at the front. Hellen and Cloutard tried to find seats as far forward as possible. They had lost contact with Sister Lucrezia and the other nuns outside the church.

"Hellen, we should separate. We would do best to watch from different perspectives," suggested Cloutard.

"I agree." Hellen touched her earpiece. "Tom, where are you?"

"Outside, looking for Guerra. François is right. Palffy had his opportunity, but he doesn't want to get his hands dirty. We have to keep our eyes peeled for Guerra. Ossana, too," Tom said.

Cloutard, by now some distance from Hellen, nodded and pointed toward the front of the basilica. "Palffy's there."

Hellen looked where Cloutard was pointing and saw the count seated in the second row, apparently reserved for VIPs. The area was cordoned off, and security was everywhere. Sitting around Palffy, Hellen recognized celebrities, politicians, business leaders. Neither Hellen nor Cloutard paid any attention to the inconspicuous man in simple priestly garb who had taken a seat next to Palffy.

Hellen and Cloutard found seats several rows apart. Moments later, the organ began to play and the mass for the Rite of Dedication began. The Pope stepped up to the altar, flanked by a large number of cardinals.

"*In nomine Patris et Filii et Spiritus Sancti,*" the Holy Father began.

Hellen's eyes scanned the basilica incessantly, searching for suspicious faces. Around the Pope, on all sides, stood a veritable army of cardinals, dignitaries, altar boys, and —of course—security. Hellen was looking toward the altar and almost cried out in horror when she saw him. One of the security men, standing directly beside the altar, had just raised a hand to his ear and was speaking into his headset. She recognized him instantly: Jacinto Guerra.

63

Noah had returned to the Command Center. Brand new, over eighty feet long and fifteen high, the monstrous mobile headquarters had been designed especially for Atlas operations and was packed with state-of-the-art technology. Black and heavily armored, the monstrous vehicle was unique in Europe; it looked like the offspring of an armored troop carrier and a freight train. On the roof were several satellite dishes, each of which could be fully retracted to allow the truck to reach its impressive top speed of almost 130 miles per hour. Today's operation was to be its baptism by fire.

As he rolled up the ramp into the huge mobile computer center, Noah felt as if he was in a science fiction movie. He rolled past the first two workstations until he reached his own and quickly brought himself up to speed. Countless monitors of all sizes covered the left wall, showing aerial views, infrared images, and feeds from various surveillance cameras and body cams. Thank God this thing's got good air-conditioning, he thought. All that equipment could make this place uncomfortably hot very quickly.

The situation was tense, but everything was unfolding according to plan. Each of the team of six in the Command Center was responsible for keeping track of a different section of the church and surrounding area via monitors. Noah was responsible for communications— his job was to make sure everyone was where they should be.

"What did the subway check turn up? Anyone or anything suspicious? Any vehicles from the Autoritat del Transport Metropolità?" Noah asked.

"Nothing. What did you expect?" said Tamás, the Hungarian officer sitting next to Noah. He sighed. "You got a bad tip. Once again, all the effort and expense is way out of proportion to the threat. Just think how much money we're burning here just to guard a few people. The things you could do with that . . ." He insinuated a female figure in the air with his hands.

"Typical Tamás," said Michelle Dubois, a colleague from France's *Groupe d'Intervention de la Gendarmerie nationale.* "Poor boy, that you have to spend a lot of money for that." Her figure was close to the outline Tamás had just made in the air. Tamás's eyes followed her as she went to the door. "I'm signing out for ten minutes," Michelle said without turning back. "I have to visit the little girls' room. And Tamás? You can stop staring at my ass any time now." She knew him well enough by now.

You want me to come along? Tamás almost said, but he managed to keep the thought to himself. He really didn't feel like having a #metoo discussion with his captain. He turned his attention back to the screen in front of him.

Noah smiled. "She's not your type, anyway," he said, patting Tamás on the shoulder.

Michelle opened the door and found herself face to face with a woman wearing the uniform of the Autoritat del Transport Metropolità. The woman shoved her back into the bus, stepped inside and swung the door shut behind her. Even before Michelle hit the floor, the woman had drawn her suppressed Heckler & Koch and put a bullet between Tamás's eyes. Noah turned around but could only watch as the woman, without a moment's hesitation, murdered his other three colleagues with perfectly targeted shots. For a brief moment, the trailer fell completely silent. The only sound was the radio traffic in Noah's ear, like a ghostly whisper in the air. Noah stared at the woman. He had never seen Ossana before, but from Tom's and Cloutard's descriptions he knew this must be her. She pressed the hot suppressor to Michelle's forehead and disarmed her. Michelle grimaced in pain but didn't make a sound. Ossana stared intently at Noah.

"One false move and she dies."

Noah had no reason to doubt Ossana. He did not move. Not because he felt any particular pangs of conscience for his French colleague—they were all professionals, after all, and life-threatening situations were part of the job. Noah just didn't want to risk Michelle's life without a plan—something that Ossana, unlike Noah, obviously had.

"Listen to me carefully," Ossana said. "You will inform all agents, one by one, that there has been a bomb threat and that the mass has to be interrupted. You will remove each agent from their post. You will issue them with new orders—each one individually, so that every agent will hear only their specific order."

Noah nodded. Ossana handed him a sheet of paper with instructions, but he could already see what she was up to. She aimed a second pistol at his head.

"Get started."

Noah began to call each of the officers, informing them of the bomb threat and assigning them a new post based on the list Ossana had given him. What Ossana didn't notice, however, was that Noah had opened the lines to Tom, Hellen and Cloutard as well. They could hear every word of his instructions.

64

Tom had slipped cautiously into the interior of the basilica. He reasoned that each of the security agents had specific orders and was focused on a certain section of the site, so he would not attract any undue attention and could easily study what was going on.

Without warning, however, he suddenly heard Noah's voice in his ear—but Noah did not seem to be speaking to him. He listened, quickly realizing that Noah was in trouble. Just as quickly, he also knew they had not been mistaken. Something very big was going down, and now it was up to him, Hellen and Cloutard to throw a wrench into Guerra's and Ossana's diabolical plan. He ran through his options. It would take some time for Noah to remove all the agents from their posts, which gave Tom a small window of time in which to get to the Command Center and stop it before it gathered any momentum. If enough of the security guards remained where they were, the situation would have no chance to escalate at all. Tom began to make his way outside.

"I'm on my way to help Noah," he said in a low voice, informing Hellen and Cloutard. Heading for the exit, he noticed a wave of unrest start to ripple through the church. People stared at their phones and whispered to each other.

Just as Tom was about to leave the basilica, he stopped. He heard someone cry out, "A bomb. There was a bomb at the public viewing."

Moments later a second person jumped up and shouted, "There's been a bomb threat in here, too. We're all in danger!"

The Pope interrupted his sermon and looked out in dismay at his audience. The cardinals around him were whispering nervously. The murmurings of the congregation grew louder, and Tom recognized Count Palffy, who now had his phone in his hand and was saying something to the man seated next to him. A woman jumped up and screamed, "Fire! The Sagrada Familia is on fire!"

That was the final straw. From one second to the next, panic broke out. Smoke began to rise into the nave from the crypt below, directly beneath the altar. As if a switch had been flipped, chaos erupted. People jumped up from their seats and tried to push their way outside as fast as they could. Images of Notre Dame burning were still fresh in everyone's memory, and the fear ran deep. Within seconds, it seemed as if those gathered inside completely forgot the meaning of Christian charity: they jostled and shoved; people fell and were trampled. All anyone was interested in was saving themselves, and to hell with everyone else. Everyone wanted to get away as quickly as possible. Collateral damage was someone else's problem.

Radio communication was impossible. Tom could barely hear himself think, let alone speak. He could forget about stopping Ossana. Tom hated himself for his decision, but Noah had to deal with his situation himself. Tom began to battle his way through the crowd. He had to get to the altar. Most of the security people were long gone from their posts, and the Pope was in mortal danger.

65

INSIDE THE SAGRADA FAMILIA

Hellen was also trying to fight her way through the crowd to the altar, but it was like swimming against the tide. She could see that Palffy was already standing next to the Pope and saying something to him. The Pope was surrounded by security guards, Guerra among them. For the first time, Hellen noticed the unassuming priest who had been sitting next to Palffy. He, too, was standing with the Pope. Now, flanked by security men and Palffy, Hellen saw the Pope move away from the altar and out of her line of sight, one of the many massive pillars of the Sagrada Familia briefly blocking her view.

"I've lost sight of them. Palffy and the Pope are on their way out," Hellen shouted into her headset. She was still more than ten yards away and struggling to make headway through the fleeing masses. "Okay, I can see them again now. Palffy's with the Pope. They're heading toward the side exit."

Cloutard heard Hellen's announcement and was confused. "Hellen, can you repeat that? The side exit? I just saw Guerra with the Pope going down to the crypt."

Tom broke in. "But that makes no sense. There's no other way out of the crypt. Maybe they went to the back of the sacristy?"

"But I can clearly see Palffy going to the exit with the Pope. I'm going to stay on him. Tom, you take Guerra," Hellen said.

But Cloutard was insistent. "Something isn't right. I swear I saw Guerra with the Pope. They were on their way down into the crypt."

Tom, meanwhile, had reached Cloutard.

"What's going on, François? Have we got two popes now? One in the crypt and one on his way outside? Can you take care of Ossana and Noah? Hellen's going after Palffy. I just hope you're right and the Pope is still here."

"We also saw the Pope being led down to the crypt. And frankly, he did not look very pleased about it." Sister Lucrezia had overheard Tom's last words. She, Sister Alfonsina, and Sister Bartolomea had spotted Tom and had followed him to the altar.

"I don't know what Guerra's up to down in the crypt, but it can't be anything good," Tom said. "If he really has the Pope, they might be planning to kill him in the crypt. The only question is: who is Hellen after?"

Cloutard shrugged. "I think I'll go and have a little talk with Ossana."

Tom nodded. "I'm on Guerra!"

He raced down the steps to one side of the altar, heading toward the crypt. What he didn't notice, however, was that the three nuns were following him.

Hellen had now made it outside, just in time to see Palffy climb into a limousine with the Pope and two security men. More security guards had cleared a path for them through the crush of people, but had not managed to clear the road completely for the car. The scene in front of the Sagrada Familia was one of indescribable chaos, everyone pushing and shoving to get outside and away from the church as fast as possible. News of the bomb threat had spread like wildfire, even outside.

"Palffy's just got the Pope into a car. They're leaving. I'll stay on them," Hellen shouted into her headset, unsure if anyone could even hear her.

The security detail had ushered Palffy and the Pope into the second of three armored Mercedes limousines. More bodyguards and the Pope's *camerlengo* climbed into the other two. The convoy started to move, though it could do no better than a walking pace for the moment. The police tried frantically to clear the streets, but with little success. The driver of the Mercedes carrying Palffy and the Pope laid on the horn, but could hardly move. Hellen ran after the car, but knew she would not be able to keep it up for long; a nun's habit wasn't built for a sprint. In a few hundred yards the car would reach the edge of the exclusion zone, and they would have open streets ahead of them. She had to think of something.

People were running to her left and right. The chaos was complete. Hellen reached the corner of Carrer de Lepant and saw the Pope's car diminishing in the distance. She turned and saw a motorbike approaching. Without hesitation she ran into the street in her nun's outfit and blocked its path, her arms outstretched. The driver hit the brakes hard, skidding and dropping the motorbike onto its side. It slid along the road for a several yards, coming to rest at Hellen's feet. The rider looked to be uninjured, and Hellen picked up the motorbike, climbed on, and sped away.

"I'll bring it back, I promise!" she called back over her shoulder.

The car with Palffy and the Pope stopped at the intersection of Carrer de Valencia. This was her chance. She could still catch up. She cranked the throttle and the machine accelerated. She hadn't ridden a motorcycle for years, but now was no time to think about that. Only one thing mattered: she had to stop Palffy and save the Pope.

66

"Do we have enough light?" Guerra checked the cell phone that one of his men had set up on a tripod. On the display, he saw the Pope on his knees, framed in front of the altar in the crypt.

The crypt itself was an impressive piece of architecture, larger than the nave of many churches. From the gilded keystone of the dome, twelve struts curved to every side, coming to rest atop mighty columns. Behind the columns, a colonnade circled the entire crypt, and several small chapels were also arranged around the almost-circular structure. At the base of each column was a stand supporting a bowl about twenty inches in diameter, and in each bowl, the eternal flame flickered. The dark-brown wooden pews, facing the simple altar, were arranged in two rows, leaving a narrow central aisle.

Guerra nodded benevolently and strode toward the altar. As he passed the Pope, he leaned down to him and said, "These pictures will go around the world. The Pope, beheaded in the name of Allah with the Sword of Peter, at the altar of one of the most famous churches in the world. We're going to break YouTube."

Slowly, he lifted the ancient sword from its chest, which lay on the altar. He flourished it skillfully over the Pope's head a few times.

"Don't worry, it's still extremely sharp," he said to the Pope.

The Pope looked up at Guerra, but with no fear in his eyes.

"What do you think you will achieve? The Catholic Church has survived worse crises. It will not make Islam stronger," Holy Father said calmly.

"Silence!" Guerra snapped. "You have no idea what this is about. Do you really think we're putting on this circus for something as banal as religion? For belief in a God? You are an old and deeply naive man."

Tom had stopped at the top of the final section of the stairs leading down and had overheard the entire exchange. Below him, on the floor of the crypt, he saw the charred husks of the smoke bombs that had caused all the chaos a few minutes earlier. He had to intervene, and there was no time to waste, but before he could move, he heard a noise behind him. He turned and saw Sister Lucrezia, Sister Alfonsina and Sister Bartolomea.

"Jesus, what are you doing here?" he whispered. "This is damned dangerous. You're just in the way."

Sister Lucrezia glared at Tom and whispered back, "You will stop cursing in this house of worship, Thomas. The Lord will look after us. We have no intention of standing idly by while the Holy Father is kidnapped, not if we might be able to do something about it."

Tom decided not to get into a debate just then. Instead, he shook his head, checked his Glock, and crept down the last twenty steps. Although the stairway was clearly visible from the altar, Guerra and his men were so focused on getting their setup right that they didn't notice Tom as he slipped down along the wall on the right side of the stairway.

Guerra continued to prowl around the kneeling pontiff, who was now deep in prayer. Tom, meanwhile, had arrived at the bottom of the stairs, which came down to the right of the altar. The stairway opened into the colonnade, and he concealed himself inside the first small chapel. On the chapel floor, right by his feet, he read "Antoni Gaudí i Cornet." The word "Cornet" was what caught Tom's eye. He was standing in the tomb of the world-famous architect. *Ah, Cornet*, he thought.

"Are you two idiots finally ready?" Guerra looked at his two assistants. "We have to make this quick. The bomb squad will get here any minute. They'll search the entire Sagrada Familia for a bomb that doesn't exist, and they'll probably start down here. Masks on, and let the games begin."

That's my cue, thought Tom. He had surprise on his side. With his pistol raised, he stepped out of his hiding place. Two well-placed shots and Guerra's two companions went down, one with a hole in his head, the other with a bullet in the chest. Tom completed his swing to the left and took aim at Guerra, but hesitated. He was facing the man who killed his parents—he had him in his sights. Tom's hesitation gave Guerra a momentary advantage: a quick turn and Guerra was behind the Pope, the Sword of Peter pressed to the pontiff's throat. But even with a sword at his neck, the Pope remained absolutely calm.

"You're tenacious, Wagner, I'll give you that. I must have been too nice to you so far, but that ends today. I'm going to finish you off myself. First I'll take care of him"—Guerra had knocked off the Pope's *zucchetto* and now grabbed him by his grey hair and pulled his head back; he pressed the sword harder against his neck—"and then you."

Guerra and Tom stared each other in the eye. Neither moved.

Suddenly, a voice rang out. "Holy Mary preserve us!" The three nuns were standing beside Tom.

Guerra laughed. He pointed with the sword at the nuns. "What's this, Wagner? Your backup?"

At that moment, Sister Lucrezia cried, "*Conquiniscere!*"

Guerra didn't understand the word, but he found out what it meant when the Holy Father, without warning, ducked forward.

Tom saw his opportunity and seized it. He fired twice, two bullets slamming into Guerra's shoulder. The mercenary stumbled backward, releasing the Pope. A heartbeat later, Tom rushed at Guerra and knocked him to the floor of the crypt. The sword slipped from Guerra's grasp. The nuns rushed over and helped the Pope to his feet. Quickly, they led him away to the stairs. Tom picked up the sword and moved around the prone and bleeding Guerra, the blade tip pointed at his throat.

"Don't do it!" the Pope, behind Tom, called out. The pontiff's voice resounded through the crypt. The authority in the leader of the Catholic church's voice took Tom's breath away, and not just his: Guerra, too, seemed paralyzed. Tom looked around. The Holy Father was standing at the base of the stairs, his arms raised as if to prevent Tom from killing Guerra. "All they that take the sword shall perish with the sword. What was true for Simon Peter on the Mount of Olives is also true for you, my son."

A deathly quiet settled over the crypt. No one stirred. Even Guerra was momentarily overwhelmed by the Pope's words. Tom looked down at the sword in his hand. He tossed it aside, into the center aisle, but immediately drew his Glock. Sister Lucrezia plucked at the Holy Father's robe.

"We have to leave, Your Holiness," she whispered.

At the same moment, Tom heard a female voice through his earpiece. "You haven't got a prayer, Wagner. More importantly, you have no idea who you're up against. You simply cannot win." Tom knew the voice. Ossana. "Might as well say goodbye to your friend in the wheelchair."

Tom heard the crackle of static and a high-pitched whistling noise; Ossana had broken the connection.

A violent blow swept Tom's legs from under him and he hit the marble floor hard. Guerra had taken advantage of Tom's inattention and knocked him off his feet with a

346

twisting kick. Tom's Glock was knocked from his hand as he fell; it skittered away underneath the pews.

Guerra leapt to his feet and threw himself on top of Tom. But this time Tom was faster. He wasn't going to drop his guard a second time. Lying on his back, Tom was able to turn Guerra's momentum to his advantage. He grabbed Guerra's arms and, using his legs, catapulted the mercenary away. Guerra landed painfully on one of the pews closer to the exit, knocking it over with a crash. Tom rolled onto his side, trying to get to his Glock, but from where he lay it was out of reach.

Despite the bullets in his shoulder and the hard landing, Guerra was back on his feet fast. If he was in pain, he didn't show it. Tom, too, was on his feet again. He saw that Guerra had pulled a knife. Tom slid the telescopic baton from his belt, flicked it out to its full length with a jerk, and went on the offensive. He attacked Guerra from the front, darting forward quickly like a fencer, and knocked the knife from his hand.

Driven back to the side of the crypt, Guerra grabbed one of the flaming bowls on its stand and pushed it over toward Tom. The burning oil flooded the floor, setting fire to the nearest wooden pews. Tom retreated in alarm, but jumped to the other side of the column and drove Guerra farther back. At the next column Guerra pushed over another bowl, then another.

Tom could go no further. Guerra moved through the center aisle, heading for the altar and the two dead men. He grabbed one of their pistols and immediately fired at Tom, who ducked for cover behind a column.

"Do you still remember?" Guerra called out.

Guerra took out his phone, and a few seconds later music began to play. Music that went straight to Tom's core, the saddest piece of music he had ever heard. His memory came back then, with none of the gaps. The music was the start of his mother's favorite piece, "Brockes Passion" by Georg Philipp Telemann. The pain that seared through him was beyond his ability to describe. Tom had been injured many times on missions, but none of his old wounds came even close to the torment he experienced in that moment. Once again, he was a little boy confronted by a wall of fire, staring at the burning car in which his parents had perished. The minor strains of the overture did the rest: Tom was unable to move a muscle. Guerra had him in his control, like a marionette on strings.

"You should have listened to my advice," Guerra shouted through the blazing flames, and he fired in Tom's direction once more.

Tom could not reply. He slid down to the base of the column, while the music in his head grew louder and louder, dragging up the pain of years, cleaving him like a scalpel. The fire only made things worse; Tom felt he was on the verge of losing his mind completely. The crypt was slowly becoming oppressively hot and the air began to burn his lungs, but Tom was helpless to overcome the pain of his memories. He could only stand there, seven years old, crying his eyes out, in front of him only burning debris. And from one moment to the next, he was completely alone in the world.

"Remember what I told you twenty years ago," Guerra bellowed, grinning like a demon. "Don't stick your nose into things that are none of your business."

The heartbreaking minor theme had now given way to an almost merry-sounding oboe. Guerra briefly closed his eyes. He felt safe. He could enjoy this moment. Eyes shut, he kept on talking. "Your mother loved Telemann, didn't she? Just before that bomb tore her to pieces, she was listening to this very piece." He pointed to his cell phone. An aria began, and the words they both heard were like a kick to Tom's gut when he was already down:

"Break, my heart, flow forth in tears."

Tom was finished. The man he suspected of murdering his parents had not only just admitted it, but seemed to have known all along who he was. And he was taking diabolical pleasure in pouring salt onto Tom's wounds.

And then, suddenly, the world for Tom stood still. A moment of clarity jolted through him like an electric shock. He had to confront his pain and fear, not bury them deep inside himself. He had to unshackle himself. His life would never again be what it once was. But to free himself, he first had to overcome himself: he had to choose to live. After that, dealing with Guerra would be a piece of cake.

In the aria, the Daughter of Zion sang, "Hear his sniveling, sighing, yearning, look how full of fear he is," and something shifted inside Tom.

Summoning all the strength and willpower he could muster, Tom made his choice. He could see where his Glock lay beneath a pew. Bracing against the column, he pushed himself to his feet and glanced around the corner. Guerra, his eyes closed, was still savoring the sounds of the music: this was Tom's chance. He launched himself from behind the column, threw himself flat on his stomach, slid across the smooth marble and grabbed the gun. He fired immediately in Guerra's direction, but the bullet went wide. The shot tore Guerra out of his trance and brought him back to the moment. Taken by surprise by the sudden change in Tom, he ducked for cover and returned fire. Both men ran, bent low and shooting at each other, Guerra down the center aisle and Tom around the encircling colonnade. Separated by burning pews, both weary, they took cover again.

"What are you up to, Wagner?" Guerra said, still goading Tom. "You can't win. We'll always be one step ahead of you. And if you think killing me will change anything, think again. We are everywhere."

67

Ossana gazed at Noah, a triumphant smile on her face. In a few moments, Tom would be dead, and she and Guerra could celebrate their success.

"It's been nice, but I've got something more important to take care of."

She stepped swiftly over the bodies of Noah's colleagues, lying on the floor of the mobile Command Center. Without warning or provocation, and with complete indifference, she fired twice into the head of Michelle, still crouched on the floor. Michelle rolled backward, lifeless as a doll, and lay still. Noah inhaled sharply. Ossana paused at the door and withdrew a rectangular block from her backpack. Noah knew what it was: C-4 plastic explosive. Ossana fixed the block to the door handle and looked back over the corpse-strewn floor at Noah. In his wheelchair, he could not possibly get through.

"You have a small chance to escape. But frankly, I don't think you'll make it," Ossana said.

"Why not just shoot me?" Noah barked at her.

"I don't shoot cripples," Ossana replied with a sneer.

She pushed the detonator into the plastic explosive, activated the timer, left the truck and closed the door behind her. Noah was trapped, with no idea how much time he had.

68

Hellen had no idea what she would do if the convoy carrying Palffy and the Pope stopped, and even less of an idea of what Palffy was up to. Why was he allowed to ride with the Pope at all? She was no expert, but that fact alone seemed to her extraordinary. She had been chasing the convoy of cars on the stolen motorbike for some time, and her mind was in overdrive. The convoy seemed to be heading toward Barcelona airport. Were they so keen to get the Pope to safety that they were going to fly him out of the country? What good would that do Palffy? Or was this all just one big masquerade?

With these thoughts going through her head, Hellen realized that the convoy was drifting apart. The last car, which had been driving the whole time just behind the one carrying Palffy and the Pope, dropped back, as if trying to get to a safe distance. Hellen could not think her suspicions through to the end, however, because the center car suddenly exploded in an enormous fireball.

Hellen managed to brake just as the inexorable shock wave reached her and knocked her off the bike.

The shock wave and the heat of the explosion shattered the windows of cars and shops on both sides of the highway. People screamed and began running in all directions, and dozens of nearby car alarms started to wail. Flames leapt high into the sky. Hellen got to her feet and stared ahead at the blazing wreck—there was no way anyone in the limo could have survived.

A car bomb to kill the Pope? Then why the sword? Had that been Plan B? Was Palffy not only the perpetrator after all, but also a victim? Was there a logical explanation at all? Her confusion only grew. Maybe she'd fallen for a diversion, and the real show was happening somewhere else?

The scales fell from her eyes. The other two limousines had disappeared. She picked up the bike, took the next exit from the highway, and raced back toward the heart of Barcelona.

69

Tom was finding it hard to breathe. The heat was getting worse by the minute. He checked his ammunition and made a decision. He took several deep, fast breaths, pumping like an athlete about to face the most important competition of his life. Two shots slammed into the wooden pew in front of him, followed by a click. Guerra was out of bullets. Tom let out a roar and leaped to his feet. Running on adrenaline, he lifted the pew and hurled it forward. Then he sprinted from cover and, using the seat and back of the pew as a kind of stairway, launched himself through the flames straight at Guerra, who was taken completely by surprise. Tom grabbed him in mid-flight, and the two men went down together, landing hard in the center aisle of the crypt. Exhausted, they both lay on the floor for a moment before Tom, bathed in sweat, his face twisted with pain, picked himself up and moved slowly toward Guerra, who was pushing himself up on the back of a pew. Tom kicked him in the face with all his strength. He waited for Guerra to regather himself a little, then swung back and slammed his fist against Guerra's temple. Something snapped inside Tom and he saw red. He was blind to the fire raging around him. He beat Guerra mercilessly, barely managing to stop himself before he went too far. Horrified at what had come over him, he retreated from where Guerra lay bloodied on the marble floor. Guerra laughed. He spat out the blood that had collected in his mouth.

"I've got another piece of advice for you," Guerra said as he rose to his feet. "Finish what you start."

Guerra was standing upright in the center aisle. In his hand, he held the Glock that Tom had dropped when he leaped on him. He took aim at the obviously exhausted Tom. For a moment the two adversaries stared each other in the eye. Guerra laughed and said, "Give my regards to your parents."

He pulled the trigger.

Click. Click, click, click.

"Mine was empty too, asshole," Tom said. "By the way, you're under arrest. You have the right to keep your mouth shut, because nobody gives a shit about what you have to say, anyway."

Tom, breathing hard, failed to notice that one of Guerra's henchmen, the one he'd shot in the chest, was not dead after all. Behind Tom, the man struggled painfully to his feet. He picked up the sword and crept slowly, silently toward Tom. Guerra immediately saw what his partner was up to. He flung the empty pistol at Tom, who ducked. Then Guerra rushed him, snarling. *The stupid act of a beaten man*, Tom thought. He dodged Guerra's charge easily, and with a deft spinning kick took advantage of Guerra's momentum and kicked him in the back with all his strength as he flew past. Tom was startled by what followed, and he wasn't the only one.

Guerra's henchman had been about to run Tom through with the sword. Instead, he drove the blade through Guerra's body up to the cross-guard. Despite the roaring flames, Tom heard the horrible sound of the sword slicing through Guerra's solar plexus. A gush of blood spilled from Guerra's mouth onto the shirt of the swords-man, who promptly released the heft and stared in wide-eyed horror at Guerra. Guerra staggered and stumbled, trying to stay on his feet, but he no longer had control of his movements. He staggered against a blazing pew and his trousers caught fire. Seconds later he was completely engulfed in flames. He collapsed with a hideous scream.

Tom stood and stared into the flames. He no longer feared them. But Ossana's words flashed in his memory: Noah, his best friend, needed his help. He raced back up the stairs.

70

ATLAS MOBILE COMMAND CENTER, A PARK BEHIND THE
SAGRADA FAMILIA, BARCELONA

Noah knew he didn't have much time. As soon as Ossana
had closed the door, he hoisted himself up and tipped
himself out of his wheelchair. He was about twenty feet
from the door. Not far for most people, but the floor of
the truck was strewn with corpses. Ossana had gone
through like a hurricane, leaving five bodies, three
toppled office chairs, a laser printer that had fallen off a
desk, and sundry other objects scattered across the floor
in her wake. For Noah, it was a special challenge, his
personal Mount Everest. With his eyes fixed on the
flashing timer attached to the C-4, he pushed past the
first body.

Cloutard had finally battled his way through the stream
of panicked people fleeing the basilica. Outside, he ran to
the first security guard he saw.

"Where is the Atlas Command Center?"

The man was clearly overwhelmed, but pointed to the back of the church. "Back there," he shouted over the screams of the fleeing people. He had braced himself against a steel barrier and was doing his best to direct the panicked masses. Cloutard nodded and ran off, jumping over several barriers and ignoring the shouts of the guards who tried in vain to stop him.

He turned a corner and there it was: the futuristic, high-tech truck.

A police barricade surrounded the small area where the enormous vehicle was parked. Cloutard dodged through the crowd and was about to climb over the barricade when he saw the rear door of the trailer open. Ossana stepped out and closed the door behind her.

Was he too late?

"STO-O-O-P!" he bellowed.

Ossana turned at the sound of his shout. Surprised to see him, she nevertheless managed a small smile. She blew him a kiss, swung herself elegantly over the police barricade and disappeared into the crowd.

Cloutard, zigzagging through the crowd, stayed on her heels. "Stop her!" he shouted, but no one took any notice. Everyone was looking out for themselves. Then a man running collided with Cloutard from one side and he momentarily lost sight of Ossana. He kept jumping in the air to see over the swarming people. Nothing.

"*Merde!*" She was gone.

Out of nowhere, a searing pain shot through his back and he collapsed. He'd been struck in the kidneys, and when he fell to his knees in pain, Ossana's knee came up and hit him in the face. He crashed onto his back. People ran over him without stopping.

Then Ossana appeared in his field of vision. She had her silenced gun pointed at him, but, unusually for her, not at his head.

"I'm glad my people in Tabarka didn't kill you. The world is so much more fun with you in it, François. But right now, I don't need you following me. For your own sake, do me a favor: get away from here as fast as you can."

Cloutard had propped himself on his hands and merely nodded. Ossana slipped the gun in inside her uniform, turned and jogged away.

"I'll get you one of these days," he shouted weakly after her.

Cloutard picked himself up again and watched as Ossana trotted past several fire trucks and emergency vehicles that were just pulling up. She disappeared into the subway. Cloutard took a deep breath. His nose was bleeding, and his back still stung.

"Did you get Ossana?" Tom cried, emerging from the church and running toward Cloutard.

Cloutard shook his head. "No. She took me by surprise. My hand-to-hand skills are limited to horizontal wrestling."

"What about Noah?" Tom asked.

"Noah?" Cloutard said, and his eyes opened wide. "My God, I hope we're not too late!"

"Fuck!" Tom cried, and he ran for the truck.

Sweat dripped from Noah's forehead. Between him and the bomb was one last overturned office chair, but its back had become wedged under the shoulder of one of his dead colleagues, and neither the chair nor the corpse would budge. Noah's strength was fading. His arms burned and he was on the brink of surrendering to his fate. Even if he made it to the door, Ossana had attached the C-4 charge to the handle—out of his reach, he knew, even as he managed to push the office chair aside with a powerful jerk, using up the last of his strength. The sweat trickling into his eyes stung like pure salt. He looked up. The timer was counting down the last ten seconds. There were only inches between him from the detonator. With a final heave, he reared up, arching his back as far as he could. He was stretching for the timer when the door abruptly opened, and the C-4 brick fell to the ground. Tom saw the danger instantly and yanked the timer leads out of the detonator. He looked at Noah in astonishment.

"You lose something? Or is that your version of the 'downward dog' pose?" Tom asked with a grin as he looked down at his friend on the floor of the truck.

"Just going out to stretch my legs," Noah shot back, no less sardonic, but obviously relieved. "Did you get the bitch?" Noah looked up at Tom and Cloutard expectantly.

"I'm afraid not," Cloutard said. "She got away. But she told me to get away from here as fast as I could. What do you think she might have meant?"

"When she left me here, she said she had something more important to do," Noah said.

"I last saw her going into the subway station. She's probably long gone by now," Cloutard said.

"The subway? But the subway's not running today, not here. Security shut down all the stations around the Sagrada Familia," Noah said.

"Damn it, I forgot to tell you. Tom, she drove through half of Europe in a car with the logo of the Barcelona public transport system. I could kick myself for losing her. If I had stayed on her, we would know more," said Cloutard.

"All the more reason to find out what she's up to. I suspect that killing the Pope was only part of the plan," said Tom. He grabbed a pistol lying next to Noah on the floor of the truck and threw another to Cloutard. "Come on, François. Looks like we're not finished yet."

71

"Where's Guerra?" Ossana asked the three men standing by the service vehicle. All of them wore uniforms with 'Autoritat del Transport Metropolità' printed on the back. One of the men shrugged and unlocked the door to a service room for her. The case was still inside, just as she and Guerra had left it a few hours earlier. She placed her thumb on the fingerprint scanner on top of the case. "Access granted" appeared on the display and a faint click signaled to Ossana that the case was now unlocked. She lifted the lid and looked inside.

"Where is that asshole? This was his fucking job." Ossana shook her head angrily, and her voice echoed through the tunnel. She took a deep breath and focused on the job before her. Not even she activated a bomb like this one every day. She set the timer and started the countdown.

. . .

Tom and François ran through the empty subway tunnel.

"She could be anywhere," said Cloutard.

"What do you think Ossana is up to down here?" Tom asked.

"A bomb, maybe?" Cloutard said. "She used my organization's network to have a package sent across Europe to San Marino, where she picked it up herself; it also fits her warning to me to get away from here. Bottom line: probably a bomb."

Tom thought about that for a moment and nodded. "Whoever dreamed this up wants to make a bigger statement. It's not enough for them to behead the Pope with the Sword of Saint Peter for all the world to see, now they want to blow up the Sagrada Familia and thousands of people with it?"

He paused. His arm shot out to the side, stopping Cloutard in his tracks.

"Do you hear that, François?"

They had reached a junction. On their right, a service track disappeared around a bend; they heard voices from that direction. They crept cautiously along the wall and saw first the service vehicle, then two uniformed men leaning against it, sharing a cigarette. A door abruptly opened on the left, and Ossana and a third subway worker came out. This was obviously a service tunnel for the subway technicians.

"*Arrêtez!*", Cloutard shouted, opening fire, but his bullets missed their mark and struck the side of the vehicle beside the smoking men. They were taken so completely by surprise that the one with the cigarette almost swallowed it. But they wasted no time drawing their own weapons and returning fire. Simultaneously, the third man also began shooting at Tom and Cloutard, positioning himself between them and Ossana to give her cover.

"Are you crazy? Are you trying to get us killed?" Tom yelled as he ducked for cover behind an electrical cabinet, pulling Cloutard in behind him. Bullets slammed into the cabinet.

"Hello darling," Ossana called. "Didn't I tell you not to follow me? Now you and your new friend will die down here, just like thousands of other people."

Tom sneaked a look around the corner of the cabinet and saw the men bundling Ossana into the service van. He squeezed off three rounds in their direction as the car started to move, accelerating toward Tom and Cloutard. They pressed themselves against the wall behind the electrical box as the car shot past. Cloutard ran after it and emptied his magazine.

"Come on, Tom! What are you waiting for? We have to stop them."

"No, let them go. We've got to deal with the bomb."

Cloutard came back and they ran to the service room.

"Tom, can you hear me?" Noah was in Tom's ear again. "I've got our comms up again."

"I'm a little busy just now," Tom replied, and with a violent kick, which Cloutard was just able to dodge, Tom broke open the door. Their fears were confirmed in the worst possible way. In the service room on a small table stood a locked flight case. On the display at the top, a timer was counting down:

14:57.

14:56.

14:55.

"Isn't that a little small to destroy the Sagrada Familia?" Cloutard wondered almost in a whisper.

"Not if it's . . ." Tom was so appalled at the idea that he wasn't able to finish the sentence.

". . . nuclear?" Cloutard did it for him.

"*What?*" said Noah, who had overheard.

"*Mon Dieu*. We have to get away from here."

"And do what? Run away? Let them vaporize half of Barcelona and hundreds of thousands of people? Make the greater Barcelona area uninhabitable for decades? No way."

Tom had already grabbed the case and was running through the tunnel, heading for the exit.

"Noah, we need the bomb squad," he shouted into the headset.

"I'll come your way," Noah replied.

"Meet me at the subway entrance. If necessary, you're going to have to disarm the thing. We have thirteen minutes and 26 seconds left." He and Cloutard ran up the stairs and immediately saw Noah rolling up in his wheelchair.

"Doesn't look good," said Noah, taking a closer look at the case. "It's got a biometric lock. We can't get in, at least not fast enough." He pointed to the display, where the seconds ticked away inexorably. "Even the bomb techs won't be able to do anything about it."

The bomb disposal technicians had arrived in the meantime and nodded their agreement.

"Well we can't sit around picking our noses," Tom said, thinking hard. "Somebody has to do something."

"Evacuate!" one of the disposal technicians threw out, fear on his face. No one replied. They just looked at him and shook their heads.

"I've got an idea." Tom hoisted the case and ran.

"Tom!" Cloutard and Noah shouted in unison. "What are you doing?"

"I've gotta get this damned thing out of here."

Stunned, Cloutard and Noah watched Tom disappear into the crowds.

"Where's Tom?" Cloutard and Noah spun around and saw Hellen. She had just jumped off the motorbike and was standing behind them.

Noah could not meet Hellen's eye.

"Tom's . . ." He hesitated. Hellen turned pale.

"Tom's what?" Hellen snapped.

"... he's got a bomb ..."

"A nuclear bomb," Cloutard corrected.

"Yes, he's got an *nuclear* bomb, and he's taking it away."

"A nuc—what!? My God! I just watched the Pope and Palffy get blown up, and now there's a nuclear bomb? Doesn't this nightmare ever end?"

"What do you mean, you watched the Pope get blown up? He was here the whole time. Tom's nuns have taken him to safety. By the way, where's your earpiece?"

Hellen shook her head helplessly.

"I lost it." She leaned on one arm of Noah's wheelchair and snapped at him, "Don't change the subject. Where. Is. Tom?"

Noah pointed to the south. Hellen straightened up and looked in the direction he was pointing. It hit her like a wrecking ball. "But that's where we—" Without finishing her sentence, she ran off.

"Hellen, wait! What are you going to do?" Noah called after her.

"*Les femmes*," said Cloutard, looking at Noah and shaking his head.

It took Tom a few minutes to reach his destination. With all the excitement, the assassination attempt and the bomb threats at the basilica, chaos still reigned on the streets. Even the policemen who had been standing guard by the plane were gone. Tom's progress carrying the bomb was slow, and Hellen caught up with him at the Cessna.

"What are you going to do, Tom?" said Hellen when she reached the plane parked on Avinguda Diagonal. He was already lifting the bomb into the plane.

"I'm going to fly this thing as far away from here as I can."

"Are you trying to kill yourself? You can't just . . . I—I don't want to lose you. Not again." Her eyes filled with tears. "I'll come with you! I'm sure I can help you somehow," she said with determination, wiping away her tears.

Tom backed out of the plane. He turned to Hellen and took her by the shoulders.

"Out of the question. I can't let this bomb kill hundreds of thousands of people. And you least of all. There's no other way." He looked at the countdown:

9:16

9:15

9:14

"I have to do this alone, and I don't have the time to discuss it."

He pulled her to him and kissed her fervently. Then he let her go and jumped into the plane, closing the door behind him.

He fired up the engine, catching the attention of people around the machine. Hellen had to accept his decision. She could only watch as Tom turned the Cessna around for take-off. Tears running down her cheeks, she began to shoo the onlookers away from Tom's "runway." It was not a difficult task: the noise and the trundling Cessna made it clear what Tom was up to. As the plane took off, Tom pulled the nose up hard and steered it toward the Mediterranean. Hellen, fearful, watched him fly away.

72

The Cessna's engine roared as Tom opened the throttle,
pushing the plane to its maximum speed. He wanted to
get as high as possible and as far from Barcelona as possible, and to do so as fast as possible. He had no desire at
all to die that day, certainly not for a plan cooked up by
Guerra, Ossana and Palffy. His body was pumping adrenaline and his pulse and breath were racing, but he forced
himself to run through his options with relative calm.

*Okay, you can't drop the bomb into the Med. You'd contami-
nate it for decades. Besides, the tsunami would probably wash
away half of Barcelona.*

He could forget about that.

And there's no way you're going to die with this fucking thing.

That was also not an option for him. He looked back and
saw the numbers on the countdown: 03:37

The seconds were slipping away. Then he looked a short
way beyond the suitcase nuke, and a smile started to

cross his face. Maybe Noah's stupid joke from that morning hadn't been so stupid after all. He reached for the radio.

"This is Niner Hotel Mike Charlie Romeo Foxtrot calling USS Ronald Reagan. Come in. We met this morning."

The radio operator on the USS Ronald Reagan grimaced. "Goddamn it, Wagner, how many times do you want your uncle to save your ass?"

"Okay, listen up. You must have heard by now what just went down with the Pope at the Sagrada Familia. Well, the brains behind their little kill-the-Pope plot also planted a nuclear bomb under the Sagrada Familia. I repeat, a nuclear bomb."

The radio operator put Tom on speaker.

"Sir, you need to hear this. It's Admiral Wagner's nephew again. He's saying something about an nuclear bomb in Barcelona."

"It's not in Barcelona anymore. I've got the damn thing here with me. I'm trying to stop Barcelona from blowing up. I need your help to get rid of it."

"You have a primed *nuclear* weapon in your plane?" The radio operator nearly choked.

The CO came on the line. "I'm all ears, son."

"It's on a timer and it's got just over two minutes left. You can help. Get those two F/A-18s that were so nice to me this morning in the air ASAP. They can dig us all out of a pile of shit."

Tom put the Cessna on autopilot and turned around to the bomb. The countdown was at 01:42. This was going to be as tight as hell. Tom hastily dug out the emergency flares stuffed in a sports bag with all kinds of other junk on the rear seats. He tore open the sports bag and tried to stuff the bomb inside it. Impossible. The thing was too big.

"Think, dammit!" he said aloud to himself. He found an old Stanley knife in the bag, which gave him an idea. He cut away one of the seat belts and used it to tie the flares to the bomb. Then it occurred to him that the flares could be ancient and might not burn at all. He was anything but a religious man, but he said a silent prayer to any gods listening that the torches would still ignite.

On the aircraft carrier, flags waved: clear for take-off. The two pilots could hardly believe that Wagner and the Cessna were responsible for them returning to the air. In quick succession, the two F/A-18s took off from the aircraft carrier. This time, though, they had already had their orders: they had one shot, and not much time to take it. The lives of everyone within hundreds of miles depended on them.

00:48

00:47

00:46

Tom scraped the striker built into the cap against the ignition surface of the flares. He let out a whoop when the first one began to burn, then hastily repeated the process with the second torch. His fear of fire and flame had been exorcized down in the crypt, but now he knew for sure that he was over it.

On the radio, he heard both pilots confirm that they were in position. He took the burning bundle and glanced at the countdown one last time:

00:13

00:12

00:11

He hurled the bomb out of the Cessna. He looked down after it, watching as it got closer and closer to the surface of the sea. The first F/A-18 launched a missile at the package, but it shot past, missing by a fraction of an inch. Tom's heart nearly gave out. Were the flares not hot enough to attract the missiles' attention? The second F/A-18 launched, and he held his breath.

A moment later, the case evaporated in a ball of fire.

He took a deep breath as he watched the smoke and debris below. It was a few seconds before he truly realized that the danger had been averted for good.

"WOOOHOOO!!!!" Tom could hold himself back no longer. He pounded his fists against the roof of the machine.

He heard cheering from the radio, too. Shorty, who'd been flying that morning when Tom had almost been blown out of the sky, had launched the missile that brought down the bomb.

"Good shooting, sir!" said Tom.

He watched as a Seahawk helicopter took off from the aircraft carrier. That would be the recovery team sent to collect the remains of the case, especially the radioactive material, he thought. Thank God his plan had worked. At some point in his training, he had learned that a nuclear weapon could only be triggered by its own detonator. If an external explosion destroys the detonator, no nuclear fission can take place. He smiled, happy to have that responsibility off his shoulders. His job was done.

"USS Ronald Reagan, come in, over," said Tom.

The CO was back on the line. "Go ahead, soldier."

"I'm signing off now. I promise not to disturb your airspace anymore. Over and out." Tom smiled as he turned the plane onto a course for Barcelona, but this time he had no intention of landing in the middle of the city.

He started his descent and brought the Cessna down safely on the water close to Port Olympic. A motorboat was already on its way to meet him and take him ashore. When Tom stepped out of the boat, Hellen was waiting. She ran to him and threw her arms around his neck.

"You are truly insane sometimes," she said. She looked deep into his eyes and kissed him. "Wagner, we've got a lot to talk about."

Tom looked around and saw his boss, Captain Maierhofer, standing next to Noah. His face was as lemonysour as usual, but even he managed to twist a grin out of it.

"Your methods are awfully unorthodox, Wagner . . . but good work."

With Hellen in his arms, Tom didn't even care that Maierhofer had mispronounced his name.

People standing around the harbor broke into applause and Tom turned to Hellen again.

"I've never kissed a nun in my life," he said, eyeing the habit she was still wearing. He wrapped her firmly in his arms and kissed her again. And this time, he wasn't about to let anyone interrupt.

73

THE HOLY FATHER'S PRIVATE CHAMBERS, VATICAN CITY

"Please come in." The Pope's camerlengo, Monsignor Girotti, led them past the two Swiss Guards and into the Pope's private rooms. "The Holy Father never receives visitors here," Girotti added, apparently to emphasize the exceptional nature of their visit.

Tom, Hellen, François and Noah looked around the barren room. They had expected pomp and opulence, but this was just the opposite. Apart from a simple bed and an equally simple wardrobe, all that stood in the large room—about 1000 square feet in size—was a plain desk by the window, which afforded a breathtaking view over the Vatican Gardens. In one corner was an unadorned fireplace, in which a fire crackled. Even summer nights in the Vatican could be chilly, it seemed. The Pope rose from his desk and approached his four visitors.

"The Lord be with you," he greeted them.

"It is a great honor, Your Holiness, to have you receive us," said Tom.

Tom, Hellen and François bowed before the head of the Catholic Church and kissed the Ring of the Fisherman on his hand. Noah, who was Jewish, refrained.

"There are, in truth, no words that can properly repay the debt of gratitude that I—and of course the entire Catholic Church—owe you," the Pope said. "You not only saved my life and recovered our holy relics, you have also averted a human catastrophe of terrible scope. And, of course, you found and recovered the sacred weapon, the Sword of Saint Peter. For these things, I thank you."

The Pope bowed slightly before the group, and the camerlengo's eyes widened considerably at the gesture.

"But that is not enough, not at all," said the Holy Father. "I would like you to be present when the sword is laid in its final resting place."

Hellen inhaled sharply. She could already guess what he meant.

Minutes later, they were following the Pope, the camerlengo and eight Swiss Guards into the catacombs below St. Peter's. Four of the guardsmen carried Noah's wheelchair. The Pope himself carried the chest with the sword as they made their way to the Vatican Necropolis.

The Vatican Necropolis is a large burial site directly under the grottoes of St. Peter's Basilica. Originally a burial site built by Emperor Caligula next to a Roman circus on the southern slope of the Vatican Hill, tradition holds that the Apostle Peter was buried there after being martyred by Nero in AD 64 or 67. In AD 324, Emperor Constantine I began construction of the first basilica dedicated to Saint Peter, located directly over the presumed site of the Apostle's tomb. The necropolis has only been accessible again since its excavation in the 1950s; the "Peter Campus" is the small area where Peter's tomb is thought to be located, and is among the holiest sites of the Catholic Church.

The Pope handed the chest to Tom, then crossed himself and lowered himself to his knees in front of the tomb of Saint Peter. He prayed in silence for a few minutes. When he was finished, the camerlengo helped him back to his feet. The Holy Father placed the chest containing the sword on top of Peter's sarcophagus, and they stood in silence for a few minutes. Each of them could feel the magic emanating from the sacred weapon, and the uniqueness of the moment.

74

"Astounding how expensive a piccolo espresso can be."
Cloutard sipped at his tiny cup. "And then it is not even
very good. We French make better coffee."

He looked around the little place where the four of them
were now sitting, just a stone's throw from St. Peter's
Square. The walls were hung with historical representa-
tions of Rome and an old map of Vatican City in a kitschy
gold frame. Cloutard, as a precaution, had not ordered
food. The odors wafting out from the kitchen told him he
would be wiser not to. In a tourist trap like this, he could
only be disappointed.

"The French make good coffee?" Tom said. "Hmm. If you
want really good coffee, come to Vienna and we'll go to
Hawelka," Tom said.

"Hawelka? Never heard of it, I'm afraid. I only know your
classics: Landtmann's, Café Central . . ."

Tom rolled his eyes. " François, next time you're in Vienna, I'll take you on a coffee-house tour—off the beaten track."

"I'd prefer a bar crawl." Noah took a swig of his Campari soda.

"Just as easily arranged. Pity we all live in different parts of the world," Tom said. He became a little melancholy. "You're really sure you want to go back to Israel?" he asked Noah.

Noah nodded. "My mind's made up," he said. Tom decided not to probe any deeper into his friend's decision.

"It will be some time before I can come to Vienna," said Cloutard. "I have to rebuild my business first."

Tom and Noah put their hands over their ears and chorused, "La-la-la-la-la-la!"

"We don't want to hear anything about it," said Tom. "We don't know anything about anyone wanting to rebuild any organization, do we?"

Noah shook his head. "I haven't got the faintest clue what you're blathering about," he said, grinning mischievously, and the three of them laughed. Hellen sat quietly, absorbed in her own thoughts.

"Then I'll just sit here and drink my . . ." Cloutard pulled a face and peered into the tiny cup. ". . . whatever-it-is."

"The whole two-popes question has been cleared up, by the way. Our surveillance cameras in the basilica showed that Palffy had a double sitting next to him, hence the mix-up. But there's one thing I still don't understand: What did those clumsy hijackers have to do with the whole thing?" Noah asked and looked around his companions.

"Those were my people," said Cloutard casually.

Tom, Noah and Hellen looked at him, dumbfounded. "More information, please," said Tom.

"A few months ago, Guerra came to my place in Tabarka and presented me with a dossier of evidence. It was solid, too, the kind of evidence that would put me behind bars for a very long time. All he wanted from me was a couple of favors to make the dossier disappear. I did not trust him in the least, of course, and began to do a little research of my own. That was when I stumbled across AF. What I did not realize was that Ossana was infiltrating my organization at the same time.

"AF?" Noah said. "Never heard of it."

"I cannot tell you exactly who or what is behind it. But the more research I did, the more curious I became," said Cloutard.

75

François Cloutard guided the Fiat Cinquecento he had rented at the airport up the narrow mountain road. He had left the village proper behind half a mile below, and now there were no more houses beside the road. He knew that every Sunday the village inhabitants walked up that same road to attend mass in the small mountain church. Cloutard had been here many times before and had walked the same route many times himself. Today, however, he was uncertain whether his journey would prove to be completely in vain.

He hoped that the man he had come to see still offered his daily audiences in the small trattoria beside the church. The Fiat groaned around the last turn, and when Cloutard had completed the final ascent, the vista he knew so well opened before him.

Cloutard turned off the engine. First, he entered the small church. He moistened his fingers with holy water from the stoup, knelt before the altar and made the sign of the cross. There were only five pews. He sat down in the last of them and prayed, "Hail Mary, Full of Grace, The Lord is with thee . . ." Only when he came to the end of the prayer did he sense the presence of another person in the church.

"So I was not mistaken. We have not seen each other for a long time", said the old, quavering voice, all too familiar.

Cloutard stood. He took a few steps toward the old man and embraced him warmly. He looked into the old man's tired eyes. His frayed, gray cotton trousers and old but well-starched shirt, the waistcoat he always wore open so that it wouldn't pull too tight across his belly, and his worn and scratched walking stick offered no clue that he was one of the most important Mafia leaders in all of Italy. For decades, from his trattoria there on the mountain next to the church, he had guided the destinies of several crime families. People came to seek audience with him not only from throughout Italy, but from all over the world. In the trattoria, problems were solved, orders given and favors requested, just as it had been in the Cosa Nostra for more than a hundred years.

"Let us go across the street and drink a grappa," the old man said. He had already turned around and was shuffling slowly out of the church. "You know if I can help you with whatever is on your mind, I'm going to ask a favor of you in return?" The old man's voice turned cold and resolute for a moment, then regained its usual warmth. "So what is bothering you?"

They sat down at a small table outside the trattoria. Benedetto poured two glasses of grappa and handed one to Cloutard. "*Salute*," said the old man, sipping from his glass. Then he leaned back slowly and folded his hands over his impressive belly.

"I am being blackmailed by someone who works for an organization called AF," said Cloutard said, his expression solemn. "Benedetto, who is behind this?"

The old man's face darkened. On his already deeply wrinkled face more furrows appeared. He reached for a small bell that stood on the table and jangled it three times. Cloutard knew what that meant. Benedetto wanted his consigliere to be present at the meeting. In the families, certain topics were only discussed in the presence of the consigliere, the adviser. Apparently, Cloutard had touched on a subject of great importance. A few moments later, an astonishingly young man appeared. He bowed deeply to Cloutard, pulled up a chair and sat down on Benedetto's right. He remained silent and awaited the old man's words.

"Shortly after the end of World War II, a meeting of businessmen and politicians who wanted to prevent another global escalation of that kind took place," the old man began, his tone almost casual. "Now, this is not one of those secret societies that the media keeps blaming for every stupid new conspiracy theory. At the time, there were just a few informal meetings. These were people who saw the world as it really is—who saw that there is no good or evil, but simply different truths and value systems. For that same reason, we also took part in those meetings. The whole thing had no name or form, and it was certainly not meant to be a world government or anything like that. The meetings petered out in the eighties, and I forgot all about it."

"But it did not peter out entirely, did it?" said Cloutard.

"*Certo*. We were simply no longer invited. The participants changed, and by the time I learned by chance a few years later that the meetings had in fact continued, it had transformed into an organization whose sole aim was the manipulation and control of the masses. We are talking here about manipulation at an economic, political and social level. They called themselves "Absolute Freedom" but they had exactly the opposite in mind."

"But this sounds exactly like the conspiracy theory nonsense served up by the tabloids and those hare-brained bloggers, someone behind the scenes pulling the strings of the entire world." Cloutard shook his head in disbelief. "It cannot be possible for something like that to have escaped the attention of the intelligence services, the national governments or the Church for decades."

Cloutard began to doubt whether it had been wise to come to the aging godfather for advice after all. Benedetto seemed to have grown old, very old. And apparently very confused. Because he kept on talking, and what he said became more and more absurd.

"Absolute Freedom has power and influence that the families, the secret services, the community of nations, and even the Vatican can only dream of. There is nothing they have not gotten their claws into. But they are astute enough to proceed with subtlety. Often, the cogs they turn are only small, but they are in very effective places. They think exclusively in the long term." Benedetto's eyes were wide, and Cloutard thought he saw something even a little crazy in the old man's gaze.

"Take all that has been happening in recent weeks with the holy relics, for example," the old man continued. "Their aim is to stir up fear and undermine the political and social climate in Europe more than it already is. At the same time, they want to incite hatred. And if you ask me, they seem to be succeeding. Holy relics are disappearing all over Europe. People are being kidnapped and killed, bombs are exploding, churches are being burned down. The people are growing more and more insecure. AF has different departments for terrorist attacks, extortion, media manipulation, election fraud, and much more. You think the Russians set up Trump for the presidency? No. They're everywhere."

Benedetto had looked around nervously as he whispered his last sentences. Cloutard had heard enough. It hurt his heart to see a man like Benedetto—a man who had spent decades as a hard-bitten criminal, true, but who had also dispensed a great deal of wisdom and justice in his life— now evidently so utterly off his rocker. He smiled at the old man and they drank another grappa. Then Cloutard stood up and said goodbye. "You have helped me very much, Benedetto," he said sadly.

Cloutard embraced the old man warmly and left the small trattoria bewildered.

At the small car park, Cloutard heard the consigliere calling after him.

"Signore, I must have a word with you," the young man said, approaching him. "The *padrone* is no longer the man he once was. He has been spouting this nonsense for some years now. He won't let anyone examine him, of course, but doctors among his friends agree. His mind is . . . muddled. He tells anyone who will listen about this Absolute Freedom fantasy, whatever the issue brought to him. Absolute Freedom is to blame for everything. But we all know that Absolute Freedom exists only in the mind of the padrone. Lately, his confused phases have been occurring more and more frequently, and have become more severe. Sometimes he cannot leave his bed. He probably will not be with us much longer. I am sorry you came all this way for nothing."

"That is quite all right, Consigliere. Benedetto is an old man. Even if he was unable to help me, at least I have gotten to see him once more before God calls his name."

Cloutard said goodbye to the young man. As they shook hands, Cloutard noted a conspicuous tattoo on the young man's arm, but made nothing of it.

A strange cloud hovered over Cloutard as he drove down the narrow mountain road.

76

A SMALL CAFÉ NOT FAR FROM ST. PETER'S BASILICA,
ROME

Noah shook his head. "Impossible."

"So I also thought," said Cloutard. "But the signs converged when I learned of Benedetto's sudden murder. I realized that something big was being planned. I had no idea they were planning to blow up half of Barcelona, but I knew I had to get out of the situation I was in, and fast."

Tom nodded. Noah, still wearing his skeptical face, also listened patiently.

"I could not simply go to the police, of course. Instead, I put all the information I could gather onto a cell phone, and I put the phone into the hands of the two dumbest guys in my organization and hired them to hijack a plane. After all the other hijackings, my hope was that the information would find its way into the right hands. I knew they would mess up the hijacking."

Tom smiled bitterly. "And I screwed up that plan when I took the phone . . . and let someone take it away from me."

"Yes," Cloutard said with a nod. "Thank God those idiots were stupid enough to say my name out loud and you were able to pick up the trail again."

Noah raised his glass. "Here's to the idiot criminals." He looked over at Cloutard and smiled mischievously. Cloutard reached into his coat pocket, took out a flask, and joined Noah's toast.

"Let me guess," Tom said. "Louis XIII?"

"*Quoi d'autre?*" Cloutard replied. He took a swig from the flask. "You know, it bothers me that Joan of Arc's shield has now gone to Blue Shield. I was going to hang it over my fireplace. Unfortunately, after the auction, Guerra made it abundantly clear to me that I had to actually deliver it. And since brute force is not in my nature, I dropped it off in Como as requested."

"Where you saw Hellen. And the rest is history," Tom added.

Hellen, who had been sitting silently the whole time, evidently lost in thought, looked up when she heard her name mentioned. Tom gently touched her arm.

"Shall we go outside for a minute?" he asked her quietly.

Hellen nodded and stood up. The tables on the sidewalk in front of the café were all occupied. Tourists and, surprisingly, a number of Roman locals sat beneath the white parasols, enjoying the magnificent view of St. Peter's. The spring sun was already fairly warm, but Hellen shivered with every little breath of wind. She looked sadly at Tom.

"We've become very close again these last few days, Tom," she said. "I've seen many sides to you that I didn't know about before. But as wonderful as you are, I can also see that it just won't work between us. Though I . . .", she faltered, tried to go on, but then sighed and left the sentence half-spoken.

Tom tried to say something, but Hellen raised her hand.

"Please, let me finish. Yes, I have changed how I think about you, and about us, too. And I am forever grateful to you for what you've done. But you and me, we're just not right for each other."

Tom nodded stoically. "You're right, I know. It just wouldn't work out."

Hellen knew it was crazy, but when he confirmed her own words like that, it only hurt more. She was confused. She wanted him, yet at the same time, she knew they had no future. And she knew he felt the same way. They stood there, abashed and uncertain, and it felt like an eternity before one of them spoke again.

"So what's next?" asked Hellen. "Will you go back to Cobra?"

Tom shook his head. "No, I'm done with that. I have no idea what I'm going to do, not yet. My uncle's invited me to his place in San Diego. I think I'm going to accept his invitation, try and get a little distance."

He looked into Hellen's eyes, already suspecting what she was planning for herself.

"What about you? Blue Shield's not really an option, is it?"

Hellen shook her head. "No. Not now. So many questions about my family history have come up in the last few days. There's so much that's unresolved. I think I'd like to take some time for that and see if I can find some answers."

She fell silent, and Tom realized how hard all this was for her.

"Tom, you know I'm no good with goodbyes. Give my best to those two inside for me. I have to go now."

Hellen took Tom in a fleeting embrace and did not wait for him to say anything. Then she turned away and, a few moments later, disappeared around the corner into Via Rusticucci. Tom felt a sudden, unfamiliar emptiness. His right hand reached into his jacket pocket, where he had put his ticket to San Diego. He took out the envelope, and from the envelope he took out the second ticket, the one he had bought for Hellen. He tore it in half, then rejoined Noah and Cloutard in the café.

77

Ossana had parked her car two blocks away. She could
have passed for a resident of the neighborhood, going for
a brisk evening stroll. The streets were silent, with no
traffic in the villa area and nobody out on the street, just
a few houses with a light on inside. Ossana glided like a
cat over the walls of the estate and walked the three
hundred yards of the tree-lined, cobblestoned avenue,
illuminated by old London street lamps, as if she did so
every day. She fished her lock-pick set out of her jacket
pocket, and in a few seconds had opened the front door.
She tiptoed into the dimly lit study.

Count Nikolaus Palffy III was standing with his back to
her, hurriedly removing several documents from his safe,
itself hidden behind a Kandinsky on the wall above the
fireplace.

"In a hurry, Nikolaus?" Ossana said in her most noncha-
lant tone.

Palffy spun around and stared at her in horror. He opened his mouth but could get no word out.

"Your plan did not work," Ossana added.

Palffy took a breath and recovered his self-possession. He squared his shoulders and spoke in a composed, authoritative voice. Those who did not know him well might have thought he had the situation under control. His gaze darted across his desk, where one of the drawers was open. Inside it was a loaded Walther PPK.

"I already have a new plan, one that will draw even more media attention. More importantly, it will bring more votes in the next elections. I'm here for some important Blue Shield papers. I need to prepare the details."

Ossana smiled. "You seem quite optimistic about the fiasco you and your protégé Guerra were responsible for in Barcelona."

"That was a setback, yes, I admit it. We lost that battle. But it was not a complete waste. We achieved our goal of fanning the flames of insecurity amongst the Europeans."

Ossana looked at Palffy calmly. Palffy approached the desk.

"Nikolaus, you failed. We put a great deal of money into your project. It was your idea. You planned it, you implemented it. But along comes a guy from Vienna with a crew of amateurs and scuttles your ship before it can even set sail. The best you managed was to switch your getaway car before you blew up with it."

Ossana strolled to the window and gazed out into the garden. In the pale light from the swimming pool, the garden had a bluish glow. Palffy edged closer to his Walther PPK.

"We made it clear to you from the very start how crucial the success of your plan was, and that we could not afford any mistakes. We are not some band of outlaws sticking up stagecoaches in the Wild West."

Palffy snatched the Walther PPK and pointed it at Ossana, who still had her back to him.

"Our concern is that you will switch sides, just to save your own miserable hide. You know about us. You know about AF. We cannot afford a security risk like that."

She turned swiftly, her Heckler & Koch trained on him. She fired once, twice, three times. Two of the bullets struck close to his heart, the third between his eyes. Nikolaus Palffy III was dead before he hit the floor.

"Amateur," Ossana muttered as she flipped through the documents Palffy had taken from the safe. They were emblazoned with UNESCO and Blue Shield logos. On a cover sheet, she read: "Rejected Blue Shield Projects." Ossana began to look through the files more closely, skimming the headings. At each one, she raised her eyebrows a little more.

"Babylon and Semiramis"

"Nostradamus and the Philosophers' Stone"

"El Dorado"

"The Golden Fleece"

"The Ark of the Covenant"

"The Tomb of Alexander the Great"

"Atlantis"

"Noah's Ark"

"The Confederate Treasury"

That was just the start. The files contained far more. Ossana had no idea what information the documents could give them, but it could not hurt to take them with her. She packed everything from Palffy's safe into her black backpack—including the amulet with the Maltese Cross, in a small plastic bag next to the documents.

When she had everything stowed in her pack, she pressed a speed dial button on her phone, establishing an encrypted connection. It rang once at the other end, and someone answered.

"The job's done, Papa," she said, turning out the light.

Ossana left the house and walked back to her car, not noticing the figure that slipped from the shadow of a tree to follow her.

———

— THE END —

OF „THE SACRED WEAPON"

Tom Wagner will return in:

„THE LIBRARY OF THE KINGS"

GET THE FREE TOM WAGNER ADVENTURE "THE STONE OF DESTINY"

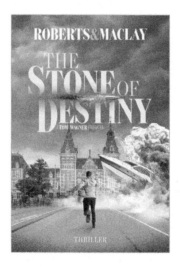

The Tom Wagner Prequel "The Stony of Destiny"
(Click here)

or visit www.robertsmaclay.com/start-free

A long-lost treasure leads to the dark history of the Habsburgs.

A breathless hunt across Europe with a shocking conclusion: the thriller "The Stone of Destiny" plunges our hero into the dark history of the Habsburg Empire and leads him to a treasure lost for centuries. A conspiracy with its roots in the final days of World War I and reaching into the present: fact merges with fiction – as always, with lots of action, surprising twists and a healthy dose of humor.

You can get the book "The Stone of Destiny" for free by signing up for our newsletter: Click here
or visit www.robertsmaclay.com/start-free

THE TOM WAGNER SERIES

THE STONE OF DESTINY

(Tom Wagner Prequel)

A dark secret of the Habsburg Empire. A treasure believed to be lost long time ago. A breathless hunt into the past.

The thriller "The Stone of Destiny" leads Tom Wagner and Hellen de Mey into the dark past of the Habsburgs and to a treasure that seems to have been lost for a long time.

The breathless hunt goes through half of Europe and the surprise at the end is not missing: A conspiracy that began in the last days of the First World War reaches up to the present day!

Free Download!
Click here or open link:
https://robertsmaclay.com/start-free

THE SACRED WEAPON

(A Tom Wagner Adventure 1)

A demonic plan. A mysterious power. An extraordinary team.

The Notre Dame fire, the theft of the Shroud of Turin and a terrorist attack on the legendary Meteora monasteries are just the beginning. Fear has gripped Europe.

Stolen relics, a mysterious power with a demonic plan and allies with questionable allegiances: Tom Wagner is in a race against time, trying to prevent a disaster that could tear Europe down to its foundations. And there's no one he can trust...

Click here or open link:
https://robertsmaclay.com/tw1

———

THE LIBRARY OF THE KINGS

(A Tom Wagner Adventure 2)

Hidden wisdom. A relic of unbelievable power. A race against time.

Ancient legends, devilish plans, startling plot twists, breathtaking action and a dash of humor: *Library of the Kings* is gripping entertainment – a Hollywood blockbuster in book form.

When clues to the long-lost Library of Alexandria surface, ex-Cobra officer Tom Wagner and archaeologist Hellen de Mey aren't the only ones on the hunt for its vanished secrets. A sinister power is plotting in the background, and nothing is as it seems. And the dark secret hidden in the Library threatens all of humanity.

Click here or open link:
https://robertsmaclay.com/tw2

———

THE INVISIBLE CITY

(A Tom Wagner Adventure 3)

A vanished civilization. A diabolical trap. A mystical treasure.

Tom Wagner, archaeologist Hellen de Mey and gentleman crook Francois Cloutard are about to embark on their first official assignment from Blue Shield – but when Tom receives an urgent call from the Vatican, things start to move quickly:

With the help of the Patriarch of the Russian Orthodox Church, they discover clues to an age-old myth: the Russian Atlantis. And a murderous race to find an ancient, long-lost relic leads them from Cuba to the Russian hinterlands.

What mystical treasure lies buried beneath Nizhny Novgorod? Who laid the evil trap? And what does it all have to do with Tom's grandfather?

Coming February 2021

THE GOLDEN PATH

(A Tom Wagner Adventure 4)

The greatest treasure of mankind. An international intrigue. A cruel revelation.

Now a special unit for Blue Shield, Tom and his team are on a search for the legendary El Dorado. But, as usual, things don't go as planned.

The team gets separated and is – literally – forced to fight a battle on multiple fronts: Hellen and Cloutard make discoveries that overturn the familiar story of El Dorado's gold.

Meanwhile, the President of the United States has tasked Tom with keeping a dangerous substance out of the hands of terrorists.

Coming May 2021
https://robertsmaclay.com/tw4

THE ROUND TABLE CHRONICLE

(A Tom Wagner Adventure 5)

The first secret society of mankind. Artifacts of inestimable power. A race you cannot win.

The events turn upside down: Tom Wagner is missing. Hellen's father has turned up and a hot lead is waiting for the Blue Shield team: The legendary Chronicle of the Round Table.

What does the Chronicles of the Round Table of King Arthur say? Must the history around Avalon and Camelot be rewritten? Where is Tom and who is pulling the strings?

Coming Fall 2021
https://robertsmaclay.com/tw5

THRILLED READER REVIEWS

"Suspense and entertainment! I've read a lot of books like this one; some better, some worse. This is one of the best books in this genre I've ever read. I'm really looking forward to a good sequel. "

———

"I just couldn't put this book down. Full of surprising plot twists, humor, and action! "

———

"An explosive combination of Robert Langdon, James Bond & Indiana Jones"

———

"Good build-up of tension; I was always wondering what happens next. Toward the end, where the story gets more and more complex and constantly changes scenes, I was on the edge of my seat"

———

"Great! I read all three books in one sitting. Dan Brown better watch his back."

———

"The best thing about it is the basic premise, a story with historical background knowledge scattered throughout the book–never too much at one time and always supporting the plot"

———

"Entertaining and action-packed! The carefully thought-out story has a clear plotline, but there are a couple of unexpected twists as well. I really enjoyed it. The sections of the book are tailored to maximize the suspense, they don't waste any time with unimportant details. The chapters are short and compact–perfect for a half-hour commute or at night before turning out the lights. Recommended to all lovers of the genre and anyone interested in getting to know it better. I'll definitely read the sequel."

———

"Anyone who likes reading Dan Brown, James Rollins and Preston & Child needs to get this book."

———

"An exciting build-up, interesting and historically significant settings, surprising plot twists in the right places."

ABOUT THE AUTHORS
ROBERTS & MACLAY

Roberts & Maclay have known each other for over 25 years, are good friends and have worked together on various projects.

The fact that they are now also writing thrillers together is less coincidence than fate. Talking shop about films, TV series and suspense novels has always been one of their favorite pastimes.

———

M.C. Roberts is the pen name of an successful entrepreneur and blogger. Adventure stories have always been his passion: after recording a number of superhero audiobooks on his father's old tape recorder as a six-year-old, he postponed his dream of writing novels for almost 40 years, and worked as a marketing director, editor-in-chief, DJ, opera critic, communication coach, blogger, online marketer and author of trade books...but in the end, the call of adventure was too strong to ignore.

————

R.F. Maclay is the pen name of an outstanding graphic designer and advertising filmmaker. His international career began as an electrician's apprentice, but he quickly realized that he was destined to work creatively. His family and friends were skeptical at first...but now, 20 years later, the passionate, self-taught graphic designer and filmmaker has delighted record labels, brand-name products and tech companies with his work, as well as making a name for himself as a commercial filmmaker and illustrator. He's also a walking encyclopedia of film and television series.

www.RobertsMaclay.com

Made in the USA
Las Vegas, NV
09 December 2021

36673830R00226